Praise for *End of the Trail*

End of the Trail may be Vickie McDonough's best book yet. Skillfully blending action and romance, she gives readers a story of families lost and found that will linger in their memories long after the last page is turned. I highly recommend this book!

—**AMANDA CABOT**, author of *Summer of Promise*
and *Christmas Roses*

The Morgan family saga continues with a heartwarming story of love and adventure with a prodigal son and rancher's niece. With a mixed cast of characters and surprises along the way, McDonough gives you a compelling story of faith to sink your teeth into and savor until the very last word.

—**MARTHA ROGERS**, event and workshop speaker,
and author

Far more than your ordinary cowboy story, *End of the Trail* touches a place deep within you, a place where lies, betrayal, abandonment, and broken promises live; a place where two young people must overcome hardship and find family, loyalty, faithfulness, and above all, love. You'll cry, you'll laugh, and you'll feel. But most of all, you'll enjoy.

—**MARYLU TYNDALL**, author of Legacy of
the King's Pirates series

From the moment Keri saves Brooks from being hanged, sparks fly and smiles abound. Vickie McDonough's romantic tale exemplifies the renewing power of love. *End of the Trail* is utterly charming.

—**CHERYL ST. JOHN**, author of *The Wedding Journey*

In this story of a loveable, but rascally prodigal, Vickie McDonough weaves an endearing story of how Brooks Morgan reconciles with his family as well as with his God. The love interest is provided by Keri Langston, a feisty young woman whose ranch Brooks wins in a poker game. McDonough deftly leads the reader through a tangled web of events that comes to a satisfying conclusion at the "End of the Trail."

> —GOLDEN KEYES PARSON, speaker and author of the
>   Darkness to Light series

End of the Trail delights with a fresh plot that takes turn of events not normally scene in historical fiction. McDonough effectively show how God turns what is meant for evil into good. A book to be treasured.

> —DIANA LESIRE BRANDMEYER, author of
>   *A Bride's Dilemma in Friendship, Tennessee*

End of the Trail is a novel of faith and forgiveness. The book overflows with surprises, intrigue, and Texas charm. Readers will love this story!

> —ANN SHOREY, author of *Where Wildflowers Bloom*,
>   Book 1 in the Sisters at Heart series

TEXAS
TRAILS

⟵ ★ ⟶

END OF THE TRAIL

VICKIE McDONOUGH

A
MORGAN FAMILY
SERIES

MOODY PUBLISHERS
CHICAGO

Edited by Pam Pugh
Interior design: Ragont Design
Cover design: Gearbox
Cover images: Veer and iStock

Library of Congress Cataloging-in-Publication Data

McDonough, Vickie.
      End of the trail / Vickie McDonough.
          p. cm. — (Texas trails: a Morgan Family series)
      ISBN 978-0-8024-0408-4
      1. Texas—Fiction. I. Title.
PS3613.C3896E53 2012
813'.6—dc23
                                          2011050522

We hope you enjoy this book from River North Fiction by Moody Publishers.
Our goal is to provide high-quality, thought-provoking books and products
that connect truth to your real needs and challenges. For more information
on other books and products written and produced from a biblical perspective, go to www.moodypublishers.com or write to:

River North Fiction
Imprint of Moody Publishers
820 N. LaSalle Boulevard
Chicago, IL 60610

1 3 5 7 9 10 8 6 4 2

Printed in the United States of America

This book is dedicated to my agent, Chip MacGregor, who came up with the idea for a series written by multiple authors and who asked me to be a part of it.

To Susan Page Davis and Darlene Franklin, my coauthors in the Texas Trails series. Thanks for joining me on this fabulous journey. It was great working with you both.

And to Moody Publishers for catching the vision of the Morgan family and buying this series. Thanks to the artists for our beautiful covers, to the editors for making our stories shine, and all the behind the scenes folks who helped bring this project to life. You all have been great to work with!

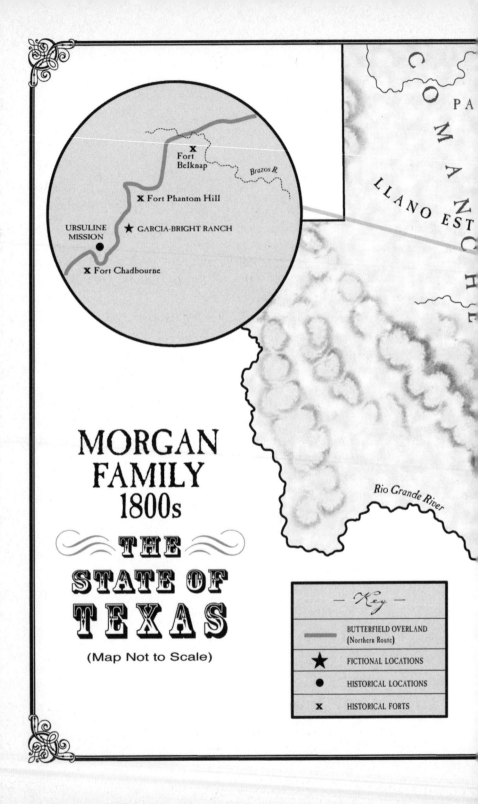

COMANCHE

PA

LLANO EST

Fort Belknap
X

Brazos R.

X Fort Phantom Hill

URSULINE MISSION
★ GARCIA-BRIGHT RANCH

●

X Fort Chadbourne

Rio Grande River

MORGAN FAMILY 1800s

THE STATE OF TEXAS

(Map Not to Scale)

— Key —

———	BUTTERFIELD OVERLAND (Northern Route)
★	FICTIONAL LOCATIONS
●	HISTORICAL LOCATIONS
X	HISTORICAL FORTS

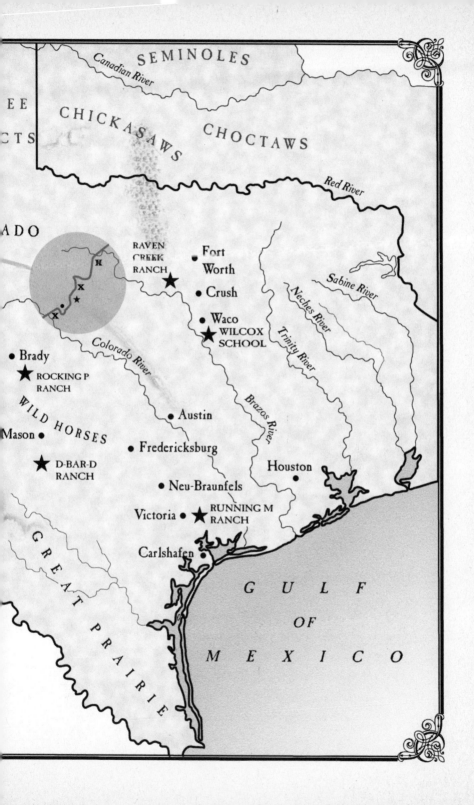

PROLOGUE

WACO, TEXAS, 1886

You're a good son, Brooks, but your father is right."
Brooks stared at his mother, halfway stunned
that she'd sided with his pa against him. "You don't
feel I do my share of the work around here either?"
Annie Morgan winced and gazed out the parlor
window, not looking at him. She might not admit in words that
she agreed, but that tiny grimace told Brooks she did. He
ducked his head, hating the feeling of disappointing his mother.
He'd always been her favorite child. He craved her warm smile,
but that was hard to be found just now. Still, he pushed aside
disturbing feelings and retrieved his charming smile—the one
his ma said could make a die-hard Texas cattle rancher invest
all his money in a herd of sheep—and squeezed between his
ma and the window.

She flicked a glance up at him then it swerved away. "Don't

try to charm me. This is all my fault. I shouldn't have coddled you so much."

His grin faltered. Now she sounded like his father. "You didn't coddle me."

"Yes, she did. She still does." Melissa's voice sounded from upstairs, followed by quick footsteps on the stairs.

He spun around, glaring at his bossy older sister. "Nobody asked you."

"I'm getting married soon, and with Josh gone off to medical college, that means you'll be the oldest sibling at home." She reached the bottom of the stairs and shifted the basket of dirty clothes to her other hip, cocking her mouth up on one side. "It's time you start acting like you're sixteen instead of six."

Brooks clenched his fist. As much as he might like knocking that know-it-all look off Melissa's face, he would never hit a female.

"That's enough, Missy. Get the laundry started and then check on Phillip. I'll be out in a few minutes." Ma turned her gaze on him as Melissa—smirking—slipped out the door. Ma's brown eyes were laced with pain and something he couldn't quite decipher. "Your sister is right, but she shouldn't have said what she did. After you nearly died in that fall from the hay loft when you were four, I kept you close. Too close. Wouldn't let you out with your father to do chores anymore. I blamed him for not watching you. He warned me not to be so overprotective, but I was stubborn and wouldn't listen."

"No, Ma—"

"Let me finish." She held up one hand, palm out. "You know how much I love you, but my coddling you has made you soft. Spoiled."

Brooks winced. Never had his ma said such a thing to him, and he didn't like the uncomfortable emotions swirling around inside him because of it. She really thought he was spoiled?

"You're nearly a man now, and you need to start acting like one. It's time that you quit taunting Phillip and helped your father more."

"But I do—"

She closed her eyes and shook her head. "Not nearly enough." She looked deep into his eyes. "What if something happened to your father? Would you know enough to take over running the ranch?"

"Of course I do." He stated the words with bravado, but inside, he felt less sure. Not sure at all, in fact.

"Well, I've said what needed to be said, now it's up to you. It's time you grow up, son."

Brooks stared at his mother. She'd never talked to him so firmly. So harshly. He felt betrayed by the person who loved him the most. He stomped outside, slamming the door behind him. If he'd been eleven, like Phillip, he'd probably have cried, but like his ma said, he was a man now—or almost one.

He did his share of work. Hadn't he just filled the wood box in the kitchen and hauled in a bucket of water? Ma had no call to lay into him like she had.

Just because he and his pa had argued after breakfast.

Because he didn't want to mend fences and shovel horse flops all his life. Josh got to follow his dream and go to medical school. Why couldn't their pa see Brooks had dreams of his own? He glanced at the barn then back at the house. Maybe it would be worth cleaning the stalls to get back on his ma's good side—and maybe then she'd make some more of those oatmeal cookies with raisins and nuts that she'd baked for the first time last week. His mouth watered just thinking about them.

Blowing out a breath, he moseyed to the barn. What he'd really like to be doing right now was fishing or swimming in the pond with Sammy or visiting pretty Sally Baxter. He ambled into the barn, dragging his boots and wrinkling his nose at the smelly hay in the floor of the stalls. His pa had left the muck there just like he'd said he would.

Jester lifted his head over the side of one stall and nickered. Brooks strode over to the black gelding and stroked his nose. "Nobody understands me, boy. I'm not like Pa. He likes working hard, getting sweaty and smelly, but I don't."

The horse nodded his head, as if agreeing with him.

"Hey, you want to go for a ride?" Casting aside thoughts of work, he bridled and saddled Jester and led him out of the barn. A long, hard gallop would do them both some good.

"Just where do you think you're going?"

Brooks jerked to a halt at his pa's deep voice. "Uh . . . riding."

Pa shook his head. "No, you're not. There's work to be done. Get back in there and muck out those stalls."

Hiking his chin, Brooks glared at his pa. "Maybe I already did."

Riley Morgan stared at him with those penetrating blue eyes. "I wish you had, but I can tell by your reaction that you haven't." He shook his head, his disappointment obvious.

Brooks gritted his back teeth together. It wouldn't matter if he had cleaned the stalls, his pa wouldn't be pleased. Nothing he did made Pa happy. "I'm sorry to be such a disappointment to you."

Phillip trotted around the side of the barn. "Pa, Pa, look at the frog I caught."

Brooks glared at his little brother. How come he couldn't do stall duty? He sure had to do it when he was Phillip's age.

His pa's harsh expression softened, and he tousled Phillip's light-brown hair. "That's a mighty fine frog, son. Did you finish weeding the corn like I told you?"

Nodding like a little cherub, his brother smiled. "Sure did, and I got some of the beans weeded too."

"Good job, son. Go in and show that nice frog to your ma."

"Look at my frog, Brooks." Phillip held up the commonplace critter.

"Ain't nothin' special about it. Just a dumb ol' toad."

Phillip's happy expression faltered.

"Go in the house, Phillip."

The boy nodded and shuffled to the house.

Brooks ire mounted. When was the last time his pa had told him he'd done a good job?

The smile on Pa's face faded as he spun back around. "That was a cruel thing to do. Just 'cause you're upset doesn't give you the right to hurt Phillip's feelings."

Brooks shrugged, feeling only a tad bit guilty.

His pa reached for Jester's reins but Brooks yanked them away and scowled, matching his father's expression.

"I want that barn cleaned out, or you can go without dinner. The Good Book says if a man doesn't work, he shouldn't eat."

"Fine. I'd rather not eat than mess with that muck."

"I guess I was wrong in giving you that gelding. A man who can't clean up after his horse doesn't deserve to have one. Give me the reins."

"Why?" Brooks backed up another step, tugging Jester along with him. The horse was his best friend.

"You stuffed yourself full of your ma's cooking this morning, but did you even give a thought to feeding your horse?"

Brooks hung his head at that comment. He'd forgotten again to feed Jester.

"Harley Jefferson came by earlier asking if I had a good riding horse for sale. I've just about decided to sell him Jester."

Brooks's eyes widened, and he felt as if he'd been gut shot. "You wouldn't."

"I don't want to, but obviously it will take something drastic to get your attention. You've got to learn to pull your weight and tend this place. It will be yours one day."

"I don't want it. Give it to Phillip since you love him so much." Brooks's frown deepened.

Pain creased his father's face, but Brooks hardened his heart against it. He was sick of being told he was no good. And he wasn't about to let his father sell his horse.

"I love you too, son, and that's why I'm working so hard to teach you to become a man. I just hope it's not too late." He shoved his hands to his hips and stared out toward the plowed field. "I joined the war when I wasn't much older than you. It's time you grow up, son."

Tears stung Brooks's eyes in spite of his resolve to not allow such sissy behavior. He was so sick of hearing how his pa had fought in the war. It wasn't his fault there was no war for him to fight in. He was sick of being bossed around. Sick of his whole family.

He threw the reins over Jester's neck and leaped into the saddle. He kicked the horse hard, causing him to lunge away from his pa's frantic attempt to grab the reins.

"Get off the horse, boy. You hear me?"

"I'm no boy. And since no one here realizes that, I'm going somewhere else where I'll be appreciated." He kicked Jester hard in the side again, and the horse squealed at the unusually harsh treatment, but he leapt forward.

"Brooks. You come back here right now. Stop!" Fast footsteps chased after him.

Sitting straighter in the saddle, Brooks ignored his pa's ranting and squeezed away the moisture in his eyes. He'd stay away a few days—maybe a week—and when he returned, everyone would be happy to see him again. At least he hoped they would. And ma would bake those oatmeal cookies to celebrate his return.

But deep within he knew the truth—they would all be happier without him. All he'd ever done was cause them trouble.

He turned Jester to the west. Maybe by the time he visited every town in Texas his family would forget how much trouble he'd been and welcome him home.

And maybe Houston would get a foot of snow this winter.

CHAPTER ONE

Central Texas, 1896

Lightning skittered across the granite sky. The boom of thunder that followed spooked Brooks Morgan's horse into a sideways crow hop so unexpectedly that Brooks had to grapple for the saddle horn to keep from losing his seat. He tightened up on the reins and guided Jester back onto the trail. He had hoped to make it to the next town before the storm let loose, but it looked like he was in for a soaking. He didn't mind a good washing down, but Jester hated rain.

Rocks crunched beneath Jester's hooves as he trotted up the trail. A gnawing in the pit of Brooks's belly made him wish for a home-cooked meal, but those were hard to come by for a drifter like him. He glanced up at the ominous sky as another bolt of lightning made him squint. Tugging down his hat, he pulled Jester to a stop atop the hill to get his bearing. The sky looked as if twilight had already set in, though it was just two in the afternoon. Another bolt of lightning zigzagged from heaven to earth, with an explosion that set Jester prancing. Rain was one thing, but Brooks had no hankering to get hit by lightning.

He clucked out of the side of his mouth, and Jester leapt forward with no more encouragement. The black horse was as game as any, but send a little rain his way, and you could almost see a yellow stripe appear on his back. They topped another hill, and a small town came into view, barely visible because of the sheet of rain that was falling between Brooks and the place. Several lights flickered, welcoming him.

He reined the horse down the hill, thankful that the rain hadn't reached him yet to make the passage slick. At the bottom of the valley, he nudged Jester into a gallop. The horse slowed when the first raindrops hit him, but then stretched out into a long-legged gait that ate up the ground. Something hard hit Brooks on the shoulder, and he glanced sideways to see who had lobbed the object, but not another soul was out in this weather. Another rock hit the back of his hand, then the sky let loose in a storm of hail.

Brooks hunkered down. Rain was bad enough, but hail could kill a man. He reached the end of town, reined Jester to a trot, and rode him right up onto the boardwalk. The horse was the only thing of value he owned, and Brooks wasn't about to let him be pounded by hail. He slid off, rubbed his shoulders where the frozen rocks had pelted him, and listened to the loud thunking on the roof overhead. A layer of white had nearly coated the street.

Jester pawed the wooden floor of the boardwalk and jerked at the reins. Brooks ran his hand over the horse's coat, checking for injuries, then patted Jester's shoulder. "You're all right, boy."

A woman with a face that reminded him of a fox scampered

out the door of a dress shop, shooing him away. "You can't have that beast on the boardwalk. He'll make a mess."

Brooks bit back the first thought that came to mind and smiled. He ducked his head, tipping his hat, and a river of water poured down onto the walkway. The woman yelped and jumped back. Brooks smiled and led Jester toward her. The horse hugged the wall, as if trying to get as far away from the hail as he could. "Sorry, ma'am." Brooks raised his voice to be heard over the clatter. "We'll just mosey on down to the café and see if we can't get something to eat."

She sucked in a breath, blinking her eyes as if she had dust in them. "Why . . . they don't serve horses at the café—and get that beast off the boardwalk before—"

Her words were drowned out by the pounding of hail on the roof overhead. He passed a barbershop and nodded to the two men seated inside, one whose face was covered in lather. He brushed a hand across his own stubble. That was something he'd have to tend to himself since he had no money for luxuries like a shave in a barbershop.

The delicious scent of bread baking—or maybe pies—pulled him to the third shop. CLYDE'S CAFÉ was painted on the window, and a light shone from inside. Maybe the place was still open, although 2:00 p.m. was rather late for lunch. Brooks glanced at the street. The hail had lightened up but still thunked against the wooden rails and walkway. If a man didn't know better, he'd think it was winter by all the white that covered the ground, instead of late summer. He dropped Jester's reins, ground-tying the horse, and opened the door of the café.

One old man sat sideways in his chair, leaning against the wall, studying him. A rifle lay across the table next to him. Brooks nodded and glanced at the empty tables.

"C'mon over and join me, if'n you've a mind to." Curious,

light-blue eyes shone out from under a set of bushy, gray eyebrows that matched the man's thick moustache. He looked tall, if his long legs were any indication, but his frame was overly thin, like a man recovering from a long illness.

Brooks flashed a grin and nodded. "Don't mind if I do. I'm gettin' tired of eating with just my horse for company." He pulled out a chair, tugged off his wet hat, and laid it on the table behind him. He yanked on his shirt, which clung to his body, and peered up at the man. "I've had my bath now. Looks like I could use a change of clothes."

The man nodded. "Smells like it too." His gap-toothed smile softened his words.

A heavyset man with a day's growth of whiskers plodded out from behind a stained curtain. "Help you, stranger?"

"Just coffee." Brooks longed to order whatever it was that smelled so good, but that would have to wait until he had more money.

"That it? Just coffee?" The big man frowned then waddled to the back room. He returned with a coffee pot and a cup, which he set in front of Brooks, and filled the cup. Lugging the pot, he returned behind his curtain.

The old man chuckled. "Clyde takes it as a personal offense if folks don't buy his food."

"Nothin' personal about it. My pockets are just a bit lean at the moment." Brooks wrapped his hands around the cup and sipped the brew. A pleasant feeling of warmth traveled through him and helped satisfy his empty belly.

The man nudged his chin toward the window that Jester stood in front of. "Nice horse."

Brooks nodded, liking the old man. "My pa gave him to me, a long time ago."

"Where's your pa now?"

"Waco." If he was still alive. Brooks pushed the barrel of the rifle back toward the wall so it wasn't pointing right at his heart.

"Know what kind he is?"

"Yep. A Morgan. My family raises them."

The man held out his hand. "I'm Will Langston. Welcome to Shoofly."

Brooks shook hands. "Brooks Morgan."

The man's fuzzy brows lifted, making his pale eyes seem larger. "Same name as your horse?"

Brooks nodded and took another sip of his coffee. "Yep. Even spelled the same."

Will chuckled. "I like you, boy." He looked over his shoulder. "Clyde, bring this fellow some of those chicken dumplin's and pie, if you've got any left over."

"I can't let you pay for my food—not unless you've got some kind of work I can do," Brooks said.

"That can be arranged. I'm in need of someone to help me while I'm in town."

Brooks studied the man, wondering what kind of help he needed. "Like what?"

Will ran his fingers over the engraving on the stock of his rifle. "I'm good at reading people, and I sense you're all right." He leaned forward, tapped his finger on the table, then glanced up, pain lacing his eyes. "There's no easy way to say this, but I'm dying."

Brooks sat back, staring at Will. That had been the last thing he'd thought the man might say. "I'm sorry."

Will pushed out his lips. "Don't be. I've lived a long life, and I'm ready to meet my Maker." He heaved a sigh that tickled Brooks's cheeks. "There are days, though, that I don't feel so well and could use some help. Nobody in this little town has the time. I thought maybe you'd be interested."

Rubbing the back of his hand against his cheek, Brooks stared at the old man. Being a nursemaid wasn't exactly the job he'd been looking for, but something about Will pulled at him. Maybe he could help out while he looked around for other work. "I reckon I could help for a bit."

Will's expression softened, and he smiled and leaned back. "Good."

Clyde set a plate heaping with chicken and dumplings in front of Brooks, then a fat slice of peach pie. Brooks wolfed down the food, hoping he wouldn't regret his decision. But how hard could it be tending an old man?

◀ ────── ★ ──────▶

WESLEYAN FEMALE COLLEGE
GEORGIA

Keri Langston swatted at the badminton shuttlecock and smacked it clear across the net to the back row. She gave her roommate, Emily Adkins, a victorious smile. While she thought the game—one brought back from England by a student returning from break—was a waste of time, she seemed to be the only woman who could play it as well as the men. Maybe she hadn't lost all her rough edges.

Across the net, Emily dabbed at her cheek with an embroidered handkerchief.

Keri watched the shuttlecock fly over her head, then heard it whiz back after being hit by a player standing behind her. It smacked Emily in the forehead. Emily's eyes went wide, she back stepped, and fainted. The gentleman behind Emily caught her under the arms, and his surprised gaze collided with Keri's.

"Let's take her to rest under one of the trees," she said.

The man scooped up her friend and followed Keri to the nearest live oak. He set her down. "Should I get some water? The headmistress?"

Keri stooped beside her friend and peered up into the

man's kind gray eyes. "Maybe some water. Emily has frequent bouts of fainting." She could hardly tell the man that Emily insisted on lacing her corset as tight as possible to make her waist extremely thin.

She waved her hand in front of Emily's face as several of their classmates gathered round.

"Is she all right?" Corrabelle Stuart asked.

"She will be." Keri swatted her hand in the air. "Y'all just scurry on back to whatever you were doing."

Charlotte Winchester leaned toward Keri's ear. "A refined lady does not say *y'all*, and we don't *scurry*." She straightened, her nose pointing up, and glided away.

Keri scowled at the wealthy young woman who'd been her nemesis ever since she first arrived at the Wesleyan Female College in Georgia. The only thing Keri liked about Charlotte was her last name—the same name as Keri's rifle back in Texas. How many times had she wished for her rifle, if for nothing else than to instill a little fear into Miss Charlotte Winchester. But no, two years at college had refined her into a lady—and a lady never shot someone who was unarmed.

The man returned with a glass of water just as Emily started stirring. Keri thanked him, lifted Emily into a sitting position, and held the cup to her friend's lips.

"Here, drink some of this."

Emily's lashes fluttered as she gazed past Keri to the young man still standing there. "Whatever happened?"

"You fainted," the man said.

"You got walloped in the head with a shuttlecock." Keri stared at the red spot on Emily's forehead. If her friend knew it was there, she'd probably faint dead away again.

"I'm heading back to the dorm to rest," said Corrabelle. "I'll take her with me."

The man and Keri helped Emily stand, then Corrabelle

wrapped an arm around Emily's waist, and the two toddled away.

"I'm Allen Dawson from Alabama." He tipped his hat. "You certainly handled that well. Calm and collected."

"Thank you. I'm Keri Langston from Texas."

"Ah, well, that explains it."

Keri frowned. "Explains what?"

"Why something like your friend's fainting didn't faze you. Being that you are from Texas, I would imagine that you're used to fighting outlaws and Indians."

Keri resisted rolling her eyes. That was all anyone in Georgia thought of Texas. "Why, that's correct. I've killed a dozen outlaws and more than twice that number of Indians."

Mr. Dawson's eyes widened; then he smiled, and his ears and cheeks reddened. "Ah . . . you're joshing me, aren't you?"

Keri just shrugged. These Georgians were an uppity bunch, most turning their nose down at her because she didn't come from a wealthy Georgian family. Just two more weeks, and she'd be returning to Texas. She couldn't wait to get home.

She meandered across the wide lawn, glad to have a day free of her studies. Two men rode up on a near-matched pair of bays. They dismounted, and Keri studied their horses. Riding was one of the things she missed most. Oh, the school had riding classes, but she'd been forced to ride sidesaddle. What a horrible torture that had been.

Someone walked up beside her, and she glance sideways.

"That's Ben Martin and his brother, Arthur." Anna Kate Howard held her purse in her hand and swung her hips, making her skirt swish back and forth. "They're from a wealthy family that lives just outside of town. They're both so charming." Anna Kate blew out an exaggerated sigh.

Keri didn't bother to explain that she was more interested in the men's horses than them.

Someone sped past them, and Anna Kate shrieked. "Why . . . why . . . he stole my handbag. Somebody stop him!"

The lithe youth dodged around the few people who'd been close enough to hear Anna Kate, then tore off across the lawn. Keri's feet moved before her brain did, and she picked up her skirt, running toward the Martin brothers. "I need to borrow your horse. Give me a leg up."

Both men stared at her as if she'd gone loco. She snatched the reins from Arthur's hand, mounted without their help, and kicked the bay into a gallop. She focused on the thief and began closing the distance, but Miss Marks, the headmistress tried to head her off, arms waving. "Miss Langston, what do you think you are doing?"

Keri reined the eager bay to the right and passed her shocked headmistress. The boy had reached the edge of the school's lawn, and if he got to the side streets, she may well lose him. But the horse was fast. She rode past the boy, heading him off, and pulled back on the reins. "You there, give me that purse."

The youth tried to dodge past her, but she reined the horse around, as if cutting a steer out of the herd and pulled in front of him again. "You're not getting away unless you give me that purse. And a crowd is coming this way, so you'd better hurry if you don't want to get caught."

The boy glanced over his shoulders, his gaze frantic when he turned back. He flung the purse toward Keri and took off running the other way. She let him go this time. She hated dismounting and returning the horse, but she didn't want to be called a horse thief. Once on the ground, she picked up Anna Kate's purse and dusted it off.

The Martin brothers were the first to reach her. "Quite excellent riding," Ben said.

Arthur frowned. "She took my horse." He ran his hands down the animal's legs as if checking for injuries.

"I'm sorry for that, but I couldn't allow that thief to steal my friend's purse."

Ben grinned. "No, we can't have that, can we?"

"But she could have caused injury to Charlemagne." Arthur walked the horse around, keeping his eye on the animal.

"Ah, lay off her, Art. Can't you see she's a hero? Uh . . . I mean a heroine." He smiled again and tipped his hat. "Ben Martin at your service. And that was the finest riding I've ever seen by a woman."

"Keri Langston, and thanks."

The crowd parted as someone struggled to the front. "Miss Langston, I need to have a word with you, right this instant."

Anna Kate followed on the headmistress's heels, panting hard. Her blue eyes sparkled. "Did you catch him?"

Keri nodded and handed the beaded bag back to her friend.

"Oh, thank you." Anna Kate hugged her purse to her chest. "All the money I have is in here."

"Then you shouldn't have brought it today." Miss Marks peered at Anna Kate through her thick spectacles, then turned her glare on Keri. "In my office, right now, Miss Langston."

The headmistress grabbed Keri's arm and dragged her through the crowd. Ben Martin tipped his hat to her with a wide grin on his handsome face. Keri ducked her head. She hated being the object of everyone's attention and could almost hear the snooty upper-society girls gossiping about what a backwoods ignoramus she was.

She had never wanted to come here in the first place, but Uncle Will had insisted she needed to learn to be a lady. Just two more weeks, and she could leave.

Two more weeks and she'd be home.

CHAPTER TWO

*W*ill leaned over the side of his bed and retched into the bucket Brooks had left there. Brooks grimaced at the stench in the room, rose from his chair, and hurried to Will's side.

"You're going to have to do more than that if you plan to set a record. I once knew a guy who'd spew a barrel full."

Will rolled onto his side, a tiny grin softening his miserable expression. "Don't plan to set no record."

Brooks patted the old man's shoulder and grabbed the pail, wincing at the foul odor. He hadn't known emptying messy buckets would be one of his duties when he hired on, but he'd grown to like Will, and the old man had no one else to care for him. He dumped the bucket, rinsed it out in the horse trough, then hurried back inside and put it within Will's reach. He stared down at the slight figure on the bed, compassion stirring in his chest. "You need anything? Food? A drink?"

"Water might be good." Will coughed and swiped his sleeve across his mouth.

"You sure you don't want something stronger to ward off the hurt?"

Shaking his head, Will stared up at him with pain-filled eyes. "I quit drinking the hard stuff years ago. Just give me one of my pain pills with that water."

"Let me run out to the well and get some cool water. Be right back." Brooks grabbed a pitcher in the kitchen and hurried out the front door toward the town square. Shoofly looked like many small Texas towns with an open square, sporting a few tall oaks, surrounded by businesses that faced the square. The town spread out several blocks in each direction, but there wasn't anything particularly special about it. The well sat on the southwest corner of the town square. He jogged across the street and dropped the bucket down, making a loud echoing splash, then he hauled it up and filled the pitcher.

He lifted his face to the sun as he carried it back. Most of his life had been spent outside, and he missed that, but he'd promised Will to stay and help him, so he would. He needed to take Jester for a ride next time Will fell asleep, or the poor horse would think he'd been abandoned. He shook his head. Maybe he shouldn't leave Will alone, even while he was sleeping. In just the week he'd been in Shoofly, the man had gone downhill. How many more weeks did he have on this earth?

His steps slowed as he waited for a buckboard to pass. The driver nodded, and Brooks did the same. He hadn't asked Will his age, but he guessed him to be in his early fifties—just about twice Brooks's age. Scrunching his lips to one side, Brooks considered that thought. If he lived to be Will's age, that meant he'd already lived half his life—and what did he have to show for it?

Shaking his head, he hurried back to the house and fixed

Will's glass of water and got a pill from the new bottle he'd just picked up from the apothecary yesterday. Will was sitting on the side of his bed when Brooks returned to his room. He handed the items to him and stood there in case Will needed him. He hated seeing the older man in pain and wished he could do more. "You want me to cancel tonight's poker game?"

Will grimaced as he swallowed the pill. He shook his head. "Since I been goin' to church the past month, I've started feeling it ain't right to be playing cards, but I promised the marshal one last game, so I'd best keep my word."

"You sure you feel up to it?" Brooks pulled his chair over and sat so he wasn't towering over Will.

"I'll feel better after I eat. You can go down to Clyde's and get us both some supper—stew or whatever soup he made—or get you a plate of something you can sink your teeth into."

Brooks nodded. "Just tell me when you're ready, and I'll go."

Will stared at him, his pale-blue eyes taking on a serious cast. "I'm grateful to you, son, for helping me. Don't know what I'd do without you."

That evening, Brooks surveyed the scene at Will's table, feeling odd serving as host to a group of men he barely knew. The marshal, town doctor, and Will sat on the only three chairs in the house, while Brooks and Earl, the barber, sat on upturned crates. A bowl of peanuts sat on the sideboard behind him, along with some sliced fruit bread he'd bought at the bakery. The men hadn't grumbled about drinking lemonade instead of liquor, probably because they already knew Will refused to allow it in his home. Brooks still wasn't sure Will should be out of bed, but it wasn't his choice to make.

He looked down at his stack of coins and paper money. He wasn't all that great of a poker player, but tonight he'd done far better than usual.

Doc Brown tossed his cards down. "I'm out. Lousy hand."

Brooks glanced at Will, the only other player remaining at the table. The older man only had a few coins in front of him. He hated to beat him, but if Will found out he folded when he was holding four queens, he'd be in trouble. He pushed his pile of coins to the center of the table. "I'll see you and raise you."

The marshal whistled through his teeth. "The kid's got both guns loaded. What you gonna do, Will?"

Tapping his few remaining coins, Will stared at his cards, then at the pot. His lips pursed, and his mouth quirked up on one side then he looked at Brooks. "Let's raise the stakes." Will reached into his vest and pulled out a rolled-up parchment. He brushed a hand along the paper and dropped it into the pot. "I'm tossing in the deed to my ranch."

Brooks's heart jolted. He didn't even know Will owned a ranch. "I can't take your ranch."

Earl snickered and nudged Brooks with his elbow. "That's right. You cain't unless you got the winning hand." The doc and marshal chuckled, shoulders bouncing.

Brooks longed to win. If he owned a ranch, maybe he could finally prove to his father that he was responsible. But guilt needled him. He didn't want to win Will's ranch. Was the man even thinking clearly enough to know what he was doing? The thought of the look of pride on his pa's face encouraged him to push the rest of his coins into the pot.

"I'm all in." He flipped his hand over. "I call you with my four ladies."

Will's expression remained sober, and Brooks's heart pounded. In less than a minute, his whole future could change. Will turned over a king, and Brooks's mouth went dry. The old man flipped up another king. Brooks's breathing deepened. When he turned over the third king, the dream of the ranch began to fade. Will glanced around the table, as if purposely drawing out the tension. Brooks leaned forward, willing him to turn over the other card and put him out of his misery. Finally, Will reached for the fourth card. Keeping it facedown, he used it to flip over the fifth—an eight of spades. Then he tossed the last card onto the pile. A two of hearts.

Brooks fell back in his chair, a stupid grin tugging at his lips as all four men stared at him. He owned a ranch—and a pot of money. It looked like his luck had finally changed.

"Well, say something, kid." Earl grinned at him, his gray eyes dancing. "How does it feel to own a ranch?"

Doc Brown's brows lifted, and the marshal sat back with a smirk on his face. Pain narrowed Will's eyes, but he looked pleased with himself. Brooks had a feeling he'd been set up, but how? And why? He grabbed the deed and slid it across the table toward Will. "I can't take your ranch."

"It ain't my ranch anymore. You won it fair and square. 'Sides, what am I going to do with it when my days are numbered?"

"Don't say that." Brooks felt the blood drain from his cheeks. "You might outlive us all."

Will chuckled but shook his head. "Don't think so. All I ask of you is that you take care of Keri."

Brooks nodded. Keri must be a horse or maybe Will's dog. How much trouble would that be? "I can do that."

The smirk remained on the marshal's rugged face. What weren't they telling him about the ranch? How bad could it be?

Will pushed up, then wobbled and dropped back to his seat. "I reckon it's time for me to say good night."

Doc Brown and Marshal Lane hopped up, and each took one of Will's arms and helped him back to his room. Earl stood and stretched, then he reached for the last slice of fruit bread. "That Raven Creek Ranch is a nice little piece of property. I hope you'll take good care of it."

"I'll do my best—just as soon as I'm done here." He winced at how that sounded. He'd stay with Will for as long as he was needed, but he sure would like a peek at the ranch. "How far is it from here?"

Earl pursed his lips, freckled with crumbs, and glanced up toward the ceiling. "Not all that far. Maybe five miles east of town."

Brooks's heart jolted. "That close?" Why, he could ride over some morning if the marshal or doc could stay with Will, but then that wouldn't be right. No, he'd just have to wait. He picked up all the cards and put them in the tin can Will kept them in and then set the glasses on the sink to be washed after the men left. He scooped the coins and dollars into an old cigar box Will had sitting on a shelf and fingered the deed. He longed to open and read it but didn't want to appear too anxious.

"Guess I'll mosey on home. See you around, kid." Earl nodded and slipped out the door.

Brooks followed and leaned against the door jamb. He was twenty-six years old, but these men still referred to him as "kid." He knew they meant it as an odd sort of endearment, but he longed to be seen as an equal. He knew he'd have to prove himself first. Maybe this ranch would be just the opportunity he needed.

⟵ ★ ⟶

Keri stood when her name was called. The pitiful smattering of applause hurt more than she'd thought it would, but what else could she expect? No family or close friends sat in back with a bouquet of flowers and wide smiles to greet her after the ceremony. Even Uncle Will hadn't bothered to come. Not that she'd gotten her hopes up, but some small speck of wishful thinking must have taken residence inside her, otherwise she wouldn't be so disappointed.

"Bless her heart," the woman behind Keri said. "The poor thing must not have any family."

Keri's cheeks burned as she dropped to her seat as the next name was called. Did the woman not know that she could hear her? Evidently the woman hadn't attended finishing school, or she'd never have made such a comment out loud.

The music droned on until the final name was called; then the headmistress recited a speech. Keri despised all the pomp and circumstance surrounding her graduation from finishing school. She suspected Miss Marks had only passed her so that she could be rid of her. She'd just squeaked through by the skin of her teeth, especially after her riding-astride incident. Her fingers were still red from scrubbing floors after classes for a week.

Sighing, Keri stared off to the side, studying the horses waiting for their riders. They were far more interesting than Miss Marks's humdrum speech. Keri didn't belong in this place with these ladies of quality, although most of them were quality only on the outside. She'd never met a more self-centered, narrow-minded group of people in her whole life. Texans were generally friendly folk, as long as you didn't ask questions that were too personal, but not these society ladies. No, a country girl was all she'd ever be and all she wanted to be. Cattle, wind, and dust were her calling, not fancy teas and white dresses. Give her trousers, a western saddle, and Raven Creek over a huge plantation or big, fancy city house any day.

Tomorrow she would leave this hated place. Just one more week until she would be home.

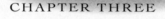

CHAPTER THREE

he evening sun had dipped below the horizon, painting the underbellies of the clouds a brilliant pink. The eastern sky darkened to a deep navy, but there was still enough light for Brooks to see his way. He turned Jester back toward town and let the horse run. After a week of being corralled, both man and beast needed a good gallop.

A bug smacked into Brooks's wind-whipped face, but nothing could ruin this ride. The heat of the day had dimmed slightly with the sun's disappearance, although sweat still beaded on his forehead. He tapped his chest, feeling the deed there, inside his shirt. He wasn't about to let the treasured paper out of sight. Four thousand acres. He shook his head, trying to grasp hold of the idea that he owned a ranch far bigger than his pa's. "Yehah!"

Hunkering down, he galloped Jester down the road under the light of a three-quarter moon. He owned a ranch. A wide grin pulled at his lips. Now all he had to decide was whether to raise cattle, Morgan horses like most of his family did, or both.

Half an hour later, with Jester brushed and bedded down, Brooks trotted up the steps to Will's house and tiptoed inside. He blinked at the darkness. Hadn't he left a lantern lit in case Will had gotten up? He crossed the parlor to the kitchen, and his knee smacked into something hard, ratcheting pain up his leg. Brooks sucked in a sharp breath and pawed his hand in the air until he found the offending item—a chair turned sideways. His heart bucked. Had Will fallen? "Will? You all right?"

He flipped the chair onto its legs, and fumbled for the tin can on the sideboard that held the matches. Why hadn't Will responded?

The match flamed to life, and Brooks froze as he stared at the disarray. The place looked as if a tornado had blown through. His gaze snapped to Will's room, concern pushing his feet forward. His racing heart settled when he saw his friend lying on his side on his bed, but it set off at a gallop again at the disorder of the room. Someone had pulled the few clothes and items Will owned out of the dresser drawers and dumped them on the floor. Will's pillow and blankets lay in a heap beside his bed. Brooks ran his hand across his cheek. Not a soul in town that he knew of would steal from Will. Everybody liked him.

Alarming apprehension tightened the skin on his cheeks. Why hadn't the noise of the intruders awakened Will? He turned back to his friend and set the lantern on the round table beside the bed. The new bottle of pills the doctor had given Will lay on its side—empty. Brooks sucked in a sharp breath. Surely Will hadn't taken them all.

He reached out his hand, pulled it back, then touched Will's shoulder. Brooks swallowed hard, dread coursing through him like a flash flood. He rolled Will over, and the man flopped limp as a chicken with a wrenched neck. Foam ran down one corner of his mouth, and his pale eyes gazed toward the ceiling, but Brooks knew they'd never see again. He pulled down Will's eyelids, as his own closed against the stinging pain. He'd grown to love the kind old man in the short time he'd known him, and he felt his loss more deeply than he would have imagined.

But something didn't fit. Will had been dying and in pain, no doubt about that, but he couldn't imagine him taking his own life. In fact, he'd been talking a lot about God and how he'd changed his life and looked forward to heaven. Could a man who committed suicide go to heaven?

Brooks backed away from the bed. He had to get the doc— no, too late for that. He needed to get the marshal and show him the damage. He needed to get out of there and catch his breath.

He hurried into the parlor and headed for the door, tears burning his eyes, but he paused and turned back to the sideboard. The cigar box that contained almost all of his money was gone.

——— ★ ———

Brooks stood beside Will's grave, holding his hat in his hands. He missed him. Missed his teasing. His bossiness. His friendship.

A man he'd never met tossed shovelfuls of dirt on top of the wooden casket the undertaker had made. Brooks had paid his last penny to have the box made, but he didn't regret his action. He only wished he'd still had his poker winnings so he could have bought Will a fancier coffin with carvings on it and fabric inside.

A heavy hand clamped onto his shoulder, pulling his gaze away from the morbid scene. The marshal shook Brooks.

"C'mon. Folks have headed home. No need to stand and watch this."

Brooks nodded, cast a final glance at the grave, and fell into step with the marshal. He'd never been close to anyone who died and it left him numb and unsettled. Will had talked about heaven, and so had Brooks's folks when he was younger, but was there really anything on the other side of the grave?

The marshal stopped and turned toward Brooks. "I've talked to Doc Brown, and he assured me Will would never take his own life."

"I don't think he would either. So, where does that leave us?"

"I have my suspicions as to what happened, but I don't have any proof yet."

Brooks skidded to a stop, relieved to know he wasn't the only person who thought Will's death was suspicious. "You think someone murdered him?"

"That would be my guess." Marshal Lane nodded. His moustache twitched then hiked up on one side as he quirked his lips. "And I have a good idea who probably did the deed."

"Who?" Brooks's hand fell to his hip, where his gun usually rested, but out of consideration for Will, he'd left it at the cabin this morning.

The marshal narrowed his eyes. "You ain't doing nothin', kid."

Brooks stiffened. "I'm not a kid. Will was my friend, and I'll do whatever is needed to capture the man who killed him."

Marshal Lane spread his feet like Brooks imagined him doing in a gunfight. "No, you won't. You'll ride out to Raven Creek Ranch and start a new part of your life. Leave the justice getting to me."

The marshal's order left a foul taste in Brooks's mouth, as if he'd bitten down on something rancid. He wanted to find the man—or men—responsible for snuffing out Will's life, but he had the sense to know that justice was best left for the lawman. "I'll head out in a couple of days. I promised Will that I'd pack up his things and take them back to Raven Creek with me and that I'd leave the place clean."

The marshal nodded. "Just don't get any funny ideas on tracking down the killer."

Brooks winced. Murderer. Killer. How had the like found his way into a sleepy little town like Shoofly?

A week later, Brooks rode Jester down the street headed out of town. He nodded to Marshal Lane as he passed the man. Though Brooks had questioned a number of people, no one had admitted to knowing anything about Will's death. He blew out a sigh. He'd hoped to find Will's killer, but it looked like the man would go free. What had the killer hoped to accomplish by murdering Will? Maybe it had just been a drifter passing through, looking for food and money.

He shook his head. He'd probably never know.

The bright September sun cast its rays across the land, already driving away the coolness of the morning. Excitement bubbled up in Brooks's gut as he nudged Jester into a trot. With the marshal's detailed instructions to Raven Creek Ranch, he should arrive at his new home in a few hours. What would his pa say if he knew Brooks owned a ranch?

The smoke of an arriving train left a trail of black intruding on the pretty day. How ironic that folks would be pulling into Shoofly at the exact same time he was leaving.

Clicking out of the side of his mouth, he tapped his heels against Jester's side, and the horse lunged forward, eager to run. Brooks's lips split into a wide grin as he considered how things had changed since he'd arrived in town that stormy day. Tonight he'd sleep in his own house on his own land.

Yes sirree, his luck was changing.

Keri disembarked the train, a tingly excitement spiraling all the way through her, down to her toes. She was finally back in Texas. Almost home.

She scanned the depot in search of Uncle Will. She hoped he'd received the telegram she'd sent from the depot in Macon informing him of her impending arrival.

When she didn't spot him, disappointment threatened to pull her down, but she refused to allow it purchase. Nothing could douse her delight at being away from finishing school and those snippy, snooty young women who were supposed to be the cream of society's crop. She shuddered at the thought of Charlotte Winchester and her cronies being the next generation of Southern women.

She made her way to the front of the depot and surveyed the town, hoping to see Uncle Will striding toward her. His letters had come less often the past few months, and his handwriting was shakier. She had no idea how old her uncle was, but he hardly seemed so old that it would affect his writing. Maybe he'd injured his hand branding cattle or trying to break a green mustang or one of a dozen other ways.

Shoofly had more than doubled in the two years she'd been gone, but it was still tiny compared to Macon, Jackson, Shreveport, and most of the other southern towns the train had taken her through.

She turned her head toward the pungent odor of cattle. Most women would be repulsed by the stink, but it reminded her of home. Pens to her right held bawling cattle, ready to head to the slaughter houses. A more pleasant scent—that of pies baking—pulled her back toward town and made her stomach rumble. The quick breakfast she'd had at the small hotel she'd overnighted in had ceased to satisfy her hours ago. The café across the street and two doors down drew her attention. With a plan of action, she spun around and strode over to the ticket agent, who stood behind a barred window.

"Can I help you, miss?" His overly large, blue-gray eyes peered out from a long, narrow face.

"My name is Keri Langston. I'm Will Langston's niece. I was hoping he'd be here to pick me up, but he must have been delayed."

With each sentence she spoke, the man's eyes grew wider. He swallowed hard, bouncing the lump of his Adam's apple. "I . . . uh . . ."

Keri waved her hand. "Just tell him when he arrives that I've gone over to Lucy's Café to eat lunch."

"But—"

Keri spun on her heel. Surely the man wouldn't mind passing on a message. If Uncle Will arrived and didn't find her, he would ask about her train, and hopefully, the clerk would pass on her message.

Quick steps brought her to the café, and she entered, taking a window seat so she could keep a watch-out for her uncle. Several buggies and tied horses lined Main Street, awaiting their owners. Two women strolled down the boardwalk dressed in calicos instead of the frillier day dresses with those ridiculous leg-o'-mutton sleeves that restricted one's movement. Keri shook her head at the loco things women went through for the sake of "beauty." She'd already shed her corset and couldn't wait to get home and don her trousers. Her poor uncle would probably have a case of apoplexy and say he had wasted his money sending her to that fancy school.

He would be right.

"Can I help you, miss?"

A young girl poured water into a glass in front of Keri, who asked, "What's your special of the day?"

"Beef pot pie or chicken and noodles. Miss Lucy likes to give folks a choice, but it's a good thing you got here before the noon rush, 'cause we tend to sell out, especially our pies."

"I'll take the chicken and noodles." She'd never mastered the art of making noodles and ate them whenever she had the opportunity. "And a cup of hot coffee." If she never drank another cup of tea, she'd be as happy as a cow in a clover patch. "So, is Miss Lucy here?"

The girl nodded. "In back, but she's mighty busy gettin' ready for the lunch crowd. If'n you know her, maybe you could poke your head in back and say howdy once you're done eatin'."

Keri nodded. "I'll do that."

She gazed around the room, spying guests at only two other tables. A man and woman sat in the corner, leaning across the table and talking softly. A young couple in love, she guessed. She sighed. Her uncle had hoped that sending her away to finishing school would help her to become a refined lady—something an old bachelor couldn't teach her—and help her land a decent husband, the last thing she wanted. Would Uncle Will be disappointed? Truly?

Hanging her head to avoid eye contact with the pair of cowboys across the room, she drew her finger across the condensation on her water glass. All she'd thought about was getting home and getting back to normal, but maybe she should take things more slowly.

Uncle Will owned a decent-sized spread of land, but it paled in comparison to many Texas ranches. Money had always been a hard commodity to come by, which was why she'd taken to wearing cast-off pants from the ranch hands. Uncle Will knew how to mend them, but he didn't know about sewing dresses, and the few times he'd bought her dresses, they'd hung on a peg in her room, adding color but not much more. She hated dresses, and many times she had wished she'd been born a boy. If she had, would her mother have found her more useful and kept her instead of getting rid of her, first chance she got?

A tantalizing scent moved her way, making her stomach complain with eager anticipation. The girl set a large bowl with fat chunks of chicken and wide noodles in a creamy yellow broth. Beside the bowl, the girl set a plate with two slices of bread. "Enjoy your meal." She smiled and spun away.

Twenty minutes later, with her hunger sated, Keri stood, eager to see a familiar face. Every time she and Uncle Will came to town, they would eat at Miss Lucy's. Keri's only disappointment in the meal had been the fact that she'd been too full to eat a slice of pie. With the café filling up, she was eager to head back to the depot and see if Uncle Will had come by yet. If not, she'd have to assume he never received her telegram, and she'd rent a horse and ride home. They could come back for her trunk—not that there was much in it that would be useful on the ranch.

She ducked behind the curtain, and the delicious scents that had teased her senses earlier failed to affect her now that her stomach was full. Miss Lucy stood with her back to her, cutting generous slices of pot pie. Dirty bowls sat next to the sink awaiting washing, while nearly a dozen pies cooled in the security of the pie safe. Outside the back door, Keri could see the girl pumping water into a bucket.

Miss Lucy turned, wielding her sticky spatula like a weapon, and sucked in an audible breath. Curly red hair stuck out in all directions, and the normally pale skin on Miss Lucy's face was bright red. Her green eyes assessed Keri. "Can I help you?"

For the first time since returning to Shoofly, Keri smiled. "Have I changed so much that you don't recognize me?"

The woman narrowed her gaze and studied Keri, then her somber expression broke into a cheerful smile. "Not little Keri Langston? Why you've grown half a foot. And don't you look like a lady!"

Miss Lucy's smile dimmed, sucking away some of Keri's delight. Was something wrong?

The cook crossed the room and wrapped her arms around Keri, giving her the welcome-home embrace she'd longed for. She hugged Miss Lucy back, tears stinging her eyes.

"I'm so sorry, Keri. Such a sad homecoming."

Stiffening, Keri stepped back and peered up. "Sorry about what?"

Miss Lucy's eyes widened. "You mean you don't know?"

Keri shook her head, but she was beginning to wonder if the stifling heat of the small kitchen hadn't gotten to the cook. "Know about what? I just got back less than half an hour ago. Came here to eat while I waited for Uncle Will. What's happened?"

Chapped hands cupped her cheeks. Miss Lucy's eyebrows drew together, her eyes filled with pain. All manner of thoughts raced through Keri's mind.

"I'm so sorry to have to tell you, but your uncle passed away a week ago."

CHAPTER FOUR

rooks couldn't keep from smiling, even when a beetle flew into his mouth. He spat out the critter and kept grinning. The farther north he rode, the happier he grew. Pecan, hickory, and oak trees stretched out their gnarly arms, offering a bit of shade from the heat of the sun. Cattle would thrive on the knee-high grasslands. Butterflies flitted from one wildflower to another. Yes sirree, the land was close to perfect.

Jester bobbed his head up, flicked his ears forward, and nickered. Brooks shook off his lollygagging and studied the two men riding toward him. Both were big and brawny, putting him in mind of a team of oxen. They were dressed like most ranch hands, and sat atop a pair of horses that made his gelding look small—which he wasn't.

Trouble came in pairs, his ma had said, and this matched set had trouble written all over them.

Brooks grinned and tipped his hat, figuring to disarm them with friendliness. "Howdy, neighbors."

The burly duo glanced at each other, and one man nodded. The man on the right pulled his rifle from the scabbard and laid it across his lap. Brooks figured they were just as wary of him as he was of them.

"Who are you, stranger?"

Brooks shifted in his saddle so that he could reach his gun faster, if needed. "I'm the new owner of Raven Creek Ranch, Brooks Morgan. Who are you?"

The strangers eyed each other again, so fast that Brooks would have missed it if he'd blinked. A grin remained plastered on his face, but keeping it there as his concern mounted was about as hard as riding a mustang bareback.

The man on the right dismounted. Brooks watched, angling Jester a bit to the right so that he could keep his gun hand out of view. A loud click pulled his gaze back to the man on the horse—and the gun that was pointed straight at him. His gut twisted, and his smile sagged. "I don't have any money, so robbing me's a waste of time."

"We didn't come here to rob nobody." The man on the ground waved his pistol at Brooks. "Get down."

Swallowing back his apprehension, Brooks dismounted. His mind raced, searching for a way out of whatever mess it was he'd just stepped in.

The Goliath on the ground reached inside his vest and pulled out a paper, which he shoved at Brooks. "Sign that."

Curious, he unfolded the paper, his heart dropping to his boot tips as he read the bill of sale assigning ownership of Raven Creek Ranch to one Saul Dengler. He'd heard of the man back in Shoofly. Dengler was one of the biggest landowners in these parts—and now Brooks knew why. He wadded up the paper and tossed it on the ground. "I'm not signing that."

Goliath backhanded him, knocking him into Jester and sending a sharp pain ratcheting through his jaw. The man picked up the paper, smoothed it out, and shoved it back in Brooks's face. "Sign it or die."

←— ★ —→

Keri patted Bob's neck and nudged the gelding into a gallop. She had been quite surprised to find her uncle's horse still stabled at the livery when she'd gone to rent one to ride home. Riding him again was like having a little piece of home—something familiar.

She scanned the area, watching for signs of things that didn't belong. She may have been gone two years, but she hadn't forgotten how hard this land could be and how one needed to stay alert—and yet she loved it.

If someone twisted her arm, she might even admit she loved her uncle. For so many years she'd cultivated her anger toward Uncle Will, all because he'd taken her away from her mother and brought her to the middle of nowhere, but she'd fallen in love with the ruggedness of Texas almost from the start. Still, it had taken a long time for her to get over being upset at her uncle. Too long, in fact.

And now she'd lost him too. She wished she had one more chance to see him—to tell him she'd missed him. He'd been so good to her—a gentle, patient teacher—even though she'd been a brat, especially at first. She'd cried for weeks and lambasted him for taking her from her mother.

All she could remember about Grace Langston was her long, beautiful blonde hair and shiny dresses. She remembered the house with all the rooms and other women who lived there. Daytime was a joy, but Keri hated the night. Nighttime meant she was locked in her room and had to be quiet so the monsters wouldn't find her. She'd hated the evenings when the monsters intruded with their deep voices and raucous laughter, sometimes causing the women to scream or cry. Sometimes she'd wake up in the mornings to find one of the pretty ladies had been beaten.

Keri shuddered. She hadn't thought of that place in years, so why now?

She ought to be happy. Yes, her uncle was gone, and she would miss him, but she'd gained a ranch. Raven Creek was now hers, and she had so many ideas to pursue and dreams she wanted to accomplish. She would raise cattle, but training horses was what she loved most. If only the ranch hands— Nate and Jess—were still there, they would surely help her. They had been her best friends, especially Nate, but things wouldn't be the same without Uncle Will. Why hadn't she realized sooner how much she'd grown to care for him ? Had her anger over his sending her away pushed aside all loving thoughts of the man who'd raised her and given her a home?

She shook her head. Yes, she would miss her uncle, but she couldn't dwell on his passing. Nothing could bring him back. She had to focus on the future. It's what he'd want her to do. She just hoped Nate and Jess wouldn't mind taking orders from a woman. Some cowboys were funny about that.

In just a half hour, she could shed her fancy dress, don her pants, and get to work making Raven Creek Ranch one of Texas's finest. She rode through a grove of trees and heard a horse's whinny. Reining Bob to a stop, she listened. The horse she heard could be wild, but if not, that meant the animal most likely had a rider, and a rider could mean trouble. She reached for the rifle she'd borrowed from Marshal Lane and waited.

"Wrong choice, mister."

Keri stiffened at the harsh tone of the stranger's voice.

"String 'im up, Harley."

Keri closed her eyes. She didn't want trouble on her first day home, but a lynching generally meant the wrong person was going to die. Any decent man would take a troublemaker or outlaw to town for the marshal to deal with.

She checked the rifle, making sure it was loaded. She'd only have two shots, so she'd have to make the best of them.

Bob shifted and turned to his right as if wanting to avoid the goings on. Maybe she should just ride off the trail and skirt around the strangers. She didn't want trouble with any of the area ranchers. She nudged Bob back the way she'd come. A few hundred yards back was a side trail she could take. Longer, but probably safer. Definitely the smart thing to do.

———— ★ ————

The noose tightened around Brooks's neck, pinching his skin. He fought to suck in a breath of air, but the rope squashed against his throat. His pulse soared as his mind raced, searching for a way of escape. This couldn't be the end—not when his future had looked so promising just a few moments earlier.

The strangers had tied his hands and lifted him back onto Jester, but not until after he'd put up a good fight. His jaw and fists ached from his effort.

He thought of his parents. They would never know what happened to him. Maybe they already thought of him as dead since he'd been gone so long. He ducked his head, wishing he'd been a better son. Wishing he hadn't ridden off in a tirade of rebellion. Wishing he could go back and do things over— do things differently.

He closed his eyes as a bead of sweat dribbled down his temple, but he refused to die like a coward with his eyes shut. Forcing them open again, he stared at the two vigilantes.

He glanced skyward. *God, this can't be the end. I know I haven't followed Your word and have broken many of Your commandments, but if You'll help me, I promise to do better. Please, help me.*

Goliath muttered something to his crony then swatted his hand in the air. Brooks's restless horse snorted and took a step backwards, loosening the rope just enough that he could gasp in a breath. Burning pain encircled his neck from the bite of the rope, and his shoulders throbbed from his hands being pulled so tightly behind him.

One too many times he'd been in the wrong place at the wrong time.

"Got any last words, mister?" Goliath tugged up on his britches, then pulled down his vest.

"This is wrong," he rasped. "Didn't do nothing."

Pine needles from the branch above—the one the other end of the rope was tied to—rained down on him, tingeing the air with a sweet pine scent. Would that be the last thing he smelled?

"I'll give ya one last chance to sign that bill of sale and live, mister. One way or another, Mr. Dengler will have Raven Creek."

At the sound of hooves on the dirt road, Brooks glanced up to see a pretty woman clad in a fancy dress, riding astride like a cowboy. She pulled her horse to a quick stop and jerked a rifle from the scabbard, aiming it toward Dengler's men. "What's going on here?"

Goliath stepped forward, hands lifted in a placating manner. "Now you just turn yourself around and forget what you saw here, ma'am."

She didn't utter a sound. She glanced at Brooks then backed the horse around the bend. He breathed a sigh of relief, thankful the men hadn't harmed her and grateful she wouldn't witness his demise.

No, not demise—death. He wasn't ready to meet his Maker—not when he had unfinished business that he needed to deal with and dreams of a ranch that would never be his now, but he closed his eyes with the woman's lovely face etched on his mind. Not an altogether awful way to die.

"All right. Let's finish this. Got supper waitin'."

Brooks's eyes snapped open. He licked his lips, trying to work up enough spit to tell them to wait. What use was owning a ranch if he was dead? "Wait," the word came out as a limp whisper.

Peering out the corner of his eye, Brooks saw Goliath lift his hand, preparing to slap Jester on the rear. Brooks tried not to move and prayed Jester wouldn't either.

"Whoa, boy," he squeaked out.

The other man's saddle creaked as he mounted and rode off, leaving only Goliath.

Forgive me, God, for all the dumb things I did and how I wasted my life.

"Let him go." Brooks heard the feminine voice a split second after he heard a rifle cock. The woman had returned!

Brooks wanted to cheer and at the same time tell her to ride for the hills.

"Untie him." The woman said in a cool, no-nonsense voice.

"He rustled my cattle and he's gonna pay," Goliath said, raising his chin in the air.

"No!" Brooks rasped.

"I doubt that," the woman said, "but even if it is true, you need to take him to the marshal and not handle things on your own. Let him down."

"Can't do that."

"Can't or won't?"

"He's a thief." Goliath eased a step closer to her.

Brooks tried to shake his head, but the taut rope held it immobile.

The woman blasted a shot from her rifle, exploding the dirt between the toes of Goliath's dusty boots. He leaped backwards, swirling his arms like a chicken with clipped wings, as he tried to regain his balance. Brooks's eyes widened, and his heart skipped a beat when his horse took half a step sideways. The rope pulled his neck up and to the side, tightening. His pulse galloped.

Was that shot deliberate or just plain lucky?

"Stay where you are, or the next shot won't miss," she hollered. "Untie that man. Now!"

Goliath gave Brooks a look that turned his blood cold. He knew the woman was about to watch him die. Brooks's heart ricocheted inside his chest. He fought to draw what he knew was his final breath.

"He—yah!" Goliath slapped Jester on the rear. The horse jumped but didn't break into a run. The noose gagged Brook's throat, choking off all hope of his gaining a breath. A shot rang out. The rope suddenly loosened and a short stub of it fell across Brook's chest and slapped Jester's shoulder. The horse took off in a quick trot. Brooks held on with his legs and fought the rope, holding his hands captive as he gazed over his shoulder at the woman. If she ran out of ammunition, she would need his help.

Brooks turned back around. "Whoa, boy—"

His forehead collided with a tree limb. The jolt knocked him backwards out of the saddle and he rolled over Jester's rump. His back smacked hard against the earth, and what little breath he'd managed to suck in gushed out. With his arms still tied behind him, they felt as if they'd been yanked from his shoulder sockets. Momentum jerked his head back, and it whacked something hard.

Pain ricocheted through his body like bouncing bullets. Church bells rang, and the canopy of leaves overhead blurred from green to black.

CHAPTER FIVE

*K*eri cocked the rifle again and aimed it at the big man. She hoped that the stranger had managed to get his horse stopped and his hands untied, but he was on his own now. At least he was still alive. The big man in front of her looked a bit dumbfounded as he stared up at the frayed end of the rope.

"What's your name, mister?"

He slid his gaze back toward her, his eyes narrowing. "Theo Kress."

"Get on your horse, Mr. Kress, and head home."

The man no longer doubted her seriousness or skill with the rifle, because he mounted up without arguing. The horse turned away as the man settled in the saddle, but Keri kept alert, watching his gun hand for movement. He yanked the reins to the left, pulling the horse back around. "Mr. Dengler ain't gonna appreciate your interference, Miss—" He squinted. "What'd you say your name was?"

"I didn't."

"No matter. We'll find out soon enough. You messed with the wrong people."

The man kicked his mount hard in the side, and the poor beast lumbered to a trot. Once the man was out of sight, Keri exhaled. She made a smooching sound, and Bob started walking. Keeping her eyes trained on where Mr. Kress had disappeared, she kept the rifle tucked under one arm and reined Bob toward home.

Should she try to locate that man who'd nearly been hanged? If he was a thief, she certainly didn't want to be alone with him out on the prairie, so she nudged Bob's sides and galloped for home.

She blew out a breath. Her homecoming sure hadn't turned out as she'd expected it to.

———— ★ ————

Birds sang. Church bells rang. A pretty, rifle-toting city woman on a horse.

What a weird nightmare.

No, not a nightmare.

Nightmares didn't cause pain.

And every part of Brooks hurt—except for his toes.

He lay on the ground and tried to catch his breath as he waited for his vision to clear. The rope still entangled his neck, making it hard to inhale a full breath of air. His shoulders ached, as did his head and a place where his hands pressed into his lower back.

A few minutes later, he wrestled to a sitting position and surveyed his surroundings. Jester grazed nearby, and all was quiet. Grass swished on the warm breeze, and birds chirped in the trees overhead. If not for the buzzing in his head and pain spiraling through his body, he would have thought he dreamed the hanging.

But that rope is still around my neck—and hands.
Definitely not a dream.
But at least I'm alive.

A glimmer on his left caught his eye. His knife lay a few feet away, most likely shaken loose when he tumbled over Jester's rump. He backed up to the weapon and managed to grasp hold of its handle. Fifteen minutes later, his hands broke free.

Brooks pulled his arms forward and rolled his shoulders, working out the kinks. He loosened the rope around his neck, yanked it off, and threw it over a bush. Sweet, life-sustaining air flowed into his lungs. He'd been close to dying a time or two, but never that close.

It had rattled him.

He gazed up through the trees to the sky overhead. Had God sent that woman to rescue him? What were the odds of someone riding up just as he was about to die—and shooting him free? They had to be enormous.

Then factor in that the shooter was a woman.

Nigh on impossible, if you ask me. And he was the only one around to ask, unless you counted Jester.

He stood, dusted off his pants, then reached up and squeezed his aching forehead. His hand came away red. He glanced up at the branch that had knocked him senseless and wished for a saw to cut it off.

From the look of the sun, he hadn't been passed out for too long. He shouldn't have trouble finding Raven Creek before dark—if he didn't fall off his horse again. At least that sharp-shooting woman hadn't witnessed that humbling event.

He mounted Jester and found his way back to the road. The woman and the varmints bent on taking his life and stealing his ranch were nowhere to be seen, but the tree was still there with the other half of the rope still dangling from it. He swallowed hard, his throat hurting where it had been squashed by that rope.

In a matter of minutes, he'd gone from happily riding toward his new home to nearly hanging to death and then being rescued and then almost being scalped by a tree. How could life change so fast?

He tried to work up a smile—to find that old part of himself—but it had been lost in the day's events. He wasn't the same man who'd left Shoofly this morning. He was a man who'd made a promise to God.

A man who had no idea how to fulfill such a pledge.

He turned his horse toward Raven Creek. Maybe God would show him what he needed to do.

⟵ ★ ⟶

Keri tugged off the last of the hated petticoats and tossed it in the growing pile on her bed. She pulled her trousers from the chest of drawers and hugged them. "You don't know how much I've missed you."

She wriggled and twisted, finally getting them up. Either she had grown during the past two years or she had gotten fat from sitting all day instead of working. Probably the latter.

She tugged on some socks and snagged her boots from the wardrobe, carrying them into the parlor so she could polish them. The room looked smaller and dingier than she remembered. Without Uncle Will lumbering around, it was lonely, too.

The rosewood sofa must be over twenty years old. It was in the house when Uncle Will bought it. The edge of the fabric had started fraying. One of the work hands must have dusted, because only the corners of the end tables had been swiped clean. A stack of wood lay ready in the fireplace, although it would be months before she'd need a fire for keeping warm. A rocker rested near the front window with a low table under it. Sparse is how Miss Marks would describe it. Sparse and shabby.

But it was home. Keri plopped down, so glad to not have anyone else telling her what to do. She owned Raven Creek now, and that thought brought a grin to her face. But her smile faded as she glanced at the closed door to her uncle's room. She wished he were still here, but wishing wouldn't bring him back. One day soon, she needed to go through his things and see if Nate or Jess could use any of his clothes, but today wasn't that day.

She quickly polished her boots and put them on. In the kitchen, she surveyed the food stocks. Someone had recently stacked a supply of canned goods on a shelf and left some potatoes by the back door. At least she'd learned to cook passably at that awful school, though it wasn't one of her favorite tasks. They wouldn't starve, but she doubted anybody would be begging for seconds.

Outside, she unhitched Bob and led him to the barn. Uncle Will had always taught her to tend to her horse before herself, but she hadn't wanted to soil her dress any more than she had already—not that she planned to wear it often. After feeding and brushing Bob, she took the saddle to the tack room. Nate's and Jess's saddles were gone, confirming her thoughts that they must be out on the range, tending the stock.

Uncle Will hadn't mentioned either man lately in his few letters, so she hoped they were both still around. She couldn't imagine running this place without their help. Did they know of his death? Why hadn't they come to pick her up at the depot?

She found a dung fork and shoved it under a pile of soiled hay in one of the stalls, then dumped the mess in the handcart. At least Nate and Jess wouldn't have to clean out the stalls before putting up their horses tonight. They must have headed out early to have not done the task this morning.

She paused. What if they had gone into town to fetch her? Wouldn't she have passed them on the road?

Hurrying around the far side of the barn, her pulse slowed when she saw the buggy. They wouldn't have gone to pick her up and not taken it. She'd just have to wait until they returned to find out.

She ambled back around the front of the barn, noticing the silence. It had never bothered her before, but after being surrounded by squealing, giggling girls-wanting-to-be-women for so long, the quiet pressed in on her. She lifted her hand to her throat and stared down the road. A small cloud of dust lifted in the distance. She set the dung fork aside and hurried back to the house for her rifle. If visitors were coming, they wouldn't find her unarmed and unprepared.

Inside, she hastily curled up her braid and set her hat on her head, covering her long tresses. She grabbed her rifle. It was just as well that any visitor didn't know she was a woman until she knew their purpose in being here.

Out on the porch, she waited, with her rifle resting lightly across her arms. Normally, she wouldn't be so tense, but the events of the day had worn on her.

It wasn't every day she returned home to discover the man who'd raised her had died.

———— ★ ————

Excitement swirled in Brooks's gut. Ten minutes ago he'd passed the entrance to Raven Creek Ranch, and as he rounded the corner, he caught his first glimpse of his new home. There it was. Not exactly what he had expected, but then he could hardly complain, since it hadn't cost him any money. The small, two-story house was sorely in need of painting and some patching, but it was far better than most places he'd stayed the past decade.

As he drew near, he noticed a man leaning against a porch post, with a rifle resting in his arms. Probably either Nate or Jess, the work hands Will had told him about, though he'd envisioned them both as larger men. He didn't blame the man one iota for being cautious, not after what he'd just experienced. In fact, he was downright grateful to the man for protecting the property. They'd get along just fine.

He flashed a grin and nodded. "Howdy."

"Who are you and what do you want?" The voice was far higher pitched than he'd expected. Was Jess still a kid? He knew Nate wasn't, from what Will had said.

He dismounted, keeping his smile in place. "The name's Brooks Morgan."

The boy shrugged. "Never heard of you." He was awful short and on the scrawny side.

Brooks took a few steps toward him, and the youth shifted the rifle toward him.

"That's far enough. If you're looking for Will, he's not here."

Halting, Brooks struggled to understand. Had they not heard about Will's death? Hadn't Marshal Lane mentioned riding out here and explaining things? Maybe the marshal had gotten delayed because of his job, but then as far as he could remember, no one had caused a ruckus in town lately.

Plastering his grin back on, Brooks took a step forward. The boy kept his head down so that his face was shadowed. The guy was rather sissified in the way he moved. Maybe he could teach the kid to act in a more manly way once they got to know each other. Brooks reached for the deed tucked safely in his vest pocket.

The rifle swerved toward him again. "I told you not to move. What do you want?"

Brooks was glad he already had hold of the parchment. He

tugged it out, keeping his other hand raised in the air. "Hang on. I've got something to show you."

"What is it?"

"The deed to this ranch. I'm the new owner."

The rifle lowered as the boy stumbled back a few steps. Evidently the marshal hadn't been by.

"That's a lie." Up came the rifle again. "You get back on your horse and get out of here, mister."

Brooks shook his head. "Can't do it. Marshal Lane was supposed to have come by and told y'all what happened. I won this ranch fair and square in a poker game with Will."

"You're lying." The boy's pitch rose. He fired his rifle at Brooks, chewing up the ground in front of him. Both he and Jester jumped.

"Hey! Watch it."

"Get out while you still can. You're nothing but a low-down lying thief. I bet you work for Saul Dengler, don't you?"

"No—"

"You tell him Raven Creek Ranch isn't for sale."

"You're darn right it isn't, because I own it."

The boy opened his mouth to say something but turned toward two men riding into the yard, guns drawn. "What's going on here?" asked the older man.

"Nate!"

"Missy?" The man's thick brows dipped together as he slid from his saddle.

Missy? Brooks eyed the youth as he hopped off the porch and hurried toward the man and fell into his arms. His mouth went dry as the youth—or rather—young woman hugged Nate back. It must have been that blow to his head or the lack of oxygen that made him miss the woman's narrow waist and shapely hips. Who was she? And why was she wearing men's pants?

She pushed back from Nate and waved a hand in Brooks's direction. "This man claims he's the new owner of Raven Creek. Would you please explain that he's wrong?"

Nate glanced up at the same time the other man, still seated on his roan horse, did. "You Morgan?" Nate asked.

Brooks gave a curt nod. "Yep."

Nate nodded back, his expression less than friendly. Brooks couldn't blame him for being wary, considering how the doc thought Will's death suspicious and how he'd won the ranch from him.

"Sorry, Missy. What the man says is true."

The young woman glared up at him. "It *can't* be true. This is my ranch now."

She raced past him, up the stairs of the house, and slammed the door.

"Whew!" Brooks grinned. "And just who was that whirlwind?"

"Keri," Nate said, scowling. "Keri Langston. Will's niece."

Keri? Why was that name familiar? Will's niece? Suddenly, the blood drained from Brooks's face for the second time that day. Keri was the name of the critter he'd promised Will that he'd take care of. A dog—or horse. Only she wasn't a critter, but a young woman. A pretty, young woman who claimed his ranch as her own.

Why did he suddenly get the feeling that he'd been set up?

CHAPTER SIX

*K*eri yanked off her hat and flung it across the room, and her braid uncurled down her back. She stomped across the parlor floor, more emotions than she could number roiling through her like swollen creek water after a storm. Tears scorched her eyes, and her throat ached. *How could Uncle Will have done this to her? He'd always promised the ranch would be hers. Why would he have risked her home on a card game?*

She grabbed a pillow off the sofa and hurled it against the wall. It bounced off with a benign thud and fell to the floor in an unsatisfying thump.

All the loving thoughts she'd had for her uncle melted under the fire of her pain and feelings of betrayal. He'd promised her many times that Raven Creek would be hers. And it was hers. She wouldn't give it up without a fight.

She marched upstairs to her bedroom and hauled her holster and gun from the trunk she'd stored them in before leaving for Georgia. She cleaned the gun, loaded it, and strapped on the holster. She snatched up her rifle and stomped down the stairs and back outside.

Good. That low-down coyote must have ridden back to town. She marched out to the barn to talk to Nate. Maybe he'd misunderstood Marshal Lane. That just had to be the case. She had nowhere else to go and no money to live on. And she wasn't leaving her home.

At the sound of voices, she slowed her pace. He was in the barn.

"Nice to meet you both. I hope you'll stay on and help me make a go of this place."

"What about Keri?" Nate asked.

Keri lifted her chin. Good ol' Nate would watch out for her. She peered through a crack in the barn wall.

The handsome stranger pushed his hat up on his forehead and rubbed the back of his neck. "Honestly, when Will asked me to watch out for Keri, I thought she was a dog."

Keri gasped. A dog? For the love of . . . And what did he mean Will asked him to watch out for her? She didn't need some lowlife gambler caring for her.

Nate and Jess threw their heads back and roared. Laughter filled the barn, making Keri's ire grow. She shoved aside the door and stomped in, waving her rifle. "What's going on in here? Don't you have any work to do?"

Silence reigned, but she could see her work hands trying to regain their composure—the Benedict Arnolds. Nate swiped his finger across one eye. Keri turned her glare on the interloper. This was all his fault. "Why are you still here?"

His lips tugged up in a stupid grin, making her want to smack his face. Suddenly, she realized she'd seen him somewhere before.

"I'm here, because I have a deed that says I own this place." He pulled it out again and waved it in her face.

She snatched it from his hand and glanced at it. Her hopes sank like a horse caught in quicksand. She recognized her uncle's signature, and a fist tightened around her chest. "It's probably a forgery."

That annoying grin was back. To make things worse, his blue-green eyes danced, and his perfectly shaped teeth, as white as any she'd seen, made for more than a handsome smile. The man was charming—and he knew it. Probably a snake-oil salesman.

"It's not a forgery. Marshal Lane, Doc Brown, and Earl, the barber, were all there the night I won the ranch. They'll tell you it was a fair game. In fact, afterwards I felt guilty for winning Will's place and tried to give it back to him, but he wouldn't take it. Said I'd won fair and square."

"I doubt that, knowing how good my uncle was at cards." The swindler probably had an ace—or two—up his sleeve. A quick thought danced across her mind. "If you feel so guilty about winning the ranch, then sign it over to me." She held out her hand, hoping against hope that he'd just give the deed to her, then ride out of her life.

"Can't do that." He shook his head. "I made Will a promise."

"What kind of promise?"

He shrugged and rubbed a raw, red line that stretched across his neck. There was only one way to get such a mark that Keri could think of. She stared at it, and the force of her sudden thought nearly knocked her off her feet. "You're *him*?"

"Who?" All three men said in unison.

"That mangy thief I saved from hanging today."

———— ★ ————

"Thief?" Nate hollered.

"Hanging?" Jess rubbed his throat and gawked at Brooks's neck.

"You're *her*?" Brooks tried to compare the mental picture of the pretty woman in the fancy dress who'd saved his life, but it didn't fit with the gun-toting, pants-wearing female staring him down.

"I should have let them hang you."

Nate yanked his hat off and slapped his pants with it, stirring up a cloud of dust. "Now just hold on a minute. Neither of you is making any sense." He pointed at Brooks. "What hanging is she talking about? That how you got that burn on your neck?"

Nodding, Brooks told the men how he'd been stopped by Dengler's men and strung up and how Miss Langston—though *Miss* hardly seem to fit her just now—had shot the rope, thus saving him, and chased off the man bent on killing him. He owed her, but he sure as shootin' wasn't giving her his ranch.

Nate glanced at Miss Langston, as if verifying Brooks's story. She nodded, but her reluctance to side with him was evident.

"And what about the cattle?" Nate smacked his hat back on and rested his hands on his hips.

"I never even saw any cattle. I rode straight here from Shoofly. You can ask Doc Brown. I stopped in and talked to him around midmorning. That certainly didn't leave enough time to rustle cattle and ride clear out here." He hoped the men believed him, because he'd been looking forward to living in his own home and not drifting anymore.

Jess, a half foot shorter than Nate and less than half his size, scratched the back of his head. "He's right, you know. Ain't enough time to ride from town and rustle cattle and still arrive this soon."

A horse leaned its head over a stall gate and nickered, as if agreeing. Jester nickered back, reminding Brooks that his horse still waited to be unsaddled, but if he couldn't win these men over to his side, both he and his horse might be leaving.

Brooks flashed a smile. He'd learned it was harder for folks to be angry with him if he grinned.

Miss Langston scowled.

Nate turned toward her, his shoulders not quite as stiff as they had been. "I'm sorry, Missy, but the paper this fellow has is for real. I don't know what got into your uncle to go and gamble this ranch, but he did, and that's all there is to it."

She made a derisive sound and frowned. "And what's going to happen to me? I've nowhere else to go."

Brooks first thought was that she could go anywhere but here, but he'd been raised better than that—and she *had* saved his life. He glanced past her at the only corner of the house he could see from this angle. Guess he wouldn't be sleeping there after all. And he had promised Will that he'd watch out for Keri—although she would be a lot more trouble than the dog or horse he'd expected to find. He forced a grin. "You can stay."

"How generous of you." She scrunched up her lips, no doubt wanting to say far more, but she nodded her thanks, spun around, and strode out of the barn. How would he ever overcome her hatred of him?

"I'd forgotten what a little spitfire she can be when she gets mad." Jess chuckled.

Nate pinned him with a glare.

"I—uh—gotta do somethin' out back." Jess scurried out of the barn as if someone had lit his pants afire.

Nate turned back to Brooks and stared at him eye to eye. They might be about the same height, but Brooks wasn't any way near as brawny as the older man. He pursed his lips and blew a loud breath out his nose. "The marshal came by two days ago and explained what all happened—about the ranch and Will." He glanced away, lips tight, but not before Brooks saw the pain in his eyes. He must have been good friends with

Will. "I knew Will was going downhill but sure didn't know he'd go so fast. I'd hoped Keri would get home to see him again."

"He didn't look too good at the end. Maybe it's better for her to remember him healthy and strong," Brooks offered.

"Maybe. I wish I'd known she was coming home. I hate that no one was there to meet her train." He shook his head. "Wonder how she found out about Will."

Brooks shrugged. "Don't know, but it must have come as a surprise. Where was she, anyway?"

Nate gazed up at the ceiling. "Will sent her to some ladies' school in the South somewhere. Missy pitched a royal fit. She didn't want to go—didn't want to learn to become a lady, but Will thought she needed to go. She'd been raised up with us three old men. What'd we know about teaching her womanly things?"

No wonder she wore pants and knew how to shoot a rope in half. "What happened to her parents?"

Nate shook his head. "Will never said. He'd already bought this place and was living here with Miss Keri when I hired on. Will hired Jess a year or two after me, and it's just been the four of us all these years." A muscle in his jaw flexed. "I'll sure miss Will. He was more friend than boss."

"I hope that's what I'll be too."

Nate just glanced at him, but the expression on his face said, *We'll see.*

Brooks lifted his hat, surprised at his desire to win this man's approval. "The thing is, I don't have much money. What I had was stolen the night Will—died." He started to say, "was killed" but Doc had found no hard evidence other than the knowledge that Will wasn't the kind of man who'd commit suicide, no matter what. "I don't know when I'll be able to pay you or Jess."

Nate nodded. "There's been times like that before. Long as

we've got a place to stay and food to eat, we're content." Nate narrowed his gaze. "But I do expect you to treat Miss Keri kindly."

There was more in his statement than was voiced, and Brooks knew it. "I didn't expect her to be here, but I made Will a promise, and I keep my promises."

Nate looked deep into Brooks's eyes, and after a moment, nodded. "You can put your horse in any of the empty stalls, and there's a spare bed in the bunkhouse. I'll get your horse some feed."

"Thanks, Nate. I'd appreciate if you'd fill me in on how things have been handled around here and maybe give me a tour of the land later."

"I can do that." Nate turned and took three steps then turned back. "Was that really Saul Dengler's men that jumped you?"

"That's what they said. They wanted this ranch. You know any reason why they'd be willing to hang an innocent man just to get this land?" He fingered the rope burn on his neck.

"No, except Dengler is a land-grabbing lout. Probably thought he could buy it from you for far less than it's worth." Nate rubbed a hand across his jaw. "We might need to keep an eye out for Missy if he's decided he wants this land. It wouldn't surprise me none if they used her to get it."

Brooks thought of the spirited woman in Theo Kress's hands, and a shiver charged down his spine. "Right. We'll have to keep an eye on her."

"She won't like it, and without Will here to keep her in line, we'll have our hands full."

"I'll keep her in tow."

"Ha!" Nate barked a laugh. "I can't wait to see that." He turned and ambled away, his shoulders bouncing with barely contained mirth.

As he unsaddled Jester, Brooks realized the ramifications of his last statement to Nate. Just how was he to handle Miss Keri Langston, a woman who could shoot him dead in his tracks if he angered her?

CHAPTER SEVEN

eri stood at the front window, staring out at the barn. She'd like to shoot that lowlife swindler in his tracks. Life here would be hard enough without Uncle Will, who kept things running around Raven Creek, but to have that—that gambling thief here was a whole different thing. If only he wasn't so good looking.

Little seemed to rile him. That incessant smile of his would get on anybody's nerves, especially someone on their last nerve, like her. What was she going to do?

If he truly owned Raven Creek now, how could she stay? But where could she go? All she knew to do was ranch work, and nobody this side of the Red River would hire a female ranch hand. Tears stung her eyes, and she swatted at them. She hadn't been this weepy since Will told her he was sending her away to school. She'd begged and pleaded with him not to send her, and when he said he had his mind made up that she needed to learn the ways of a woman, she'd avoided him and refused to talk to him until she left. She hadn't even given him a good-bye hug—and now it was too late.

She blew out a raggedy sigh. "Oh, Uncle Will."

A knock pulled her from her thoughts. She swiped her sleeve across her eyes and walked to the door, hoping her nose wasn't red. She pulled it open, and there *he* was.

"What do you want? Come to claim the house now? Just let me get my stuff, and I'll sleep in the barn with the horses."

His lips twitched, and his blue-green eyes danced. "No need. I've already put my gear in the bunkhouse."

Didn't hardly seem right that the owner of the ranch had to sleep with the hands, but she wasn't about to mention that. "Well, good, 'cause I'm not leaving."

His eyes took on a serious look. "Neither am I—just so you know."

"Fine." She hiked her chin. "What do you want?"

He lifted his hat and ran his fingers through his thick hair. She noticed a nasty looking bruise with a gash at his hairline. "How did you get that? Did Kress pistol-whip you?"

He touched the red gash and winced. "No."

"The other man do it?"

"No."

If she wasn't mistaken, his cheeks had turned a bit red. "Well, how did you do that?"

His mouth twisted up on one side. "I ran into a tree, all right?"

She tried not to smile. "Why didn't you steer your horse around it?"

His eyes rolled up and he lifted his brows in a cocky manner. "Maybe because my hands were tied behind my back."

"Oh." She pressed her lips together, but the vision of his horse trotting down the road while he still had his hands tied hit her as funny. A giggle worked its way out. Then a snort. "Sorry."

"You don't look sorry."

She fought for composure. It was wrong to laugh at a person in dire straights, but after the day she'd had, it was either laugh or cry—and she wasn't about to cry in front of *him*.

"Fetch some fresh water from the well out back, then sit down in one of the porch rockers while I get our basket of medicines and bandages." Keri shook her head. It was no wonder he grinned all the time like a crazy person, since he'd probably been knocked loco from that blow on the head.

He lifted one eyebrow, and she realized how she'd just bossed him around. Instead of making a fuss, he merely asked, "Why do you want me to sit on the porch?"

"Because that wound needs to be treated, or you might get an infection, and—" *Die.* She left off the last word. As mad as she was that he'd outsmarted her uncle and somehow won the ranch from him, she couldn't wish anyone dead, especially someone who smiled as much as he did, no matter how he irritated her. She walked through the house to the small closet that had always held their medicine basket.

Back outside, she set the basket down and surveyed the man's wound. Her hands shook as she held back his thick brown hair. "Turn the chair so the sunlight shines on it." He did as ordered, and she cleared her throat, hating the way it sounded froggy.

"It's fine, I'm sure. Don't fret yourself over it."

She lifted her chin. "I'm not fretting. I'd do the same thing for Nate or Jess—have many times, in fact."

He grunted but held still. She washed the wound, applied some salve, and wrapped a clean bandage around his head. When she finished, she stepped back, admiring her work.

He lifted his eyes to hers, and up close like she was, she noticed how long and thick his dark lashes were. His nose was straight and his face square, angling down to a solid chin covered with an intriguing stubble. With the sunlight glinting off his brown hair, she noticed reddish accents. He really was a nice-looking man, but she needed to remember that this *nice-looking man* stole her ranch.

"So, you think I'll live?"

"Unfortunately." She busied herself cleaning up the medical supplies.

He stood and grabbed his hat off the rocker spindle. "Look, Miss Langston, if I had anywhere else to go, I'd sign the ranch over to you faster than a rattler could strike, but the fact is . . . I don't. This is my home now."

"But it's my home too. Has been for over eleven years—if you count the years I was gone." She wasn't about to tell him she, too, had nowhere to go, and she didn't at all like the fact that they had something in common.

"I'm not asking you to leave, but I do hope we can come to some kind of amicable agreement."

"Like what?"

He shrugged and she noticed just how wide those shoulders were. He must have done some heavy work somewhere to have earned them.

"I don't know. Maybe you could cook and do our laundry."

She snorted. "All the men here wash their own clothes. Uncle Will insisted on that."

He frowned, but it disappeared behind a grin. "Fine then, Missy, you can do the cooking and tend the garden."

"That's women's work." She wagged her finger under his nose. "And don't call me *Missy*. Only Nate calls me that."

"Fine."

"*Fine!*"

She realized that she was only inches from his face. His breath mingled with hers, and up so close, she could see gray flecks mixed with the blue and green in his pretty eyes. She stepped back. One foot slipped off the edge of the porch, and he grabbed her flailing arm, pulling her back up to the level floor.

"Careful now."

He stood only inches from her and could have taken advantage—he was certainly strong enough—but gently released her. Keri ducked her head. She didn't want him to be nice to her. How could she be attracted to the very man who'd stolen her ranch?

"Fine. I'll cook and do the gardening, but if you think that's all I'm doing, you're mistaken. I'm as good a wrangler as I am a shot, Mr.—" She blinked, searching her mind for his name. It sounded like some kind of water, didn't it? "What did you say your name was?"

"Brooks." He grinned. "Brooks Morgan." He tipped his hat. "A pleasure to meet you, *Missy*."

She flung a roll of bandages at him as he jogged down the porch steps. "I said don't call me that."

His chuckles drifted back to her as his long-legged gait moved him toward the barn. She sagged against the porch railing. Her homecoming sure had turned out differently than she'd expected.

———— ★ ————

Keri stood and stretched her back. Weeding four rows of beans made it ache with a passion. She pressed her fists into the small of her back, reminding herself how good these beans would taste this winter, once they'd been harvested and canned. At least she hoped she could can them. She'd enjoyed the beans the cook back at the women's school had prepared so much that she'd talked the woman into showing her how to can, and she'd even helped in the process come harvest time.

She leaned on the hoe and stared across the field to where

a trio of horses grazed. If she'd stayed with her mother, would she have learned things like cooking and sewing? She didn't remember much about her mother or where she lived, except that she lived in a big house with lots of other women. They'd always eaten good food, thanks to a Chinese man named Li Pan. Keri smiled at the memory of the aptly named small cook who often chased dogs and bums away by waving a frying skillet in the air and mumbling a string of foreign words she couldn't begin to repeat.

"Happy to see me?"

Keri's smile dimmed as *he* rode up, leading a wide-eyed cow behind his horse. "What's that?"

He pushed his hat back on his forehead, that ever-present grin in place. "You mean you don't know what a cow is?" He shook his head. "How's that possible since you grew up on a ranch?" He dismounted and stood before her.

"Ha ha." Keri curled her lip at his lame joke, wiped the sweat from her brow with her sleeve, and glanced down at her dirty pants. "I mean, why is she here? She's not one of our cows."

"No, I traded a steer to a man down the road for her. She's a milk cow—one tame enough we can milk without getting our teeth kicked in."

She lifted her eyebrows. "And whose job will that be?"

He shrugged. "I reckon we can take turns. I just had a hankering for butter on those fine pancakes you make, and I like a glass of milk now and then." He leaned closer, making her heart break from a trot into a gallop. "Don't tell anybody, though." He smiled and winked.

She watched him amble toward the barn, his horse and the cow following. Butter would taste good, and though she wasn't one to drink milk, there were plenty of other things she could use it for. Some custard would taste delicious, if she could figure out how to make it. All she knew for sure was that it contained milk, eggs, and some spices.

Dusting off her hands, she walked to the barn and into the open stall where Mr. Morgan led the cow. She noticed a diamond-shaped brand with a roughly shaped J in the center on the cow's shoulder. "That's the Diamond J brand, and I don't want any trouble with our neighbors. Why do you have their cow?"

"Because Mr. Jackson gave it to me."

Keri narrowed her eyes. "I've known Reese Jackson most of my life, and while he may be an honorable man, he's a tight-fisted ol' coot and wouldn't even give a cow to one of his own children. What did you do, smile it away from him?"

His head jerked toward her and his lips lifted. "Something like that."

"Aren't you ever serious?" She crossed her arms.

"Where's the fun in that?"

"Oh, come on. You can't run a ranch just by joking around. It takes a lot of hard work, and if you don't work and make all your hands do everything, they won't like you or respect you, and that affects output. Unhappy cowboys are restless and move on. I don't want to lose Nate and Jess. Do you hear me?"

He stared at her over the cow, his eyes dancing. "What do you think of the name Moo-linda?" He chuckled. "Get it?"

Was he serious? "I think that clobbering you took to the head jiggled something loose in your brain. That's the dumbest name I ever heard for a cow." She stomped from the stall.

"Huh-uh. What about Bossy? Now that's a dumb cow name. I mean, have you ever seen a bossy cow?" He followed her. "How about Moo-randa? Or Moo-tilda?"

The names were so absurd, she almost cracked a smile, but she wouldn't give him the satisfaction. She passed an empty stall and stared at the mess in the corner then spun around, nearly colliding with *him*. "Who mucked this stall?"

"I did. Why?"

"Because it's not clean. Just look at that horse flop in the corner." She spun around, hands on her hips. "If you're going to do a job halfway, you might as well not bother doing it."

His brows lifted. "Overlooking one measly flop isn't doing a job halfway."

"It's not doing it thoroughly either." She grabbed a shovel off the far wall, marched into the stall, scooped up the offending item and carried it outside. Glancing over her shoulder, she called out, "Uncle Will always said if you're only going to do a job partway, you might as well not do it at all."

———— ★ ————

Brooks leaned against the barn door, more than a little irritated with *Miss Fancy Britches*. Her scolding reminded him of the ones he used to get at home from his pa. He didn't know how he'd overlooked that horse flop, other than the barn had still been in shadows early this morning when he'd mucked out the stalls. He didn't like her high-and-mighty attitude, but instead of making him angry like his pa had when he'd scolded him more than ten years ago, Keri's tongue-lashing made him— what? Yeah, he was embarrassed and a bit irritated, but he wished he had done a better job—to prove to her that he wasn't the lazy no-good she thought him to be.

He checked the four empty stalls for anything he might have skipped over this morning in his eagerness to get to breakfast, but things looked all right to him. He pulled the list he'd made earlier of chores that needed doing from his shirt pocket and studied it. Wood needed chopping, as always. A number of places on the house and barn needed repair. The house needed a paint job in the worse way. One porch step was loose. A window on the rear of the house was cracked and needed to be replaced. He blew out a sigh. Had there been so much to do back at his pa's place? No wonder the man was always needling him to work. It would take one man weeks to do it all, and this list didn't even include repairing fences that seemed an almost constant issue to be dealt with, as well as tending the cattle and the small herd of horses at Raven Creek.

Brooks searched the barn until he found a hammer and some nails, then walked to the porch. He bounced on the bottom step, listening to its creak. Upon closer inspection, he found a crack that angled across one corner. He could nail the board more securely to its brace, but eventually, it would have to be replaced. "There's no time like today," his pa used to say.

After prying up the loose board, he headed back to the barn to find one that he could use as a replacement. He paused and stared at the house, then allowed his gaze to rove across the closest pasture and to the barn. This all belonged to him. It was a huge responsibility, especially since he had other people to support and watch out for. His thoughts had turned to his pa numerous times in the few days he'd been at Raven Creek. For the first time in his life, he finally understood why his father had pushed him hard to pull his own weight.

He hadn't been fair to his father. Riley Morgan was a good man, and he deserved a better son than Brooks had been. Maybe his younger brother Phillip had become that man. Brooks winced. He'd wronged his family by riding off and never letting them know what had happened. Waco wasn't all that far from Raven Creek. Maybe it was time to make amends.

CHAPTER EIGHT

*K*eri pulled out a pot and smacked it down on top of the stove with a loud, satisfying clang. If her uncle was going to lose the ranch to someone, why couldn't it have been a man who knew ranching and was efficient, not a bumbling two-bit gambler.

Moo-tilda. She shook her head at the crazy cow name but couldn't help the grin it brought to her face. It was so ridiculous, she halfway liked it, not that she'd tell *him*.

She blew out a sigh at the empty bucket and grabbed the handle. The stew wouldn't cook without water, and even though *he'd* promised to keep the bucket filled, there it was, empty again. If he spent as much time working as he did grinning, this place would be in spiffy shape in no time.

As she stepped onto the porch, a wagon pulled into the yard. Keri started to go back for her rifle, but then she noticed a woman sitting next to the driver. She wore a pink gingham dress with a matching sunbonnet. When she saw Keri, the woman waved. She looked familiar, but Keri couldn't place her.

Then she glanced at the man, and her heart dropped down to her boot tips. Carl Peters. The man who wanted to be her beau, once upon a time. She had tried to discourage him on numerous occasions, but he kept coming back like a pesky rodent.

She walked across the porch, and Mr. Morgan came out of the barn. He suddenly dropped his tools and flapped his arms like chicken wings. He yelled something at the same time the buggy creaked to a halt. *What was the crazy man doing?*

Keri jogged down the steps to greet her guests—but her foot hit air instead of the bottom step, and she fell—flat on her face. The bucket flew through the air, colliding with the buggy's wheel. The horse squealed and sidestepped away from her. Carl shouted. The woman screamed.

Pain knifed through Keri's ankle, stealing her breath. Her elbow and chin hurt where they collided with the ground, and dirt filled her mouth. She lifted her head and spat it out, but had little success.

She suddenly realized just what a spectacle she'd made. Rolling over, she stared at the bottom step—or rather—where the step had been. What in the world?

Brooks slid to a halt beside her just as Carl jumped from the buggy. A man tugged on each of her arms.

"Are you all right?" they asked in unison.

"Stop pulling on me, and just let me sit here a moment." She grabbed her ankle. It hurt, but not too horribly. The stiffness of her boots probably saved it from worse injury.

"Carl, come help me down. Perhaps I can help." The woman from the wagon waved her hand.

Carl stared at Keri with a sympathetic gaze, then his blond brows dipped as he looked at Brooks. He stood and strode back to the buggy.

"Who's that?" Brooks's gaze followed Carl.

"An old acquaintance."

Brooks grinned. "So, not a beau."

She scowled at the ninny. "Where is my step?"

"Dead and gone. I just removed it and had returned to the barn for a slat to repair it. I was only gone a few minutes. I'm sorry, Missy. I never meant for you to get hurt."

She leaned close. "Stop calling me that, and help me up, so I can greet my guests properly."

He did as ordered, but that didn't silence him. "You need to be resting that ankle, not entertaining. What if it's broken?"

"It's not, so hush." Keri allowed Brooks to help her up, then leaned on his arm and found him more than secure enough to hold her up. Standing on one leg and holding her injured foot off the ground caused her to have to press against *him*—the one man she longed to stay away from.

But now Carl was here, and suddenly Brooks Morgan didn't seem half as bad.

Carl escorted his sister Ellen toward them, his gaze ranging from concerned to curious. "Are you all right?"

"Yes," his sister said. "That was quite a tumble you took."

"I'm fine, thank you. I just wasn't aware of the fact that someone had uprooted my bottom step."

Brooks cleared his throat. "Uh . . . that was my fault. I was in the middle of repairing it."

"And who are you?" Carl asked, his brows lifted nearly to his hairline.

"Brooks Morgan." He smiled. "I'd shake your hand but they're full right now. I need to get Keri off her feet."

"Perhaps we should come back another day, Carl. Miss Langston needs to rest after taking such a tumble."

Carl frowned, then released his sister. "Just a moment, Ellen." Keri's pulse took off running as he approached. "Let me help get Miss Langston inside first."

As he drew near, Keri could smell the strong odor of his bay rum cologne. Brooks stiffened. "I can get her in the house without help."

Offering a placating smile, Carl reached for Keri's other hand, but Brooks stole her breath away when he lifted her into his arms. He smiled and winked. Up so close those eyes looked like the beautiful ocean water.

"Put me down," she hissed.

"No." He waggled his brows. "Carl, would you be so good as to open the door?"

Huffing a frustrated breath, Carl stepped up onto the second step and onto the porch. "Why don't you hand her up to me? That would be the easiest thing."

As much as Keri wanted out of Brooks's arms, she wanted to be in Carl's even less. In fact, slim as he was, she wasn't certain he could hold her. But before she could voice her opinion, Brooks hoisted her more tightly against him and took the steps as if she weighed no more than a five-pound sack of sugar.

Carl shoved the door open, albeit not so gently, then stepped back to allow Brooks to carry her inside. Brooks carefully laid her on the sofa, but she swung around into a sitting position. Her ankle ached, but she wasn't about to lie down in front of these two men.

Stepping inside, Carl removed his hat. "How can I help, Miss Langston?"

Keri sat straight, forcing her mind off her aches and pains. "Thank you for your offer, Mr. Peters, but I'm sure I'll be fine."

He nodded, his lips pressed into a thin line. Chilly blue eyes stared back. "Ellen will be disappointed. She was looking forward to hearing about your adventures in Georgia."

"Please give her my apology, and tell her we'll do it another time."

Brooks stood beside the door like a butler but she had the feeling he was more protector than servant. Carl turned and pinned a glare on him. "Just who are you?"

Grinning, he held out his hand. "Brooks Morgan."

Carl shook his head and shrugged. "Is that name supposed to mean something to me?"

"It means I'm the owner of Raven Creek."

Cold blue eyes assessed Brooks. A muscle twitched in the man's jaw. "If you own this ranch, why is Miss Langston still living here?"

Keri started to rise, and Brooks saw her grimace and then fall back against the sofa. "Because this is my home."

Mr. Peters set his hat atop his head and parked his hands on his hips, brows lifted in an arch. "You mean Mr. Morgan, here, owns the ranch, but he lets you live here?"

Keri lifted her chin, but Brooks could see the uncertainty in her eyes. "What's wrong with that? He stays in the bunkhouse with the other men."

"I can think of a lot of people who might think the situation improper."

Keri gasped and hopped up on her one good foot, wincing as she managed to stand. "What an awful thing to say, Carl. I would think you know me better than that."

"Who knows how much a woman can change in two years? I don't guess you learned much at that lady's school if you're still going around dressed in men's pants."

"And I think you need to leave." Keri dropped back to the sofa, eyes narrowed to tiny slits.

"You heard the lady." Brooks stepped in between Carl and Keri. "She wants you to leave her house."

Mr. Peters snorted. "Her house. I thought you owned this place. It's a strange set-up you have here—and not at all good for Miss Langston's reputation."

Brooks grabbed the man's fancy shirt. "The situation here is just fine. Nothing improper is going on at all. Miss Langston gets to keep her home, and I own the ranch. If I find out you're spreading rumors, you'll answer to me. You hear?" He gave the man a shake.

Carl Peters was only an inch shorter than Brooks, but the fact that the man had to glare up at him gave Brooks plenty of satisfaction.

"I've planned on courting Miss Langston for many years. Just make sure you stay out of *my* way. I'm not a man to trifle with." He tipped his hat at Keri. "Get some rest and get to feeling better. I'll be back in a few days to see how you're doing." The man spun on his heel and exited the house.

Keri moaned, but Brooks wasn't sure if it was from pain or the thought of Peters returning. He stood guard at the door as the man helped the woman into the buggy before stomping around to the other side. He cast another searing gaze at Brooks, then slapped the reins on his horse's back.

Leaving the door open, Brooks turned back to Keri. She lay in the corner of the sofa, her eyes shut but her brow was pinched together. "Are you in pain?"

She nodded.

Brooks hurried to her side and lifted her injured foot onto the sofa. "We need to get that boot off. If it swells too much, it may have to be cut off."

"No!" Keri's pretty blue eyes pierced him. "Uncle Will gave them to me."

He knew without her saying that the boots were special. "All right. I'll see if I can get it off. It might hurt a little."

She nodded and bit her lower lip.

Brooks stared at her thin leg, hesitant to touch her. But he couldn't help her if he didn't. He knelt on the floor in front of the sofa, wrapped her leg under his arm, and tugged on her boot. She hissed, but remained quiet. It looked like the ankle had swollen, but he had good hopes it wasn't broken, because she'd be screeching if it was. He took a firmer hold of her leg and the boot and pulled harder. The boot loosened and broke free. He dropped it on the floor and removed Keri's sock. The ankle was swollen, for certain, but it didn't look oddly shaped or broken. He blew out a sigh of relief.

"That hurt." Keri's voice cracked, and he turned in time to see her swipe her eyes.

"Sorry, but it had to come off."

"I know." She exhaled a sigh. "Do you think you could turn loose of my leg now?"

Brooks glanced down and realized her leg was still under his arm, and he'd been gently massaging the area just above the injury. He dropped it and jumped up, heat marching up his neck. "Sorry."

A soft smile lifted the corners of Keri's lips. "It actually felt good." But fast as a snap of someone's fingers, the smile faded. "Why didn't you warn me that you'd removed that step?"

He rubbed the back of his neck, then shrugged and shook his head. " 'Cause I just didn't think about it. I'd just pulled up the step and headed to the barn to find a replacement when that buggy drove up and you came out of the house. I'd planned to repair it right away, but you were too fast for me."

Keri wiggled her foot. "It's just a sprain. Should be good as new in a few days."

Brooks relaxed, but he still felt awful. "Can I get you something to eat or drink?"

"No, but if you could fetch the bucket I dropped and fill the pot on the stove, I'd be beholden to you. I need to get some beans cooking."

Glad to have something to do, Brooks backed toward the

front door. "Like I said before, I'm real sorry about this, and I hope you aren't hurt too bad."

She waved a hand in dismissal, and he scurried outside, feeling lower than a rat's belly. He found the bucket lying in the yard, pounded it hard against the porch rail a few times to loosen the dust and grass, and headed to the well. The well bucket made a splash, but when he hauled it up, the pail was only a little over half full. He poured the water into Keri's bucket and dropped it down again.

He gazed up at the brilliant blue sky with not a cloud in sight. They needed rain. Nate had told him the creek was starting to dry up, and there sure wasn't enough water in the well to satisfy a thirsty herd of cattle. A crow cawed overhead, and he glanced up again. "Lord, if'n You've a mind to send rain, we sure could use some."

When he returned to the house, he knocked, even though he'd left the door open. He stepped inside, and Keri was balancing beside the sofa on one foot. He set down the bucket and hurried toward her. "What do you think you're doing?"

"I—well—" She turned her head toward the wall. "This old sofa is hard, and things are poking my—"

Brooks tried hard not to grin. "Would you like me to take you to your bedroom?"

Her head jerked back, cheeks flaming. "Don't you dare laugh. This is all your fault anyway."

"You're right. I should have told you that I'd removed the step, but I thought you were still upset after our talk in the barn. I didn't want to disturb you and thought I could finish the job before anyone noticed."

She gazed up at him, looking so alone and vulnerable. "I guess you could help me to my room."

He smiled, then hoisted her up in his arms.

"Hey, I said *help*."

"Trust me, this is the least painful way." He carried her into the other room and looked around the kitchen. An empty pot sat on the stove and some carrots, two onions, and a bowl of unpeeled potatoes sat on the worktable. Looked like they'd be having stew tonight. Fine by him.

The only door led to the outside, and he glanced at Keri's face. It was so close he could see a faint line of freckles across the bridge of her nose, and her vivid eyes held his gaze. Brooks swallowed hard. If he kept staring at her, he would end up kissing her. He spun around so fast, Keri grabbed his shoulders with both hands. "Where is your room?"

"Upstairs." She batted her eyes and gave him an innocent smile. "Sure you want to carry me?"

Ignoring her snide comment, he hustled through the parlor and up the stairs that hugged the wall, swallowing back a grunt. Keri's floral scent washed over him. Every muscle in his body was tense, and though she was small and light, carrying her up a mess of stairs still winded him. And how was she going to get back down if she needed to?

At the landing, Keri pointed to the door to the left. Inside was a beautiful room—definitely a female's room—painted a pale green, with white curtains fluttering in the breeze. He set her down on her bed and stepped back, feeling more uncomfortable than the time he accidentally walked into a house of ill repute when he was running an errand for his employer. He backed into the hall. "I'll—uh—be—uh—downstairs. Holler if you need me."

Without waiting for an answer, he spun and headed downstairs. He hoped Nate and Jess returned early today. Then one of them could watch the lovely Miss Langston. Like a ghost from a haunting dream, her scent clung to him, teasing him. He appreciated her saving his life, but he'd never thought about her as anything except Will's niece—an unexpected burden—albeit a pretty one. One that he'd promised to take care of. She had been trouble since they met. Snippy. Bossy. Sassy.

But then he held her in his arms—and none of the rest mattered.

CHAPTER NINE

he horse squealed and kicked the back of the stall. Thump. Thump. The scent of something burning seared her nostrils. Was the barn on fire?

Keri bolted upright. Pain charged up her leg, and her room came into focus. She blew out a breath and straightened her leg, being careful not to twist her ankle. No fire, just a dream. She swiped sweat from her cheek where it had lain against the pillow.

Thump. Thump. "Miss Keri, are you awake?"

Keri's heart bolted like a horse from a starting gate. What could Brooks Morgan want at her bedroom door?

He jiggled the handle, and she searched for a place to hide. She wasn't ready to see him again. Not after the shameless spectacle she'd made earlier. But she had nowhere to hide, so she sat up straight and lifted her chin in the air. "What are you doing up here again?"

He gently kicked the door open, and wearing a worn apron,

held up a tray, complete with a glass holding a trio of bent daisies. "I brought dinner."

"Is that what I smell burning?"

His grin did odd things to her stomach. Or maybe it was just hunger that was swirling in her belly.

"Yes and no. Can I come in?"

"Where's Nate and Jess?" She glanced past his shoulders, which all but filled the doorway.

"They haven't come in yet. They rode out to one of the far pastures today, so it may take a bit longer for them to get back."

She waved him in and used her good foot to push up in the bed. He set the tray in front of her, and the savory fragrance of stew and corn bread teased her senses, although the stew looked a bit dry and the corn bread overly brown. Using the spoon, she lifted some kind of meat. "What's this?"

The rascal's eyes lit up. "I could tease you and say it's frog or armadillo."

Keri turned up her nose and stared at the pink meat. "Looks like ham."

"It is. I rode over and bought a smoked ham off the Jacksons. They tried to give it to me when I told them what happened, but I knew you wouldn't like that, so I paid for it with my last dime."

She glanced up and smiled. "Stew tastes a heap better with meat in it. Thanks."

He nodded, eyes dancing. "My pleasure, ma'am. Do you need anything else? I'd hoped to have some fresh milk, but it's a bit early to tend to that task yet."

"Water is fine."

He pressed his lips together and nodded. "My pleasure." He nudged his head toward the door. "There's a mess in the kitchen that needs cleaning, and besides, I've no hankerin' to get buckshot, which is what will happen if Nate finds me up here." He pretended to tip his hat, which he wasn't wearing, then ducked out the door.

She lifted the flowers to her nose and realized she hadn't heard Brooks's footsteps going downstairs. He peeked back in the doorway, and she jumped, spilling water on her shirt. "What?"

"I forgot to ask how your foot is."

"It's sore, no thanks to you."

"Probably will be for a few days. Sorry."

She glared at him to hide her embarrassment at being caught enjoying the flowers. "Stop saying that."

"Yes, ma'am." He disappeared, and this time she heard him clomping down the stairs.

Keri let out a sigh. Why did he irritate her so? He was only being nice—after causing her to almost break her leg. But he was really nice. And easy on the eyes. She was even starting to get used to his smiling all the time.

And how did a person do that?

For the first time, she wondered about his past. *How could Brooks Morgan grow up to be such a charming rascal?* He was older than she was—by a good five or six years, if she had to guess. But most times, he acted like a kid. Or an idiot.

And then he went and brought her supper in bed. And three flowers—with a lady bug on one.

How was she supposed to stay angry with him when he did nice things like that?

She spooned a tiny taste of stew into her mouth; it was bursting with flavor. She took a bigger bite and enjoyed the salty taste, then pinched off a square of corn bread. Surprise, surprise. She never would have thought Brooks Morgan could cook such a decent meal.

Brooks stared into his coffee and listened to Nate's theory at supper.

"The water is just about all dried up, except in a place or two that's deeper than most." Nate ran his hand up his forehead and into his thick, gray hair. "I can't say as I know what to do."

"And you think Dengler's behind it?"

Jess had been cramming the stew into his mouth like a starving man, but halted his spoon midair and glanced at Nate at the mention of Saul Dengler.

Nate nodded. "I suspect he's blocked the flow upriver."

"Is that legal?" Brooks snagged another piece of corn bread. It was a bit overdone but still edible.

Shrugging, Nate took a bite of his food. "Don't know as there's any law against it, but it goes against all that's good. No decent man keeps water from another."

Brooks leaned back in his chair and rubbed his index finger across the mark on his throat that had nearly healed. "Guess we all know what kind of man Dengler is."

Jess leaned forward, his brown eyes gleaming. "Did he really try to hang you?"

Nodding, Brooks sipped his coffee and remembered how close to death he'd come. "Not him, but two of his men. They wanted me to sign over the ranch to Dengler."

Nate held his cup with both hands and stared into it. "Faced with life or death, most men would have happily handed over the deed." He glanced up, his pale blue eyes serious. "How come you didn't?"

Brooks walked to the stove and grabbed the coffee pot while contemplating his response. For the past week, he'd been the odd man out. They resented his presence and the fact the he won the ranch from Will when they all expected it to go to Keri. He may own the deed to the land, but it was obvious that she ran the ranch and still held the ranch hands' loyalty.

Most of his life, he'd joked his way out of one situation and into another. He hadn't minded being a loner, because a loner had no ties and could move on whenever he wanted. But for the first time since leaving home, he wanted to belong. Belong to this tiny crew of three.

He refilled each man's cup then sat down and looked at Nate. "It's been ten years since I've had a home. This place was important to Will, and Will was my friend. It became important to me before I ever laid eyes on it."

"Important enough to die for?" Nate held his gaze.

Brooks nodded. "If that's God's will." He didn't flinch, but held Nate's stare, and something in the older man's gaze softened.

"I reckon Will knew you were man enough to hang on to this place."

Brooks sat up a bit straighter. Other than Will, few men had ever respected him, and Nate's acceptance meant more to him than there were words to explain.

"So, what are we going to do about Dengler?" Jess pushed his plate back, corn bread crumbs and dots of stew broth covered his chest.

Brooks looked at Nate, who seemed to be waiting on a response from him. "I say we go over there and blow up his dam."

———— ★ ————

"You can't blow up Dengler's dam." Keri stomped across the kitchen, instantly sorry when pain shot up her leg. After two days of resting it, she was going loco and had to leave her room.

Brooks flipped pancakes that circled the skillet. "He's blocked the flow of water from Raven Creek land. What else can we do?"

"We could try talking to him."

Brooks spun around, holding up the spatula like a weapon. "Are you crazy? Do you know what kind of man you're talking about?"

She shoved her hands to her hips. "Of course I do. I'm the one who's lived here most of my life."

Brooks turned back to his pancakes, and Keri studied his back. He was tall, with wide shoulders that tapered to a narrow waist and long, denim-clad legs. His light-blue shirt was tight at the shoulders, and his straight, brown hair hung down to his collar. She spun around on her good foot and moved to the doorway. She was getting far too familiar with this man. He'd stolen her dream, and she wanted to hate him for it but was finding it harder and harder to stay mad at him, especially when he was such a good cook—and she seriously disliked cooking.

The skillet clanged as he moved it off the stove and onto the wooden counter. "Breakfast is ready. Would you mind ringing the bell?"

Keri stepped outside and ran the clangor around the iron triangle. Jess stuck his head out the barn door and waved. "They're coming," she said as she stepped back into the warm kitchen.

"Sit down and rest your foot."

"You don't have to baby me."

He grinned and shoveled three pancakes onto her plate. "Don't think I didn't notice how you grimaced a few moments ago. I've had a sprained ankle, and you just have to rest them and let them heal."

"I'm going loco with nothing to do. I need to keep busy."

He took hold of her wrist and tugged her toward her chair. "You need to sit down and eat. Maybe I can find something to occupy your time."

She plopped down, her mouth watering at the warm scent drifting up from the flapjacks. "Like what?"

"I don't know, but I'll think of something."

Nate and Jess tramped in, dripping wet from their recent scrubbing. They took their places, and Jess smiled at Keri. "Good to see you up again."

"Thanks." She glanced at Nate. "Anything new on the water situation?"

"No, sad to say. It's only getting worse. We're going to have to do something or our cattle will be breaking down the fence to get to water."

"So, what should we do?"

Brooks poured coffee then took his seat. "I've been thinking on that. Does Dengler attend church?"

Keri and both ranch hands stared at Brooks like he'd suddenly turned rabid. "Why would you ask such a thing? What's that got to do with anything?"

Brooks slathered some of the butter Keri had churned yesterday onto his pancakes. "Because image and reputation is important to a man like Saul Dengler. I'm thinking if he's a churchgoing man, we can confront him in a crowd, which saves us from gettin' hurt and does serious damage to Dengler's image."

Keri glanced at Nate, not a little surprised that the plan was so good.

"It could work." Nate sipped his coffee and seemed to be studying on the idea.

After applying butter and molasses, Keri bit into her pancakes. "Mmm . . . pure heaven on a plate."

Nate cleared his throat, and she opened her eyes. "What?"

"Nothing."

Keri glanced at Jess then at Brooks, whose wide grin told her he was pleased by her comment. "Well, I'm not going to lie. They are good. Better than mine even." She ducked her head, feeling her cheeks heat. If she wasn't careful, Brooks might think she liked him or something. And that was just plain absurd.

Three days later, Keri stared at the dress laid out on her bed. One of the reasons she didn't like attending church was that women had to wear dresses—their nicest dresses. When she was younger, she and Uncle Will hadn't attended church because there hadn't been one close enough. Occasionally, a traveling minister would pass through the area, and families would gather together for a service. The thing she liked most about those had been eating the delicious food and desserts cooked by the ladies. They rarely tasted such delectable fare.

She wrangled on her dress and stared at herself in the hand mirror. She supposed she didn't look half bad. *What will Brooks think?* He hadn't seen her in a dress except for that first day when she shot him down from the tree, but he hadn't known who she was then. Shaking her head, she fastened the buttons, quickly fixed her hair in the style she'd worn at school, then hurried downstairs.

The men waited on the porch and stood in unison as she came out the front door. Nate whistled through his teeth. "If I'd known you looked that pretty in a dress, Missy, I'd have burned those pants of yours."

She smiled and glanced at Brooks, whose gaze was fixed on her. A warm blush rushed to her cheeks, and she looked away, but not before she noticed how handsome he looked in his fresh white shirt and clean black pants. He'd even polished his boots.

Nate helped her down the porch while Jess unhitched

their horses. Brooks stood at the side of the buggy waiting. Nate handed her off to Brooks, who smiled and lifted her into the buggy. Keri adjusted the tie of her hat and fanned her face with her hand. Oh bother. She'd left her gloves upstairs.

What did it matter? Everyone in town knew she ran around in men's pants and probably thought her utterly uncouth. After all, she lived on a ranch with three men—none of whom she was related to.

The buggy creaked as Brooks climbed on board. He grabbed the reins and clucked out the side of his cheek to the horse. She could have driven herself and knew he'd be more comfortable on Jester, but she appreciated that he wanted to escort her. Nate and Jess rode up ahead, a short distance away.

The day was perfect. The sky was a vivid blue, and clouds as white as Brooks's teeth dotted the sky. Birds chirped in the trees they passed on their way to the road. The only thing that marred the day was that she was headed to church.

CHAPTER TEN

*B*rooks leaned close to Keri. "You look lovely today. I could get used to seeing you in dresses."

She frowned at him and shook her skirt. "Well, don't. They're bulky, hot, and awkward when riding a horse."

He chuckled. "You can take the girl out of Texas, but you can't take Texas out of the girl."

She nudged him with her elbow. "Not funny."

"But true."

They rode on in silence for a while, but Keri kept sighing. "Care to tell me what's bothering you?" he asked.

She shrugged and didn't say anything, so Brooks kept quiet. He wondered about the church. Would it be like the one he had attended with his folks when he was young? A large woman playing a pump organ followed by a skinny preacher shouting at them?

If he hadn't made that promise to God the day he nearly died, he probably wouldn't be headed to church now.

But he had.

And he was.

"I don't like to attend church." Keri's whisper was so low that he almost didn't hear it.

"And why is that?"

"I don't know." She shrugged again. "Maybe because some 'good' church ladies tried to take me away from Uncle Will when he first brought me here."

Brooks clenched his teeth. He could easily see some well-meaning busybodies meddling in Will's affairs. It was an unusual situation for an uncle to raise his niece without the aid of a wife. "I'm sorry that happened."

"Yeah, well, me too. I was a scared little kid. Didn't know why my ma gave me to my uncle and why he brought me to a strange place."

"That must have been hard."

"I guess. It was a long time ago."

Up ahead, he saw Nate and Jess pull into the churchyard. The bell rang out a cheerful greeting, and people, buggies, and horses filled the yard. His stomach swirled. He understood Keri's apprehension. He hadn't been in a church in over a decade and didn't know what to expect. "Well, we'll face it together. I promise not to leave your side."

Her gaze jerked from the crowd of happy people to his, and he could see the worry there. "Truly?"

He nodded and reached over and squeezed her hand. "We're a team. Hangings or church, we'll face them together."

Brooks chuckled at Keri's wide-eyed expression, parked the wagon, and jumped down. He lifted her out of the wagon, catching her gaze and holding it as he set her on the ground. "Don't worry. I suspect these are good folks for the most part."

She nodded and took his arm. The majority of the crowd had made their way inside the white, steepled building, and they followed, going slowly because of Keri's limp. He swallowed the lump in his throat. Why should he be nervous? Yeah, it had been over ten years since he'd stepped inside a church—back when he still lived with his parents—but he'd made a promise to the Almighty, and he aimed to keep that promise.

"Welcome." A man clad in a black coat greeted them with a warm smile and an outstretched hand. "Glad to have you folks today."

Brooks couldn't quite bring himself to respond, "Glad to be here," so he smiled and shook his hand, then guided Keri inside. They settled in a pew near the back, beside an open window that allowed the light breeze to offer its cooling touch. Nate and Jess slid in on Keri's right side. Brooks looked around the crowded building but saw no sign of Dengler or his henchmen, not that he expected to.

"Still don't know why we had to come to church," Jess mumbled, loud enough that Brooks heard. A stern-faced man on the row in front of them turned and glared at Jess.

Brooks focused on the front where a thin woman with a pile of hair as tall as a horse's knee sat, playing a familiar tune on a pump organ.

A few minutes later, the man who'd greeted them in the back strode down the aisle to the front, turned, and smiled. He was younger than the reverend at the church back home and introduced himself as Pastor Damian Griffith. He led two songs, singing with boisterous gusto and a joy Brooks had witnessed in few people. Then the man prayed for the congregation—a blessing on the people, their homes, and their crops and herds.

He glanced up with a big smile, and said, "Praise be this day—the day the Lord has made. I want to open with a passage from Job 8. 'Can the rush grow up without mire? Can the flag grow without water? Whilst it is yet in his greenness, and not cut down, it withereth before any other herb. So are the paths of all that forget God.'"

Leaning on the pulpit, he stared out at the crowd. "I know it's hard for us water-deprived Texans to understand this talk about rushes. And I can't begin to explain what a flag is, except for the kind that waves in the air." Soft chuckles echoed off the crowd. "But we all understand what it means for a crop to wither in the field for lack of water—and that's what I think this verse is referring to.

"Man without God is like a field of wheat, cotton, or corn without rain. We dry up. Wither. We're not good for anything. Man needs God like our bodies need blood. Like our bodies need water—only in a worse way. Life here on earth is temporary, shorter for some than others. We need to make our lives count for something, people."

Brooks stared out the window at the leaves flapping in the wind. He thought of the past ten years—wasted years he'd spent drifting from town to town, job to job. Not accomplishing anything lasting. Why had God allowed him to live when he'd wasted the life he'd been given? Was that why God had given him a second chance? So that he could change and be a contributor to society?

"Don't leave here without making things right with God, folks. Don't leave here without asking forgiveness for your sins and asking Jesus to save you."

Heads bowed as Pastor Griffith prayed. Thoughts swirled through Brooks's head and emotions spun in his gut. The man had given him plenty to think about, but he wasn't ready to stand and walk down the aisle. The moment Pastor Griffith said, "Amen," Jess slid to the far side of the bench and all but ran for the exit, pulling a smile to Brooks's lips. Nate followed after him, albeit a bit more slowly. Jess reminded him of himself, back when he was a boy at church. He couldn't wait to get outside after the service and cozy up to the girls who had attended with their families.

Keri looked up at him and smiled, not seeming nearly as nervous as she had been, and with her at his side, he had no inclinations to gawk at the other women. None could come close to being as pretty and challenging as she. He stood and offered his hand, helping her up. "Ready to head home? Or did you want to visit?"

She glanced around the church, then shrugged. He suspected she'd like to mingle but was afraid—for some reason unbeknown to him. Maybe it was because she'd been gone so long and didn't know many folks. Or maybe it was the awkwardness of their situation. He hadn't stopped to think how his owning the ranch and allowing Keri to stay there would look to others.

A big man paused in the aisle, allowing them to exit the row, and they filed outside. Keri hobbled toward the buggy, but Brooks paused to allow a trio of giggling young ladies to pass in front of him. The last to pass, a pretty thing in a purple dress with a huge bow on the back of her head, glanced up at him and batted her lashes. Her cheeks turned red and she rushed to catch her friends. Pretty, to be sure, but far too young for him to take a second glance. He shook his head and angled for the buggy, where Keri waited. Nate and Jess must have already left for home, since their horses were gone.

"Keri?" A homely woman in her early twenties, Brooks guessed, hustled their way. "Is that really you?"

Turning, Keri smiled. "Yes, Lulu, it's me."

The two hugged, and Keri became more animated than Brooks had ever seen her.

"How have you been? What's happened since your last letter?" Keri asked as she held the woman's hands.

"I'm wonderful." The woman's hazel eyes turned toward

Brooks, red painted her pale cheeks, and she leaned toward Keri. "I'm expecting our first child."

Keri squealed and bounced then wrapped her arms around Lulu. "I'm so happy for you and Miles." She glanced over her shoulder at him, and then leaned close to Lulu's ear. "When is the happy occasion expected?"

That was it. Feminine talk was not for him. Brooks walked to the far side of the buggy and checked the harness, not that it needed checking. He untied the horse and readied things for the trip home. As he walked back around the buggy, a man strode in his direction, his gaze honed in on the women. Mr. Lulu, he presumed.

"So, who is this?" Lulu wagged her eyebrows at Brooks, and he responded with a grin, knowing what she was thinking and knowing she was wrong. The man, shorter than Brooks by several inches, but stout and hardy, caught his gaze.

Keri cleared her throat. "Um . . . this is Mr. Morgan."

"And?" Lulu lifted her brows, her eyes wide.

Keri cast a quick, beseeching glance his way. He grinned and held out his hand to the man. "Brooks Morgan."

"Miles Dunn. We own a farm a few miles south of Raven Creek."

"A pleasure to meet you both."

Keri stepped in between Brooks and Miles. "Yes, and you both must come over and have dinner sometime."

"I'd love that." Lulu nodded but cast another curious glance at Brooks. "We have so much news to catch up on."

Miles tugged on his wife's elbow. "C'mon, darling. Your folks are waiting."

Keri hugged her friend again, then hurried to the buggy, as if not having the strength to face anyone else. Brooks lifted her up and then took his seat.

"Whew, that was a close call."

He cast a sideways glance at her as he smacked the reins across the horse's back. "What was?"

She elbowed him. "You know. They nearly found out that you own the ranch and that I still live there."

"And what happens when they come for a visit? Don't you think they'll find out then?"

"Oh, dear." Keri twisted her hands together. "What will we tell them?"

He shrugged. "How about the truth?"

"But you heard Carl."

He huffed out a breath. "Carl said that because he was upset. He sees me as competition and is jealous that I'm around you all the time."

Keri stiffened. "Why, that's absurd." She lifted her index finger in the air. "Number one—I have no interest in Carl Peters as a beau. Never have but can't seem to get the idea through his stubborn head. Number two—there's nothing between us that he has to be jealous about."

Brooks's heart took wing at her first declaration, but plummeted to the ground like a shot bird after the second. She had no reason to like him, not after he'd won her family home away from her, but he'd thought things were leveling out between the two of them. He wasn't used to women not liking him, but he should have known better than to allow himself to be attracted to Keri Langston. He'd promised to take care of her.

And that's what he would do.

But he wouldn't allow any false hopes that there could be more between them.

———— ★ ————

Brooks dumped another load of split logs into the wood box in the kitchen and dusted off his hands.

"Thank you." Keri glanced over her shoulder from where she stood in front of the stove. "Dinner is about ready."

"Sure smells good."

"We'll see. Can you holler at Nate and Jess?"

She faced the stove again, and Brooks took a moment to study her. The dress she'd looked so pretty in earlier had already been cast aside in favor of tight trousers, which left no course for a man's imagination. A blue calico shirt with tiny white-and-yellow flowers was loosely tucked into her waistband, and a long braid hung down her back instead of the fancy piling she'd worn to church. It was a shame she wasn't interested in him in the least bit, because he found her more fascinating than any woman he had met in a long while.

Footsteps clomped on the back porch, and the door banged into his back. Brooks jumped and moved out of the way.

"What are you doing?" Jess fussed.

"Just thinking is all."

"Well, can you go think somewhere that ain't in the way?"

Brooks grinned and slipped out the door, nodding at Nate as he passed by on his way to the well. Both men had disappeared after the church service. Brooks suspected they'd gone to the bunkhouse to play a game of cards on their day off. He blew out a sigh. Things were getting better between him and his workhands, but he still wished they'd be more friendly. He washed off his hands and his face and shook off the water.

Pastor Griffith's sermon had rattled him. It was almost as if the man was preaching to him—that part about forgetting God. That's pretty much what he'd done the past ten years. And he'd tried to forget the family who had loved him.

He'd been a stubborn, rebellious youth who thought he knew best. Thought he had it harder than others.

He'd been wrong, but he was also too stubborn to admit it and to return home.

Blowing out a sigh, he headed back to the house. How did a man go about reconnecting with a lost family and a God he'd never really known?

The door creaked as he entered the kitchen.

"I'm just sayin'. Don't know why we had to get up early and sit through that boring church preachin' on our only day off. Thought we was goin' there to call out Dengler. He weren't even there." Jess poured some cream into his coffee. "It was just a waste of time, if you ask me."

Nate took the plate of biscuits Keri handed him and glared at Jess. "Nobody asked you, so stop your bellyachin'."

Shaking his head, Brooks pulled out Keri's chair and waited for her to take her seat. She limped toward him, carrying a large bowl of yellow, creamy stuff. He took it from her and set it on the table. "You need to sit. Is there anything else that needs to be put on the table?"

"Just the greens, but I can—"

Brooks took her by the shoulders. "I'll fetch 'em. You sit."

She gave him a grateful smile and dropped into her chair. He could have kicked himself for not thinking about her foot still hurting. This was the first day she'd cooked since her injury, and that was after attending church and wearing those dressy shoes that were bound to pinch any woman's feet.

He set the greens on the table and took his seat. Jess reached for the biscuits, and Brooks cleared his throat. Three sets of eyes turned toward him, and Jess pulled his arm back. "Would y'all mind if we asked God's blessing on our meal?"

Jess shook his head. "First you wrangle us into goin' to church and now you want to pray. What's next? Baptizing in the crik?" He chuckled and elbowed Nate. "I'd like to see that, since there ain't no water in the crik, lessn' you count Raven Crik, and we all know that black water ain't no good."

Nate bumped Jess back. "That's enough from you." He

turned his gaze on Brooks. "I think askin' the Almighty's blessing couldn't hurt nothin'."

Brooks nodded and bowed his head, but his heart raced like he'd just run all the way to church. He searched his mind for a prayer from his past. "Heavenly Father, we . . . uh . . . thank You for this fine meal and . . . uh . . . ask that You bless the hands that fixed it." He glanced up but each face was still turned downward.

Nate peeked out one eye. "You're s'posed to say Amen when you get done, aren't you?"

Brooks shrugged and curled up his lips. "Amen, I reckon."

"I'm gonna have to start wearing one of them halos instead of a hat if'n I get any more religion." Jess reached for the plate and snagged two of the fluffy biscuits.

"What's that yellow stuff in the bowl?" Nate asked, pointing his knife toward it.

"Creamed chicken. I thought it would taste good layered over the biscuits." Keri cut a biscuit in half, then spread butter on both sides and spooned some of the creamy sauce over it.

Brooks's mouth watered at the delicious aroma filling the room. He ladled some greens on his plate and passed the bowl to Keri, along with a smile. She took the bowl and shook her head, her lips dancing at the corners.

"I'm sure glad you learned to cook at that school, Missy." Nate took a big bite of chicken and biscuits and closed his eyes. "I thought Will was dumb as the backside—uh, well . . ." A deep red stained his ears. "Sorry, Missy. Been around this lughead for too long." He jerked his thumb toward Jess. "Anyway, I thought Will was just plumb loco for sending you away to that school, but I'm sure glad you learned to cook."

"I managed to miss the last two years of my uncle's life." Spoons halted in midair.

"Uh . . . I'm sorry 'bout that, but Will had his reasons for sending you away." Nate ducked his head and tucked into his meal.

"No, I apologize. It's not your fault Uncle Will sent me to school. Maybe if I'd acted more ladylike, he would have let me stay." Keri pushed her food around on her plate.

Brooks searched for a more cheerful topic. "What all do we need to do this comin' week?"

"Horses need shoein'," Jess mumbled around his food.

"Cattle need to be moved to the north pasture," Nate said.

"I still need to go to town to get my trunk, not that there's much in it I need. Just a bunch of fancy dresses."

Brooks's mind took off on a trail that it shouldn't—thinking how pretty Keri must have looked in all those dresses. He imagined a rainbow of colors: blue, green, purple, pink, and in each one, she was prettier. "I can—" He cleared his throat then took a drink of the lukewarm coffee. "I can ride into town and fetch it. I want to talk to Doc and Marshal Lane anyhow."

"I'll go with you." Keri pierced him with a look that told him arguing would be a waste of time. "We're running low on supplies, and I can get them then."

"Maybe we should all go," Nate said. "I don't much like the idea of the two of you alone on the road, not after what Dengler's men did."

Brooks shook his head. "Someone needs to stay here. We're already spread thin, and I don't want to leave the ranch unattended."

"Just be sure your rifle's loaded." Jess snagged the last biscuit.

The man sure could eat for someone so skinny. Biting back a grin, Brooks ate the last of his meal, enjoying each bite. The fare was simple but tasty and satisfying.

Keri pushed back in her chair, and Brooks reached out, grabbing her wrist. "Where do you think you're going?"

She blinked, surprise etched in each pretty feature of her face. "Just to get the pie. You do want pie, don't you?"

He nodded. "I do, but you stay seated and finish your food. I can get it."

"But—"

He tweaked her nose, gaining a chuckle from Jess. "No buts, Missy."

She scowled, and he read her mind, but she scooted forward and picked up her spoon.

Grinning, Brooks took the pie off the stove and set it on the counter then divided it into four equal slices. Keri wouldn't eat but half of hers, and then she'd save the rest for a midafternoon snack if she got hungry. She sure was a handful. He could well understand Will feeling inadequate to raise and educate such a willful female. Why, it wouldn't be much different from him raising a girl. Even though he'd had an older sister, he wouldn't know where to start. His admiration for his old friend grew another notch.

After he served everyone and sat back down, talk returned to the work they needed to accomplish this coming week, but the idea of traveling all the way to town with just Keri along didn't stray far from his thoughts.

CHAPTER ELEVEN

rooks stared at the tiny buildings as they drew near Shoofly. The day was warm with just enough clouds overhead to keep things from getting too hot. The grass on both sides of the trail swished in the light breeze, but his enjoyable trip to town sure hadn't gone as expected. Keri had climbed aboard the buckboard this morning and promptly opened a book and hadn't talked to him except for when they'd taken a short break.

She was expecting to buy a wagonload of supplies, and he didn't have a dime to his name. Too bad all his money had gotten stolen. He sure could have used it.

Heaving a sigh, he pulled the wagon off to the side of the road. Keri looked up from her book, lifted the brim of her hat, and squinted. "Why are we stopping here?"

Brooks fiddled with the reins, straightening them and then twisting them again. He'd never needed much money and mainly survived by his wits and muscle. Maybe he wasn't cut out to be a rancher. Wasn't that one of the reasons he'd left home?

"Is something wrong?"

He sighed again and turned in the seat. "I know you had your heart set on buying supplies, but the truth is, I don't have money for that."

She stared at him for a moment, then smiled and waved one hand in the air. "Is that all? We always charge them to the ranch account."

Brooks's hopes lifted for a moment, then sank. "But that was in your uncle's name. I don't have an account, and the store owner isn't about to open one up for someone he hardly knows."

Keri wrinkled her brow and blinked several times. "But it's still the ranch account. Why should that change just because the owner did?"

He wanted to think like she did, but obviously she wasn't talented in the business end of the ranch. Still, he couldn't bring himself to dash all her hopes. "I reckon we can go talk to the man and see what he says."

She gazed up, uncertainty worrying her pretty eyes. "What if they say no? What will we do? I don't know how much longer we can get by on what we have left."

He reached over and squeezed her hand. "Things will work out. There's some beans, flour, and a few canned goods in the bunkhouse, leftover from when Nate and Jess had to fend for themselves. I can always hunt meat for us. We won't starve, but I'd sure miss those pies of yours if we have to go without sugar."

She smiled. "And we've got to have coffee, or you'll never get those cowboys of ours out of bed each morning."

Cowboys of ours. Brooks clucked to the horses pulling the buckboard with a smile on his face and in his heart. It was just a slip of the tongue on her part, he knew that, but just having her associate the two of them together had made his day.

"Let's get my trunk first, and then we can see how much space is left. I hope there's someone to help lift it onto the buckboard."

Brooks flexed his right arm. "What? You doubt my masculine ability?"

Her cheeks flushed and her eyes widened. "No, that's not at all what I meant. It's quite heavy, that's all."

He tucked in his lips, pleasantly pleased with her response, and guided the wagon down Main Street. His heart clenched as he passed the small house he'd lived in with Will. A woman came out the open door and tossed a bucket of soapy water into the street. Evidently, the old coot who owned the place had already rented it. He'd hoped to visit the place again, but it wasn't to be.

At the train station, Keri handed the clerk her claim ticket, and fifteen minutes later, with the help of a brawny freight worker, the oversized trunk was loaded, taking up nearly half of the wagon bed and sinking his hopes of impressing Keri with his strength.

"What's in that thing, anyway?" he asked.

She shrugged. "Mainly my gowns, some books I bought to read on cold winter nights, and my unmention—" Her cheeks grew a rosy red, and she turned her face away. "That's about all."

She'd almost mentioned her *unmentionables*. He helped her back aboard, biting back a grin, and then drove to the marshal's office. "Do you want to wait in the buckboard while I talk to the marshal?"

Pinning him with a stare, she asked, "Would you like to wait in the wagon while *I* talk to Marshal Lane?"

"Uh . . . no, ma'am." He lifted her down and escorted her into the marshal's office.

The marshal stood and tipped his hat. The office looked

just the same as the last time Brooks was there—bare wood and wanted posters lining several walls. An old stove sat in one corner beside a door that led to two cells in back.

"Good to see you folks." The marshal's gaze focused on Keri. "How are you getting by, Miss Langston? This rascal treating you good and fairly?" Marshal Lane held out his hand, indicating for Keri to sit in the chair by the wall and winked at Brooks over her head.

"Most of the time, I suppose."

"If he's not, I can lock him up for a few days and straighten him out."

"Thank you, but no. I'd lose my backup cook if you did that."

The marshal chuckled and rubbed his moustache. "Things been quiet up your way?"

Keri looked at Brooks, and his hand went to his throat, tracing the line that was barely visible any more.

"Oh, I don't know. Mr. Morgan, here, would have been dead if I hadn't happened along at the exact moment I did."

Marshal Lane straightened in his chair, his gaze flicking between Keri and Brooks. "What does that mean?"

"It was Dengler's men," Keri stated.

"Better let me tell the story since you weren't there for the whole thing." The look she threw over her shoulder told Brooks she didn't like being hushed, but she nodded.

He relayed all the details about his near hanging.

The marshal stood and paced to the door and back. "When did this happen?"

"The day I first rode out to the ranch."

"The day I first returned home," Keri said at the same time.

"Why are you just now telling me?" He pulled a rifle from the rack on the wall and checked it for ammunition.

Brooks pushed away from the wall he was leaning against.

"Because I was wounded, and anxious to get to the ranch, and I didn't want any more trouble with Dengler until I knew how things stood."

"Sounds like they came darn close to killing you and stealing Raven Creek. That's not something I can overlook."

"If I can, why can't you?" Brooks locked gazes with the marshal. "Men like Dengler have ten men to replace the two you'd arrest, and those ten would be gunning for us. We're better off to turn our face the other way and try to get along."

"I've been waiting for a long while to pin a crime on Saul Dengler."

Brooks nodded. "I'm sure you have, but he'll just hand over those two men and deny he knew anything about the attempted lynching."

"Maybe. But I can make those men talk."

"True. But will a forced confession hold up in court?"

The marshal brushed the back of his hand across the bristle on his jaw. "Probably not." He spat at a spittoon in the corner then wiped his mouth on his sleeve. "My apologies, Miss Langston."

"Has there been any headway in finding out who killed my uncle?"

Marshal Lane dropped back down in his chair. "Nobody said that Will was killed, Miss Langston." His gaze slid past Keri and latched onto Brooks. He cleared his throat. "I can tell you that the doctor suspects foul play, and so do I, especially since there was also the robbery that night. I believe someone was looking for something."

Keri slid to the edge of the chair and leaned toward Marshal Lane. "I can tell you for certain that my uncle would never take his life, especially knowing I was returning home so soon." She ducked her head.

Brooks heard a sniffle from Keri's direction, and his heart

seized up. He rested his hand on her shoulder and gave it a gentle squeeze. "I agree. Will was in a lot of pain, but you know as well as I do that it didn't affect his outlook."

Keri jumped up, her fists balling at her side. "You've got to find the person responsible, Marshal. My uncle was a good man."

The marshal rose. "I agree, but we need to have some patience in this instance. Men like to brag about such things, and time and whiskey loosens lips. We'll find out what happened sooner or later."

Keri nodded and wiped the corner of her eyes with her forefinger. "All right. I will try. We appreciate your efforts on our behalf." She walked out the door without looking at Brooks, but he couldn't help noticing that she'd said "we," not "I."

He shook Marshal Lane's hand again, and the marshal clapped him on the shoulder. "You all be careful out there. Far as I know, Dengler and his men have never hurt a woman, but the rest of you could be in danger, especially since his land borders yours."

"We'll keep a watch out." Brooks rubbed the nape of his neck. "Any idea why Dengler would want Raven Creek? It's a good-sized piece of land, but he's blocked the water, and things are drying up. I don't know as there's anything more special about it than any other land around here."

"Dengler's just land hungry. He doesn't need a reason. I think it's his goal to own all the land in this county."

Brooks bid the marshal good day and strode outside to find Keri. She stood at the end of the walkway, her arm wrapped around a post as if she needed support. He closed the distance between them. "You all right?"

She shrugged, then sniffed. "Someone killed Uncle Will. I just know it in my gut." She wiped her eyes with a fancy, embroidered handkerchief edged in lace then turned. Her lips and chin wobbled, and her pretty eyes were red, matching her nose. "I just keep thinking about his last moments and wondering if he was fighting for his life. Was he—worrying about me?" She fell forward, and Brooks wrapped his arms around her, holding her close in spite of the spectacle they made.

"Shh . . . we'll find out who did this, I promise."

Keri jerked free, leaving his arms empty. "Don't make promises you can't keep, Mr. Morgan."

———— ★ ————

Keri marched down the boardwalk along Main Street, trying to gain hold of her emotions. Just a few weeks ago, she'd been so excited about returning home, but little did she know then that everything had changed. She had no family. The house she lived in no longer belonged to her. She couldn't live on Mr. Morgan's generosity forever, but what could she do?

Sniffling, she took a moment to study the town. Several new buildings had been added at the far end of the street and in the middle where it looked as if there may have been a fire at one time. There were few new businesses, although—lucky her—a dressmaker shop had opened up across the street. Maybe the owner would be interested in purchasing some of her dresses.

Footsteps approached then Brooks stopped beside her. "Something wrong?"

"Why do you ask that?"

He leaned on the railing and stared down. "I don't know. Given the fact that you were crying . . ."

She lifted her head. "Having watery eyes isn't crying."

A tiny grin pulled at his intriguing mouth. "It isn't?"

"Are you laughing at me?"

His grin broke forth fully, revealing his straight, white teeth. "No, ma'am. I'm smarter than that."

"Hmpf." She crossed her arms and turned her back to him. He was nothing but a big kid, always joking and never taking things seriously. The ranch would probably fail within the year with him at the reins.

"We should tend to the rest of our business and then head out again. I don't want to be on the road after dark, not with Dengler's men out and about."

She nodded and started down the stairs and across the alley. She passed the bank, then stopped suddenly as an idea sparked.

"Whoa, there," Brooks said, bumping into her back. He lightly grabbed her shoulders. "Give a guy some warning when you're going to rein in."

"Why don't you go see how things stand at the store? I want to go into the bank and check on my uncle's account. It's possible he might have left some funds there." She fished her supply list out of her handbag and handed it to him.

"You sure you don't want me to wait out here for you?"

She shook her head. "The store is just a few shops away. I'll be fine."

Brooks looked up and down the street as if checking for a problem, then he gave a single, curt nod. He tipped his hat, but she read the worry in his eyes. "See you in a few minutes."

She reached for the knob of the bank's door and watched him walk away. He was thoughtful to be concerned for her welfare, but it annoyed her at the same time. She scanned the streets, wondering what he'd been looking for. Several buggies and buckboards sat in front of stores, and a half dozen people— no one she recognized—strolled the street. Mr. Morgan's anxiety was contagious, and she didn't like worrying about something that might not even happen.

She pushed open the door, and the strong odor of furniture wax greeted her as did the clerk behind the sleek, wooden counter. A barred, glassless opening protected him from thieves, although it would do little to stop a bullet.

"How can I help you, ma'am?"

Keri sighed under her breath. Someone else she didn't know. She walked over to the window. "I'm Keri Langston, niece of Will Langston. I'm sure you've heard that he passed on."

The man nodded, his brown eyes filled with sympathy. "May I offer my condolences, Miss Langston."

"Thank you, sir. I was wondering if my uncle left any funds in his account."

The thin man frowned. "Hmm . . . let me take a look." He crossed to a cabinet on the wall behind him and ran his finger down the row of drawers, then opened one and thumbed through the cards. He pulled one out and stared at it, then returned to the window. "Well, I can tell you that your uncle did leave some money in his account, but since your name isn't on it, I regret that I can't give it to you."

Keri blinked, trying to comprehend what he'd said. "There's money, but I can't have it?"

He nodded.

"But I'm his only surviving relative."

The clerk ducked his chin. "I'm sorry. If you have a will or a handwritten letter stating that you're to inherit Mr. Langston's holdings, then I could give it to you."

Keri narrowed her gaze. "And just how am I supposed to get that when my uncle is dead? Murdered, in fact."

The man's eyes widened and he swallowed, causing his large Adam's apple to bounce. "I'm sorry. I hadn't heard that."

"Is Mr. Powell in?" Maybe the bank manager could help her.

"No, ma'am. Mr. Powell sold the bank last year and moved to St. Louis to tend his ailing mother. Mr. Arnold Michaels is the proprietor now."

Fat lot of help another stranger would be. "And what happens to the funds if there is no will?"

"Usually the money goes to the town account after a year if no one claims it."

"I see." Keri pursed her lips. She considered having a crying spell like women at the school had done when they didn't get their way, but she doubted it would have an impact on this hard-hearted soul. "I'll just have to see if I can find the will."

"Keri?"

She spun around at the familiar voice. She'd been so engrossed in her conversation that Carl Peters had walked in without her hearing him.

"Is there something I can do to help you?" he asked.

"How could *you* help?"

"Well . . ." He puffed out his chest. "I work here now." He glanced at the clerk. "Explain the situation to me, Matthew."

Keri waited while the man relayed their conversation. She hoped Carl could help her get access to her uncle's funds, but she hated to be indebted to him. Carl listened to the man, then he took hold of Keri's arm and walked her to the far side of the room.

"I'm sorry, but without the will, our hands are tied." He leaned in close, and Keri forced herself to hold her ground and not step back. "If you're having hard times, I could loan you some money."

"Thank you, but that won't be necessary. We'll manage."

Carl reached for her hand. "I could make things so much easier for you, if you'd just let me. I have a big home now on a large section of land a short way from town. It's filled with beautiful furniture."

Keri tugged her hand away. "I'm not ready to make a decision yet, Carl. I need to head home. Thank you for your offer of help."

She spun around and marched out the door, barely containing her emotions. How could Uncle Will gamble away the ranch and then leave her no money to live on? Did he not care for her enough to provide for her? Maybe his talk and smiles were just lies? Pulling her handkerchief from her sleeve, she dabbed her eyes before opening the door.

What a burden she must have been to her uncle—a bachelor who never married. A bachelor who suddenly had a young girl to raise. She hung her head, the pain of it all more than she could bear. Her mother had given her away. Was it too much to hope her uncle had loved her—at least a little?

She opened the door and waited for an approaching man to pass by.

"Keri, wait." Carl took her arm and pulled her back inside the bank. "I don't think you understand. I've just about gone loco the past two years that you've been gone. Do you have any idea how much I've missed you?"

Evidently far more than she had missed him.

"Now that you're back, I'm hoping we can pick up things where we left off."

"And just where was that?"

He blinked and stared at her, as if her response surprised him. "I had asked your uncle for your hand in marriage, but you left before I even got to tell you."

CHAPTER TWELVE

*K*eri's heart jumped, like a horse clearing a stream. She stared up at Carl. "Did Uncle Will give you permission?"

Carl scowled for a moment, then resumed his normal placating gaze. "He said I'd have to ask you. That he wasn't going to agree when he wasn't sure how you felt."

Some of the tension flowed out of her. At least he hadn't agreed. "So many things have changed. I'm not ready to consider marriage at this time, Carl."

"I can wait, but I hope to not wait much longer. You need help on your ranch, and I don't like that drifter hanging around there."

She tightened her fist until her nails bit into her hand. "Did you not understand me that day you visited? I no longer own Raven Creek. That *drifter* does."

He looked as if he'd been slapped. "Then why are you still living there?"

"Because I have nowhere else to go."

He snatched her hand again. "Then marry me. I'll buy back your ranch, and we can live there and cast Mr. Morgan out on his backside."

Keri's hope rose at the thought of getting ownership of Raven Creek, but was she willing to pay the price? Could she marry a man she cared nothing for, just for the sake of keeping her home?

She lifted her chin. "Thank you for such a generous offer. Let me consider it for a while."

"Why? Marry me *today*."

"Carl, my uncle just died. It would be improper to marry so soon. And you have no guarantee that Mr. Morgan will sell. He's already come close to dying for that ranch."

Carl's eyes narrowed and his gaze turned chilly, making Keri wonder what had caused such a reaction. "All right, Keri. I'll wait. But after two years, I'm no longer a patient man."

She stepped back, not liking the iciness of his gaze. He had no right to demand anything of her. She'd made him no promises. The harness of a wagon jingled, pulling Keri's attention away from Carl. Brooks stopped the wagon and hopped down, scowling. Relief made her knees weak. "Excuse me, but I need to go now."

She slid around Carl and hurried down the steps. Brooks lifted her into the wagon, and she noticed he must have had better luck at the mercantile than she had at the bank.

They were a good two miles out of town before her heart resumed its normal pace. Brooks hadn't said a thing, but she'd notice the muscles in his jaw twitching.

She leaned back in the seat and stared out at the passing scenery. A cluster of oak trees shaded them for a moment from the warm afternoon sun. Sweat trickled down her temple, but she wasn't sure if it was from the heat or her recent marriage proposal. Had Carl truly asked her uncle if he could marry her? Why hadn't Uncle Will told her?

Two years ago, the issue of her attending finishing school had come up rather suddenly, and her uncle had been adamant about it. Could Carl's proposal have had anything to do with that?

Maybe his purpose in sending her had been to keep her away from Carl. But why?

Carl's family ran a prosperous ranch on the far side of town. What objections could Uncle Will have had to her marrying him?—not that she wanted to.

"You all right?" Brooks sidled a glance her way.

Keri sighed. "I wish people would quit asking me that."

He was quiet for a while. His elbows rested on his knees, and the reins dangled loosely from his fingertips. "It's just that you looked a bit uncomfortable when you were talkin' to that Peters guy."

"My ankle was hurting some." That was the truth, but certainly not the whole of it.

Brooks turned in the seat and snagged her gaze. "If he's pestering you, you let me know. I'll take care of him."

The thought of Brooks Morgan walloping Carl wasn't altogether unpleasant, and she had no doubt that he could. His shoulders were substantially wider than Carl's, and she'd felt the strength of his muscles each time he lifted her in and out of the buggy. A tiny smile teased her lips. How odd that this man who'd stolen her home was willing to become her champion.

———— ★ ————

Brooks stewed on what Peters could have wanted all the way home. Keri was being tight-lipped and not talking, which left him to speculate, although seeing how Peters had her cornered up against the wall, it was obvious what he wanted. *Keri.*

He wish now that he'd thought to ask Marshal Lane about the man. He had no real reason to dislike him, except for a gut feeling and the way Peters acted around Keri—like he owned her. If she were sole owner of the ranch, he might understand Carl Peters wanting to marry her—so he'd gain a sizeable ranch as well as a mighty pretty gal. But something just didn't sit right. Peters reminded him of a fox slinking around a henhouse.

Brooks clamped his back teeth together. Why should he care if some man wanted to marry Keri? If someone did, at least he'd get to sleep in his house for once.

But the thought of her marrying someone else rubbed him as raw as old, dried leather. He didn't like the idea at all.

He felt Keri stiffen beside them as they rode into the ranch yard. A horse was hitched out front, and a man sat reclining in a rocker, holding one of the cups from the kitchen.

Nate paced in front of the house and hurried toward them as soon as he saw them. His cheeks were red from the exertion of his pacing, and his shirt was sweat-stained. "Sorry to be the bearer of bad news, but Saul Dengler is here."

"What is that man doing on my land?" Keri lifted the brim of her hat and stared toward the porch, her body rigid.

Her land? Brooks had no idea how he was going to get her to understand the land was his now, but he had worse things to deal with now. "Did he say what he wanted?"

"Nope. Just that he wanted to talk to the owner."

"Tell him I'll be right there as soon as I park the wagon."

"Tell him we'll both be there." Keri hiked up her pert little chin, and her expression dared him to disagree.

Brooks exhaled loudly and clucked to the horses, driving them around to the back of the house. Unloading the food supplies would be easier that way, and he'd just as soon not let Dengler know any more of his business than the man already did.

After parking the wagon and helping Keri down, Brooks checked to make sure his gun was loaded, then followed her through the house to the porch. Dengler stood when he saw her and smiled, reminding Brooks of a weasel that had stolen the last hen from the coop. Brooks glanced at Nate and nodded his thanks for keeping an eye on the man. Nate moseyed back toward the barn, but Brooks had a feeling he'd keep his rifle handy in case there was trouble.

"Welcome back, Miss Langston. I trust you had a good time while you were away."

"There's no point in polite social talk, Mr. Dengler. Why don't you just tell us why you're here?" Keri plastered her hands to her hips and tapped one toe.

"There's no reason to get in a huff. I've come as a neighbor paying a call on another neighbor."

Brooks stepped in front of Keri. "Friendly neighbors don't block the downstream flow of a river. You denying that you did that?"

Dengler stroked his short beard and lifted his gray brows. "Which river would that be, Mr.—"

"The one that runs through Raven Creek land. The one that's nearly dried up, thanks to you." Brooks mentally forced himself to relax his hands. "And the name is Morgan."

"Well, Mr. Morgan, just make sure you keep your cattle off my land. I don't want my Herefords mixing with those scrub cattle of yours." He glanced at Keri. "Or are they your cattle, Miss Langston?"

"They're *ours*," she responded.

"So." Dengler glanced down his foxlike nose. "You two are married then?"

Brooks glanced at Keri, growing uneasy with the direction Dengler was leading the conversation. They could throw insults at him all day, but he didn't want anyone besmirching Keri's reputation. "That's none of your concern."

Dengler's lips curled up in a vile smirk. "I see how it is."

Brooks vaulted toward the man, and Keri screeched. He shoved Dengler against the wall, knocking the man's hat off. "You see nothing. I think it's time you go."

Dengler stiffened and glared at Brooks. "Careful, Mr. Morgan. I'm not a man to trifle with."

"Why are you here?" Brooks growled out, giving the man's lapels a shake.

"If you'll release me, I will show you." Brooks turned loose of the snake, and the man brushed his lapels, then pulled a paper from his vest pocket and held it out. "From what I've heard, this goes to you."

He shook the folded page open and scanned it. A bill of sale. For Raven Creek. For twice what the last offer was. Brooks passed it to Keri. "Why do you want this little piece of land so bad? You've already got more than ten times the acreage we have. You couldn't possibly need this land."

"Doesn't matter if I want it or need it."

"It matters to me." Brooks tugged the paper away from Keri, wadded it up, and tossed it in the dirt.

Dengler's jaw worked as if he were struggling to chew up a tough piece of meat. "If that's the way you want it." He nodded at Keri and stomped down the porch steps to his horse then turned. "That's my top offer, and don't expect to see it again."

Keri rushed to the porch and placed both hands on the rail. "Our answer is no—today, tomorrow, and next year. And you can expect the marshal to be paying you a visit soon."

Dengler mounted, and his horse turned toward the road. He reined it back around, his expression dark. "The marshal has no beef with me."

"No, but I'd bet he'd like to talk to the two men who tried to hang Mr. Morgan, all because he wouldn't sell Raven Creek."

Brooks moved up beside her and shushed her. She seared him with a scalding gaze.

"Those men no longer work for me, Miss Langston. I don't tolerate workers who do what they did." He tipped his hat. "Good day."

Brooks's skin crawled as he watched the man ride away. He had a strong hunch that Dengler had gotten rid of the men who'd tried to hang him—not because of their heinous deeds but because they'd failed to accomplish their mission.

"You shouldn't goad a man like that, Missy."

She spun on him and slugged him in the arm. "Stop calling me that. Only Uncle Will and Nate have ever referred to me by that name."

He grabbed her arms and pulled her close. Her warm breath fanned his face. "What name would you like me to call you?" Sweetheart. Sugar. Honey. That's what he'd like, but he doubted she'd be too happy. At the alarming thought, he released her suddenly and stepped back, bumping against the porch rail. What had gotten into him?

Keri rubbed her arms. "I suppose since we see each other every day and work together, you might as well call me by my Christian name."

He grinned, partly because he was glad to have permission to use her real name and partly to hide his confusion over his attraction to her. He'd learned long ago that if he smiled, most folks smiled back and went on about their business and didn't stick their nose in his.

"Well, the sun's setting, and I'd better get something cooking, or we won't have anything to eat." Keri shuffled toward the front door.

"And I need to get the wagon unloaded. Don't want to

leave food out overnight, or the critters will get it." He whistled for Nate, and the man walked out of the barn, followed by Jess. They were good men. He wished they would drop their guard and fully accept him, but he knew he'd have to earn their respect. Maybe bringing home a wagonload of food supplies was a move in the right direction.

———— ★ ————

Brooks hunkered down and ran to the next bush, hoping to get a better view of the dam Dengler had built. He'd sat there so long, the birds had started chirping again, but suddenly, they stopped. Brooks stiffened and looked over the hill. Had someone seen him and come after him? The grass rustled behind him, and he spun around, falling backwards as he drew his gun. Keri crawled through the brush, and her blue eyes widened when she saw him aiming a gun at her.

"I told you to stay back with the horses," he hissed. "I nearly shot you."

"I want to see what's happening." She scooted up beside him, and for once, he was thankful she didn't have a dress on. She rose up and peeked over the ledge. "What did you see?"

Brooks jerked her back down behind cover. "You want to get that pretty head of yours shot off?" he whispered in her ear. His lips touched her skin, sending delicious tingles charging through him.

"You looked." She didn't seem affected by his nearness in the least.

"Yeah, but I have my hat on, which shades my face so they can't see me as well as they can see you."

"I have a hat too."

"Yeah, with a bright red ribbon on it."

She frowned and leaned back against a boulder. "So, what did you see?"

"They've blocked off the flow with a bunch of big rocks, then filled it in with dirt, best I can tell. There's not even a trickle on our side."

Keri clenched her fist and pulled a face. "Those lowdown skunks."

Three gunshots rang out in the distance. Brooks shoved Keri down and covered her with his body. If they hadn't been in danger of getting shot, being out here all cozied up to her would have been a pleasant affair. A horse whinnied, then Brooks heard what sounded like several horses riding away.

"Get off me, you brute." Keri shoved her elbow in his gut.

"I will, but you stay down." He peeked up over the top of the ledge and watched three riders as they stirred up a cloud of dust. It looked as if they'd headed in for the night. He rose up a bit higher and searched the area. He'd only seen the three horses earlier, and there were no signs of anyone else. "You can come up now, but keep low."

"Why, thank you, kind sir."

He grinned and held out his hand. She smacked it aside and shinnied up beside him sticking up her head like a turtle. "I say we come back tonight and dynamite that dam."

Brooks chuckled at her spunk. "They'd just build it back."

"And we can blow it up again. It takes a lot less time to demolish a dam than to build one."

"True, but it's also a good way to get shot."

She turned a frown on him. "I suppose you've got a better idea."

He nodded. "I reckon I do. It will assure you of water at all times, and it's a heap safer than using dynamite."

CHAPTER THIRTEEN

*T*hree days later, Keri stood on the porch and watched a pair of wagons, each carrying two men and a load of wood and metal, pass by. She'd seen little sign of Brooks the past few days, other than at meals, but had watched him and their hands herd a half dozen cattle down the road the day before yesterday.

She'd poked and prodded to get him to tell her what happened to the cattle, but he just smiled and had said to cook a passel of food for lunch and dinner the next few days. A horse nickered, pulling her gaze to a buggy coming down the lane. Keri shielded her eyes from the glare of the sun and saw Lulu waving as she pulled up to the house.

Smiling, Keri jogged down the steps and tied the horse to the porch rail. "This is a nice surprise."

Lulu climbed down, lifted out a package wrapped in brown paper, and hurried toward her, enveloping her in a hug. "Miles is coming over to help Brooks and the other men and said I could come for a visit. I thought you might could use some help baking for the men."

"You have no idea how happy I am to see you. My cooking has improved a lot, but I'm not sure I'm up to cooking for a crew of men, even a small crew. Three is bad enough."

They shared a laugh, looped arms, and Keri escorted her friend up the steps.

"Here." Lulu shoved the package at Keri.

"What is it?"

"Open it and find out." Lulu almost bounced on her tiptoes in her barely contained excitement.

Keri untied the twine and unwrapped the paper, revealing some brown tweed fabric. She unfolded the garment and shook it out, holding it up by the waistband. "A split skirt?"

Lulu nodded. "Yes. Isn't it a wonderful creation? I've been wearing them when I ride astride—well, before I got pregnant. Miles insists I use the buggy for now. I thought you might like to have one of my pairs."

The garment looked like the lower half of a dress to her, but she didn't want to hurt her friend's feelings.

"Don't look so bewildered. It's a skirt that's made rather like a big, loose pair of trousers. It makes riding astride so much easier than in a dress or skirt, but it also allows you the modesty of a female. Now that you're a woman, Keri, it would be better if you didn't wear men's pants."

Keri turned her back to Lulu so she wouldn't see her frown. Pants on women weren't acceptable in polite society and places like town and church, but they were far more practical dress when one lived on the ranch.

"Don't be upset at me. But there are things you don't understand about men. I've learned about them since I've been married." A becoming blush stole onto her cheeks. "Men like to gawk at women and fantasize about what's under all those yards of fabric."

"Lulu! For heaven's sake."

Holding up a hand, Lulu continued. "It's true. God made men different than women. That's why they stare at us so much. And when you wear pants, there's nothing left to guess about."

Keri hadn't considered that. It was true that her shape was very obvious in the cut of the tight pants she wore, but she'd worn them most of her life and they felt comfortable. Still . . . she sure didn't want men looking at her and thinking things they shouldn't. "Thank you. I'll consider what you've said." She held her hand out, motioning at a porch rocker. "Have a seat and I'll take your horse to the barn."

"Oh no, I can tend him."

"Sit." She gently pushed on Lulu's shoulders. "Jess is out there and can unhitch the buggy and groom your horse. Brooks likes to have a man around the house during the day, for some reason unbeknownst to be me."

"Oh he does, does he?" Lulu waggled her brows and flashed a wily smile. "Sounds like a man protecting his woman."

"Lulu! Don't say such things. It's nothing like that."

Ducking her head, a shy grin danced on Lulu's lips. She peeked up with an ornery grin, her hazel eyes twinkling. "Surely you've noticed what a handsome man Mr. Morgan is."

The words to deny her friend's comment were on the tip of her lip, but uttering them would be a lie. "Oh, of course I know he's good looking, but he's a ninny. Grinning all the time like a kid who snuck a whole pie from his ma's pantry and ate it all by himself."

"It's good for a man to be happy and smile a lot. Miles is that way. Makes for a good marriage." A pink blush rose up her cheeks.

Keri leaned back against the railing, half embarrassed to confide in her friend. "I had a marriage proposal yesterday."

Lulu popped up and scooted to the edge of her chair. "Honestly? Do tell. Was it Mr. Morgan?"

Rolling her eyes, Keri shook her head. "No, for heaven's sake. Why would you think that?"

"I've seen the way he looks at you."

"How?" She hated the way the word came out in an embarrassed giggle.

"Like a man who cares for a woman."

"No, you're mistaken. That man doesn't have a serious bone in his body and only cares about himself."

"Uh-huh."

She wagged her finger at her friend. "Don't uh-huh me." She stood to go and tend the horse but Lulu grabbed her arm.

"Wait! Don't leave me wondering. I'll just die of curiosity, and then poor Miles would be a widower. Who asked you to marry him?"

Now she wished she hadn't said anything, but then again, what would it hurt to talk to a friend about the situation? She needed another person's perspective. "It's Carl Peters."

Lulu rested her hands in her lap and worry crinkled her brow. "I thought he repulsed you. Have things changed?"

Staring down at her boot tips, Keri blew out a sigh. "Many things have changed, but not how I feel for Carl."

"I don't understand." Lulu rose and came to stand beside her. "If you still don't care for the man, how could you consider marrying him?"

Turning to face away from the house, Keri grasped hold of the railing as if were a tether, holding her in place. "It's a bit of a thorny situation."

Lulu placed her hand over Keri's. "I'm a good listener, if you need someone to talk to."

Raw emotions swirled through her, and she fought to maintain control, but her eyes burned and tears ran down her cheeks. "Oh, Lulu. I don't know what to do. Uncle Will lost the ranch to Mr. Morgan in a card game. I came home from school expecting for things to go back to the way they used to be, and found Uncle Will dead and my home lost to a charming stranger with a huge, irritating grin."

Patting Keri's back, Lulu cooed words of encouragement. "It's not all bad. Mr. Morgan must be letting you stay in the house."

"That's true, but what happens when he gets tired of sleeping with the men and decides he wants to live in the house he owns?"

"I don't know, but God does."

Keri stiffened and stepped back. "God doesn't care about what happens to *me*. Isn't that clear?"

"No, it isn't." Lulu shook her head. "God loves you. You're His child—His daughter—and He cares as much for you as if you were His only child. He gave His own Son to die for you."

"I've seen little evidence of God in my life. My mother gave me away when I was a young girl, and the uncle who raised me gambled away my home and didn't care enough to make sure I had enough money to get by. And now, I may be forced to marry a man I don't love, just to have a place to live."

Lulu stroked her hand across Keri's head and her hair. "It sure sounds like your life is in an uproar, but God's light shines the brightest when times are the darkest. Trust Him, Keri. He'll never abandon you."

Hmpf. Everyone she'd loved had abandoned her. Why would God be any different?

←— ★ —→

Brooks lifted his hat and wiped the sweat off his brow. He hoped his plan would work. It had to work. Unless God sent a deluge of rain for a week, the water-pumping windmill was his only option to get water for his herd and their needs.

Keri drove the wagon down the hill, and a trail of dust lifted into the air behind her. For the past three days, she had ridden out with an afternoon snack and some water or lemonade, but the biggest treat was seeing her again. He'd missed working around the house, but he was needed out here to help. Other than the team from the windmill company doing the installation, he was the only other man who'd worked on one before. One of the many different jobs he'd held over the past ten years.

He glanced up, proud of their progress. Jess and Daniel, one of the installers, were up at the top of the tower, attaching the fan blades. If the rest of the installation went as planned, they should be ready to test the windmill before supper.

Keri pulled the wagon to a stop, set the brake, and climbed down before he could get there to assist her. She'd forsaken the pretty boaters' hat she wore that first day he'd seen her for a frayed, straw western hat. Pushing back the brim, she gazed up at the tower. "Wow, that thing is tall."

Brooks was enamored with the paler skin under her chin that the sun hadn't touched and couldn't tear his gaze away. Would it feel as soft as it looked? He shook his head. Where were these crazy thoughts coming from? He needed to focus on something more within his reach. "What'd you bring us to eat?"

She sashayed to the back of the wagon. "I made something called a marble cake and brought some milk to drink with it." She lowered the tailgate, and Brooks caught a whiff of something sweet.

"Sure smells good."

Keri glanced at him and smiled. He captured her gaze with his and couldn't break away. His heart thundered. He had the overwhelming urge to kiss her.

"Yoohoo! Miss Keri. Lookie up here!" Jess hollered from the top of the tower.

She blinked finally and glanced up, past him to where Jess stood near the top of the tower. Brooks turned and scowled at the man for interrupting a most pleasant moment and for horsing around on the tower. The installation team had warned them about such things.

"Miss Keri." Jess leaned precariously over the side and waved his arm back and forth. "I ain't never been up this high afore."

Keri waved back then cupped her hands around her mouth. "Be careful."

Instead of waving, Jess's arms suddenly started pumping, and the next moment, he tumbled over the rail, plunging down. Keri shrieked. She spun around, burying her face in Brooks's chest. He wrapped his arms around her, and then he started chuckling.

She glanced up, horror marring her pretty features. "You're laughing?" She shoved him so hard and back stepped. "Jess is dead and you're laughing?"

He struggled to keep a straight face, then just pointed at the tower. Slowly, as if afraid to look, she turned back and gazed up. Jess swung back and forth, tied to the tower by a rope that the installers had insisted they use. Daniel leaned over the side and was giving Jess orders to stop kicking and grab hold of the tower. Jess did and started the climb back to the top.

Keri leaned against the side of the buckboard and put her head on her arm. "I thought he was dead."

Guilt for laughing washed over Brooks. He should have considered that she'd just lost her uncle, and losing a hand who'd worked at the ranch since she was small would be traumatic. He walked up behind her and rested one hand on her thin shoulder. "I'm sorry."

She spun around and slugged him in the chest, tears swimming in her eyes. "You should be. That scared me half to death." She whacked him again, softer this time. "Why didn't you tell me he had a rope on?"

"It happened so fast, there wasn't time."

"You had time to laugh." She pushed away from him and stomped to the back of the wagon. She pulled half a dozen plates from a basket and started slicing the cake.

"There's a piece missing."

"I didn't eat it, if that's what you're wondering. I gave it to Nate. He's hoping you hit water today because some of the garden is starting to wither up."

The crew gathered around the wagon, and Brooks handed each man a plate with a generous slice of cake on it. Then he poured milk for those who wanted it. Jess and Daniel ambled up to them a few minutes after everyone else.

"Did you see me flying like a bird, Miss Keri? Thought I was a goner for a minute there."

Keri sent a scolding glance at Brooks, then softened her expression for Jess. "You scared me half out of my wits."

"I know just how you feel." Jess rubbed the side of his head then his eyes lit up and he reached for a cake plate. He shoved a huge bite into his mouth. "Hey," he said, spitting crumbs like a Gatling gun shooting bullets. "This is a heap good. How'd you make it diff'rnt colors?"

"I'm glad you like it. I made two batters and darkened one with molasses and some spices. Then you take turns spooning in the two batters. Lulu gave me the recipe."

Brooks closed his eyes as he took a bite and enjoyed the sweet flavors. Keri's cooking seemed to improve each day. A man would be lucky to have a wife like her. He clenched his jaw, set down his empty plate, and walk away from the group.

The men, obviously sensing the end of their work, joked

and cut up with one another. Laughter rang out among them. He was glad they were in high spirits, as he was. He felt certain they'd gain victory over Saul Dengler without resorting to violence. It felt good to know that he'd outsmarted the vile man.

He walked over to the tower and gazed up at the crisscross web of wood and metal. Giving it a shake, he smiled at its solidness. By tomorrow, they should be watering their cattle.

"So, how did you pay for this monstrosity?" Keri stopped beside him and put her foot on the lowest crossbar and raised up her arms, grabbing a bar just over her head.

"We sold a few head of cattle—six to be exact."

"Six head isn't a few."

"We can spare six. If we don't get water soon, we'll be selling the whole herd for less than market value. Is that what you want?"

"No, of course not. It's just—what if you spent all this money and this thing doesn't work?" She ducked her head. "What if it's just a big waste of effort and money?"

"This isn't the first windmill in Texas; you know that."

She cast him a sideways glance then rolled her eyes. "Of course I know that. I wasn't born yesterday. What I meant was, what if there isn't water down there?"

Brooks grinned to hide his disappointment. "You have no faith in me."

"Ah. Something we finally agree on." She laughed, as if making a joke, but the words still stung.

"I'd better get back to work."

"Wait!" She grabbed his arm as he stepped back. "Tell me how this contraption works."

If he couldn't impress her with his ingenuity and his brawn, maybe he could impress her with his know-how. "The windmills work by pumping water from the ground. When the wind blows, it spins the sails—those metal blades at the top—which makes that rod in the center of the tower go up and down, and that pulls water up from the ground. Then it spills out into the troughs and that storage tank."

She pushed away from the tower. "Well, let's hope it works. We've got a lot riding on this contraption."

"I'm praying it works."

"*Hmpf.* I sure hope you aren't disappointed come tomorrow." She peered up at him for a moment, then turned and walked back to the wagon.

Brooks blew a heavy breath out his nose. He hoped they wouldn't be disappointed too.

———— ★ ————

Keri pulled the pot roast from the oven, flooding the room with its delicious aroma. She made a slit in the top with a knife to check its doneness. Juice ran down the side of the large hunk of meat, and she slid it back in to finish cooking. She returned to the table to cut out the rest of the biscuits, thinking about the tall water tower. It had been impressive.

And she hadn't been very nice to Mr. Morgan. When she first learned what he was up to, she'd gotten upset that he'd sold some of her uncle's cattle to buy the monstrosity, but in spite of her snide comments to him, she'd been impressed with the solidness of the tower. If it worked, it would solve one big problem. They'd have water for the cattle again—and that would be a blessing.

After cutting out the biscuits, she cleaned her hands and went out to take her laundry off the line. Timing her wash to get dried before the men returned was challenging at times, but she didn't want them viewing her unmentionables, especially *him*.

Heat rose to her cheeks at the thought. She quickly

removed her laundry, then carried it upstairs to her room, folded some, placed others in a basket to be ironed, and then walked over to the window. In the distance the tower rose up, tall and shiny. The fan on top was spinning in the warm, late afternoon breeze. It was quite an impressive structure, and she certainly had never expected to have one on her property. Tiny figures moved around the base of the tower, so she knew she had some time before the men returned.

She started back downstairs, but paused and glanced at the door to her uncle's bedroom. There were things in there that needed tending to, and what if he'd left a will tucked away in a safe spot? She needed to know, and she couldn't ignore the room forever.

Pushing the door open, she was immediately hit with her uncle's scent, laced with a mustiness from the room being closed up for a while. It was as if he just left the room. She breathed in, remembering the fun times they'd had together, once she'd gotten over being angry with him for taking her from her mother. They were never very close but she'd had no one else.

She pushed back the curtains and opened the windows to allow fresh air in. Uncle Will's room was tidy as always. Tomorrow she'd strip his bed and wash the sheets and his quilt. Opening the tall wardrobe, she stared at her uncle's clothing. She recognized all but two of his shirts. Leaning against the door, she sighed. *Why hadn't he told me he was ailing?* She would have hopped on the first train home and taken care of him. They could have spent his last months and weeks together.

Shaking her head, she pulled one shirt after another off the hangers and tossed them onto the bed. Nate might be able to use some of the shirts. Keri tugged one of the newer shirts off and held it up. Odd, it looked smaller than the older ones. Grabbing a red plaid flannel, she held the newer blue one in front, and sure enough, it was several sizes smaller. She hugged the shirts, relishing in her uncle's scent that still clung to them and feeling sad that her robust uncle had lost so much weight that he had to downsize his clothing. He'd always been such a stout, hardy man. Tears stung her eyes at the thought of him withering away.

Loud shouts rang out in the distance, and she tossed the shirts on the bed and ran to the window. From this angle, she couldn't see the water tower. She hurried to her room and leaned on the window sill. What if Brooks had been hurt—or killed?

The tiny figures were dancing and hooting. She counted them to make sure everyone was accounted for, then relaxed, a smile tugging at her lips. They must have struck water.

Keri smiled, and she knew Brooks was smiling too. Then her grin dipped.

She shook her head, not liking her train of thought. She couldn't let herself become attracted to the man who had stolen her ranch. No way, no how.

And one thing was for certain—now that he'd been successful with the windmill venture, he'd be even harder to live with. She could imagine how big his smile was just now. How come it didn't irritate her as much as it once had?

CHAPTER FOURTEEN

*K*eri hung the last of her uncle's shirts on the clothesline and stretched her back. The shirts snapped and popped in the breeze, waving like flags. With the bedding done yesterday, all that remained to be done was to sweep and dust the room. She'd tackle that this evening after supper when it was cooler or tomorrow morning. What she really wanted to do now was to go for a ride.

Fifteen minutes later, she'd saddled Bob and was galloping down the trail toward the windmill. It rose up tall and shiny, changing the shape of the landscape she'd known for so long. The blades spun in the gusty breeze, making a faint swooshing sound. So much water had pumped out that the trough had overflowed, running in a stream down the hill where it had formed a small lake. Cattle surrounded it, and a few stood ankle deep. Joy flooded her heart to know that Dengler's cruel and selfish scheme had failed. All thanks to Brooks.

She turned Bob to the south and galloped him for a while,

enjoying the wind whipping in her face and whipping her clothing. Back at school, on the rare times that she got to ride —sidesaddle, of course—they were only allowed to walk their horse. It was boring and she always ended up with a cramp in her hind end and right leg, but at least she was on a horse for a few glorious moments. She'd dreadfully missed riding and needed to ride more, now that she was home. Some part of school must have rubbed off on her, because she had become far too domesticated—cooking and cleaning instead of riding out with the men each morning like she had most days before she'd gone to Georgia. She suspected her uncle allowed her along so he could watch over her, since he didn't like leaving her alone at the house. At least Brooks had finally relaxed his rule about that. He hoped that their troubles with Dengler were a thing of the past, but she wasn't as certain. Men like Dengler didn't stop until they got what they wanted. He thought blocking their water meant they'd be forced to sell out, but he was wrong.

Up ahead, she saw the men working the fence line and rode toward them.

Brooks saw her first and started walking her way. He smiled, pulled off his hat, and swiped his sleeve across his forehead. "You're the prettiest cowpoke I've seen all day." His shirt was sweaty and dusty, but he was still one of the best-looking men she'd known. And nothing seemed to get him down in the dumps, not even a hangman's noose. "D'you bring us a snack?"

Keri waved at Nate and Jess, who were rolling up fence wire, then glanced down at Brooks. "Sorry. Just out for a ride." As far as she could see, the fence line was intact. "Nice job."

"Thanks. We're about done here. If you want to wait a few minutes while we pack up, I'll ride with you."

She nodded and dismounted, then walked Bob around while the men loaded the wagon. Brooks's horse grazed under a tree where the other two horses were hobbled, and in the leaves above, a bird chirped a cheerful song. Things were so quiet—so peaceful here. Here a person could fully relax, unlike back in Georgia where something was always going on. If not classes, then it was social gatherings—teas, recitals, and poetry readings. There was nowhere she could get away from people. She'd been surrounded by a sea of humanity.

But here, in almost every direction she looked, there were no people—not even a building. Just nature. And quiet. She dropped down in a patch of clover and began looking for four-leafed ones.

If she married Carl, she'd have to leave all this. She knew he owned land, but she'd never been to his home. If it was anything like his clothing, it would be a fine home, she was certain. As much as she longed to stay here, she had to face the truth: she no longer belonged here. She didn't belong anywhere. Sighing heavily, she tried to imagine herself as Mrs. Carl Peters. Keri Peters. The name did nothing for her. There was no expectancy or excitement.

"You ready to ride?"

Keri jumped. She had been so engrossed in her thoughts that she hadn't heard Brooks sneak up on her. "Oh, uh . . . sure." He held out a hand, and she allowed him to pull her up, and when he started for his horse, she dusted off her backside.

Instead of mounting his horse, Brooks waited beside Bob. He gave her a leg up, then handed her the reins with a smile and a wink. Butterflies took wing in her stomach as she watched his loose-legged gait take him to his horse.

He rode up beside her and stopped. "Ready?"

She nodded and urged Bob forward with a quick tap to his sides, then she bent over and nudged him harder. The horse broke into a trot, then a gallop, as they passed the wagon. She waved her hat and tossed a big grin at Nate and Jess. Brooks quickly caught up with her and they rode side by side, almost as if they belonged together.

When they neared the house, she slowed Bob to a walk, and Brooks did the same. She sidled a glance at him. "You've never told me how you met my uncle."

"It was an accident actually, or maybe it was all ordained by God."

"What do you mean?"

"Well, you see, there was this little hailstorm, and Jester and me was looking for a place—any place—that offered some protection. Right about the time the hail started, we rode into Shoofly. I rode Jester up on the boardwalk, left him there, and went into the café. All I had at the time was enough money to buy a cup of coffee. And there sat Will, all by himself, and he invited me to sit and eat with him. Even paid for my dinner. He sure was a nice, ol' man."

Keri ducked her head. That sounded like something her uncle would do. "Then what happened? How'd you get from eating with my uncle to owning his ranch?"

Brooks explained how Will offered him the job of helping him out and how they became friends. "Your uncle was mighty sick. Much sicker than he let folks know, and I think that's why he hired me."

"I don't understand why he never told me. I could have taken care of him."

Brooks pursed his lips and shook his head. "He wouldn't have liked that, Keri. Will needed a man tending him. He'd have been embarrassed to death to have you see him as helpless as he was at times."

She shot a glance at him. "How long had he been sick, do you know?"

He shrugged. "For a while. He moved into town so he could be closer to the doctor, at least that's what he told me."

They paused at the pond and let the horses drink.

"You were right about the windmill."

He smiled. "I do believe that's the first time I've heard you say those words."

"Which words?" She scowled.

"You were right." He chuckled, his shoulders dancing with mirth.

"Well . . . enjoy them, because it might be the last time I say them." She reined Bob toward home and rode off at a fast clip.

Brooks quickly caught up with her.

"Do you think Uncle Will could have been ill before I left?"

"Could be. Maybe that's why he sent you to that school in the first place. So you wouldn't watch him go downhill."

Keri dismounted in front of the barn, then led Bob in. It made sense that her uncle sent her away because he knew he was ill and was only going to get worse. But she wanted confirmation. Tomorrow, she'd ride into town and talk to Doc Brown.

She had to know for certain why her uncle sent her away, just like her ma had.

———— ★ ————

Doc Brown pursed his lips and stared at Keri, his eyes brimming with sympathy. "There's no easy way to tell you, Miss Langston, but your uncle had cancer."

Keri sucked in a sharp breath as tears pooled in her eyes and then cascaded down her cheeks. She wanted to believe the tears were from the pungent odors in his office, but she knew that wasn't the truth. Her uncle had been sick—dying—and he'd never uttered a word to her.

"How long had he known about it?"

"Over two years."

Two years? Keri thought back to the day she left for school. Just under two years ago, Uncle Will had suddenly decided she needed to learn to be a lady and had rushed her off to that awful place. It all made sense now. She ducked her head, thinking of all the letters she'd sent home, pleading for him to allow her return to Raven Creek. She had fussed and fumed over being sent away. She had thought he was just tired of messing with her, but truth was, he was protecting her. He hadn't wanted her to see him when he was sick. "Did Uncle Will know about this before I went away to school?" she asked, to confirm her theory.

Doc Brown pursed his lips and nodded. "He and I talked about his illness at length. I told him that it would probably be a long haul and not too pretty at the end." He glanced out the window. "I'm sorry if that's hard for you to hear, but I think you deserve to know the truth."

"I appreciate your telling me. I just wish Uncle Will had been honest with me. It hurts to think I missed the last few years of his life." She stared out the window at the wagon Brooks had driven to town. She'd been snippy to him because he'd insisted on escorting her when she wanted to ride alone, and she had refused his offer to accompany her in the doctor's office. Now, she wished she hadn't been so petulant.

"I know Will was trying to protect you by sending you away to that school."

Keri fiddled with her handkerchief and stared into her lap, guilt weighting her down. "There were so many times I hated him for sending me away to that place."

"Was it so bad?"

She shrugged. "Probably not for most people, but I hadn't grown up normally, at least not like the rest of the girls. I missed Uncle Will, Nate and Jess, my horses, and my pants."

Doc chuckled. "I'm surprised to see you wearing a skirt today."

"I'm trying to fit into society—kind of." She leaned forward. "Don't tell anyone, but it's really a split skirt, so I can ride and still maintain proper propriety. At least that's what Lulu Dunn says."

Doc Brown squeezed her hand in a paternal manner. "Well, you look very pretty. Your uncle would be mighty proud of the lady you've become."

"Thank you." She stood. "I've kept you long enough. I appreciate your candidness, Doc."

He nodded and walked to the door and opened it. Keri paused just inside. "Mr. Morgan thinks that Uncle Will might have been—" She swallowed hard, finding the hateful word more difficult to verbalize than she'd expected. "Um . . . murdered. Have you found any more evidence of that?"

He placed a hand on her shoulder. "I wish I could say I had proof, but I suspect your uncle was smothered."

Keri gasped and lifted her hand to cover her mouth. Her heart felt as if someone had squeezed it tight in an angry fist. How could anyone overpower the strong man she remembered? But then, he probably wasn't the same man she'd seen last Christmas. Even then, he had been thinner than she could ever remember him being. Had Uncle Will fought back against his attacker? Had he been frightened?

The doctor eyed her with compassion. "There's more, I'm afraid."

Keri nodded for him to continue. She held her hands together, trying to stop them from trembling.

"I also believe someone forced Will to swallow all of his pain pills. I'd just refilled the bottle. I don't believe he suffered much, if any. With that many pills in his system, he pretty much would have just gone to sleep."

Keri squeezed her forehead with her fingers, trying to understand all he said. "But why would anyone want to kill Uncle Will? As far as I know, he didn't have a single enemy." Tears burned her eyes, but she struggled to maintain her composure until she was alone.

The doc rubbed his chin. "I didn't think he did either. It could have just been a drifter passing through."

Keri glanced outside to where Brooks had parked the wagon across the street. He was nowhere to be seen. "Speaking of drifters, what is your opinion of Mr. Morgan?"

The doctor leaned against the door and crossed his arms over his chest. "I think your uncle was mighty fortunate that Brooks Morgan came along when he did. Not many men I know would have taken such good care of a sick, old man like Brooks did. He quickly earned the respect of anyone who knew Will."

She certainly hadn't expected such a response as that. "One more question, and I'll quit pestering you. You were at that card game when Brooks won the ranch, right?"

He nodded.

"Do you think he cheated?"

The doc burst out laughing. Embarrassed, Keri stared at the waiting room chairs on the other side of the room.

"That boy was the worst card player I think I've ever seen. It was just dumb luck that he won the final hand. He cleaned us all out. I think Will thought he'd won. That's the only way I can see him turning loose of the deed to Raven Creek." He shook his head. "Felt real sorry for him when all his money got stolen the night your uncle died. He probably lost nearly a hundred dollars."

Keri breathed in a deep breath. The doc's story matched up with the marshal's, only Doc Brown filled in a lot of the cracks in Brooks's story. "Thank you, again."

She stood at the edge of the boardwalk. How many times had she resented her uncle for sending her to that school? He'd known he was dying and had done it to protect her. To keep her from witnessing him growing weak and incapacitated. Guilt seeped into every pore of her body.

The door opened and Doc stepped out. He rubbed his chin again. "I've been wrestling with something. Don't know if I should mention it or not."

"I'll die of curiosity if you don't, now that you've mentioned it. What is it?"

"It's just speculation, mind you. But I think Will might have purposely lost the ranch because he'd grown to care so much about Brooks. Maybe Will thought you needed a man to care for you, what with Saul Dengler so set on having Raven Creek."

"Why, that's absurd. I'm more than capable of running the ranch myself."

The doc held up one hand, palm out. "Now I said it's just my opinion, but I've talked with the marshal, and he feels the same."

Pushing back her irritation at such an unbelievable theory, she nodded and walked down the steps and across the dirt road. Was it actually possible her uncle lost the ranch to Brooks on purpose?

She walked behind a wagon, and a dog lurched up, paws on the sideboard, barking viciously. She jumped sideways to keep from being bit, and stepped in something soft. Squishy. The dog seemed content to stay in its wagon, snarling and growling. Keri glanced down at her dress boot covered in manure. "That's wonderful. Can my day get any worse?"

"Hey, Keri." Brooks took the steps two at a time, grinning like a possum, and waved toward her shoe. "Looks like you weren't watching where you were going." He took her elbow and led her to the steps. "Put your foot up there."

She did as ordered, holding on to his shoulder for balance. He whipped his handkerchief from his pocket.

"Wait, you can't use your handkerchief for that. What if you need it?"

He waggled his eyebrows. "That's why God made sleeves." Bending down, he wiped the crud off the top and sides of her boot. He straightened and held the hanky away from his clothes. "Just scrape the rest off on the step."

"Thank you, Sir Galahad." She did as ordered—again. A cowboy on horseback rode past them, chuckling. Keri felt like flinging a present at him, but the image of her schoolmistress collapsing from apoplexy held her in check. Her day just kept getting worse and worse.

Brooks took the soiled hanky and tossed it in the alley, then hustled back to her, smiling ear to ear. "It's a good thing we got you cleaned up."

"And why is that?" she said, wrinkling her nose at the pungent odor surrounding her.

"Because we can't have you smelling like manure when you see your mother."

CHAPTER FIFTEEN

*K*eri grabbed Brooks's sleeve. "Don't ever tease about a thing like that."

He blinked and looked surprised. "I'm not joking. The marshal sent me to get you. Said there was a woman in his office looking for you, and she said she was your ma."

Brooks's face blurred, and Keri's knees buckled.

"Whoa, hang on, Missy. Have a seat on the step."

He turned her around, and she stiffened, regaining her composure. "I can't sit *there*. It's filthy, and besides, I'm fine."

He narrowed one eye and stared at her as if gauging her steadiness.

"I said I'm fine. Now, take me home."

"Uh . . . didn't you hear me? I said your ma is at the marshal's office."

She stomped her foot, spun around, and started to go around the wagon, and set off the snarling dog again—the dog she'd already forgotten about. Keri leapt back, bumping into

Brooks. He grabbed her, swung her around, and walked her away from the horrible creature. "Dogs like that shouldn't be allowed in town. Good thing it's tied up."

"He's just protecting his master's goods."

"He nearly bit my face off."

Brooks trailed a finger down her cheek. "Now that would be a crying shame."

Keri ignored the delicious sensations his touch stirred in her and nudged him in the side. "Stop joking."

"I'm not. C'mon." He guided her up a relatively clean set of steps and turned her in the direction of the marshal's office. She suddenly stopped, and he had to take a step sideways to keep from bowling her over. He pulled her to the railing to allow another couple to pass. "What's wrong now?"

"Are you being serious? About my mother, I mean?" What could she want? Keri wasn't even certain her mother was still alive, and if she was, why hadn't she come sooner?

Brooks's smile faded. "Why would I joke about something like that?"

Keri shrugged and rolled her eyes. "Oh, I don't know. You joke about everything else, why not that?"

"You look like her, you know?"

"Who?"

"Your mother. You have the same blonde hair, blue eyes, and pretty face. Similar but different, but if you ask me, she don't hold a candle to you."

A tiny grin pulled at her lips, but it quickly disappeared. She crinkled her forehead. "What do you say to a mother who gave you away? And why is she here now, after all these years?"

"Guess you'll have to ask her yourself."

← ★ →

Keri's nervousness was visible in her expression, the way she worried her lower lip and fidgeted. He could well imagine feeling the same way if his parents had suddenly showed up and were waiting to see him. He brushed his hand down her shoulder to her lower back. "We'll wait out here until you're ready to go in."

She nodded and crushed the lacy handkerchief in her fist. "It's just . . ." She glanced up with pain-filled eyes. "I never expected to see her again. What do I say to her? How do I keep from screaming at her for abandoning me?"

"A mother doesn't give her daughter away unless there's good reason." He turned her to face him and rested both hands on her shoulders. "Take a deep breath."

She scowled and tried to jerk away. "What good will that do?"

"It will help to calm you. Steady you."

She brushed one hand off his arm. "I am calm."

Brooks couldn't help grinning. "Calm as a rabid dog."

She gazed up at him, a combination of irritation and a wisp of humor on her pretty face. "Be careful, or I just might bite you."

Chuckling, his smile widened. "I look forward to that."

She smacked his chest. "You're a rascal, you know that?"

"So I've been told on more than one occasion, Miss Langston."

She gazed deeply into his eyes. "Thank you for being here."

He gently brushed the back of his finger down her cheek. "Anytime, darlin'."

⟵ ★ ⟶

Keri stared up at Brooks, and felt as if their gazes were locked together. Why did being with this varmint feel so right? Why couldn't she feel as comfortable with Carl, a man who could give her anything she wanted, except for Raven Creek? She shook her head and broke the connection with Brooks. All that was thought for another day. Her mother was waiting. "I guess I'd better go see what *she* has to say."

"Play nice, Keri."

She seared him with a scorching glare. "Let's hope *she* plays nice."

"I'll wait for you outside."

"No!" She snagged his sleeve. "You come too."

She tugged him along, not listening to his objections that he wasn't family and shouldn't be there. At the marshal's door, she paused, her heart hammering faster than it ever had. She wiped her damp palms on her skirt and glanced over her shoulder at Brooks.

"It will be all right. Go on in."

She took a deep breath—though it did little to calm her—and opened the door. Over the years, she'd tried to hang on to the mental image she had of her mother—a smaller woman, with thick yellow hair, and pretty blue eyes that only seemed to light up when they looked her direction. She remembered rosy red cheeks and fancy dresses. Keri looked into the shadows of the room and found a woman dressed in a plain, gray traveling dress and jacket. Gone were the rosy cheeks and colorful dress. The poofy hair had been pulled back into a tight, neat bun, and her eyes remained somber, but as they landed on her they ignited with light. The woman stood but didn't approach her.

Marshal Lane tipped his hat. "I'll give you folks some privacy."

"Do you know me, Keri?"

"How could I know you when I haven't seen you in eleven years?"

Grace Langston dipped her head. "Fair enough. But I'm hoping to make amends for that, if you'll let me."

Keri walked to the window, staring out at the street. The wagon with the beastly dog drove by, and the stupid mutt sat on the seat behind his owner, his tongue lolling and a contented grin on his face. She suddenly felt a kindred spirit to that beast. Happy as a tick on a hound dog one minute then snarling at a stranger—her own mother—the next.

She leaned her forehead against the warm glass. What was she going to do? How could she relate to this stranger from the past who'd abandoned her—the stranger she had focused her anger and hurt on for so many years?

Brooks leaned against the wall, keeping quiet but encouraging her with his eyes.

Taking a deep breath, she turned and faced her mother, all manner of emotions roiling through her. "Why have you come? Why now?"

Grace Langston offered a weary smile. As Keri stared at her mother, she realized how tired—how old her mother seemed. Surely she couldn't be as old as she looked. Hadn't she been a pretty and young woman when Keri stilled lived with her?

"I've made many mistakes in my life, and I'd like a chance to make amends."

Keri crossed her arms over her chest and lifted her chin. "How do you make up for giving away your child?"

Her mother looked down and wrung her hands. "It was for the best, Keri. You couldn't stay with me much longer."

"Why not?"

Her mother's tired, blue gaze shot upward. "Surely your uncle explained things once you were old enough to understand."

"He never explained anything, and I wasn't allowed to even ask questions about you."

"I'm sorry. I thought you knew." Her eyes blinked rapidly, and she glanced at Brooks.

He straightened. "I can step outside, if you want me to."

"No. You stay." Keri held up her palm, then looked back at her mother. "I want you to tell my why you sent me away."

Grace wrung her hands in her lap. "You were seven and such a beautiful little girl. It tore my heart out, but I had to let you go, for your own protection."

"I don't understand." *What protection? From whom?* Keri's thoughts ran rampant like a freshly caught mustang trying to escape a paddock.

Her mother closed her eyes. "Are you going to make me say it out loud? I've tried so hard to put the past behind me."

"Just like you did me?"

Grace stood and crossed the small room. "No, darling. You're the only good thing in my life."

Keri backed up, bumping into Brooks. He touched the small of her back, and she deeply appreciated his touch and comfort.

Grace reached out a shaky hand and touched Keri's. She flinched but didn't pull away.

"I sent you away, darling, so that you didn't end up living a life like mine."

"And what kind of life was that, *Mother*?"

Her mother's eyes widened with incredulity. "You really don't know."

Keri shook her head.

Grace's eyes blurred and tears ran down her cheeks. "I—I . . ." She glanced up at Brooks then back to Keri. "I'm sorry, dear, but I lived in a bordello—a brothel. I was a prostitute."

Keri gasped and fell back against Brooks. She lifted her hand to her mouth. "C—can't breath." She turned and grappled with her collar, her face pale. "Out! Gotta get out."

←— ★ —→

Keri flung the door open so hard that it banged against the wall and rattled the windows. Brooks rushed outside, but paused on the boardwalk. Keri needed some time for things to soak in, and her mother could probably use some encouraging words, though her news shocked even him. Keri climbed onto the wagon bench, snatched up the reins, and released the brake. She slapped the reins on the horse's back and they lurched forward. They trotted down the street then broke into a gallop as they cleared the edge of town. He turned back into the marshal's office. Guess he'd be renting a horse to get back home.

Grace Langston sat in Marshal Lane's chair again, her face etched in despair, but she wasn't crying. Her nostrils flared—the only other indication of the struggle going on inside her. The wooden wall behind her was papered in WANTED posters of hard men with hard expressions, but none of them equaled Keri's mother's expression.

"I never should have come here. I just—"

He hated awkward situations like these, but the woman needed some comforting. He squatted down in front of her, resting his backside on his boot heels. Reaching out, he laid his hand over hers and cleared his throat. "I think it's a good thing you came."

Her gaze darted up, a speck of hope brightening her despondent expression. "Why would you say that? And just who are you?"

He smiled and stood, then leaned back against the desk. "My name is Brooks Morgan. I'm the owner of Raven Creek Ranch, and I said that because I think Keri needs you."

Grace shook her head. "She'll never accept me. You saw her reaction. And how did you happen to become the ranch's owner?"

"It's a bit of a long story."

She held out her hands, and the corner of her lips turned up in a weak smile. "What else have I got to do?"

Brooks snagged the other chair, flipped it around backwards, and set it several feet from hers. He told her the story about the hail and meeting Will and how they became friends and how he won the ranch in the card game. "And that's about it."

She pressed her lips together and shook her head. "I don't buy it, Mr. Morgan. If Will was anything, he was a planner. He would have wanted the ranch to go to Keri. It's the only real home she's ever known."

"Maybe she remembers more than she let on."

Shaking her head, she reached down and picked up her satchel and set it on her lap, her grasp tight on the handle. "I've ruined Keri's life. I shouldn't have come."

"No. I think you did the very thing you set out to do—you saved her. She just hasn't figured that out yet." Brooks smiled. "But she will. She's smart and tenacious and one of the best shots I've ever seen."

Grace lifted one brow. "And just what is your role in Keri's life, Mr. Morgan?"

In his effort to comfort the woman, he realized he might have just shown his cards to her. "Uh . . . I'd guess you'd say I'm her landlord."

"She still lives at the ranch?"

"Yep." He stood, flipped the chair around and set it against the wall. "How did you find out about Will's death? If I'd known about you, I'd have let you know so you could have come to the funeral."

She stood. "I received a telegram informing me of Will's demise."

He reached for her satchel. "Let me get that, ma'am. We'd best get headed home so we beat the sunset."

She blinked and stared up at him. "I don't understand."

"Will's room is empty. There's no point for you to stay in town when we've got an empty room."

"We?"

He grinned. "Yeah, Keri and me."

That brow lifted again. "Just what is your interest in my daughter, sir?"

Marshal Lane peeked in, saving Brooks from making a quick evaluation of his relationship with Keri. "Is it safe to come back now?"

"Yep, it's all yours. Thanks for letting us use your office, Marshal."

Brooks offered his arm to Keri's mother and slowed his pace for her shorter gait.

"Don't think this conversation is over, Mr. Morgan, but I'll let it go, because I so appreciate your kindness and help in understanding Keri. I'm just not sure that my going to the ranch is the right thing."

"Keri needs someone to love her—someone who isn't going to leave her."

"I can't promise that—no one can. And besides, unless my guess is wrong, she already has someone there who loves her."

Ignoring her comment, Brooks escorted Keri's mother to the livery, where he rented a buggy. He lifted her up to the seat, still wondering if she meant Nate and Jess loved Keri or if she was referring to him. The buggy creaked and dipped as he climbed aboard. "Do you have a trunk at the station?"

"No, this is all. There's nothing from my former life that I care to have except for my daughter."

Brooks guided the horses out of town. The thing that pestered him was why Grace hadn't just left her career and come to the ranch with Keri. Maybe one day he'd know her well enough to ask, but that wasn't today.

Grace was—or had been—the kind of woman his mother had warned him to stay away from. And he had, though at times he'd been sorely tempted to seek out a woman's comfort, but those Scriptures she'd read to him as he grew older—verses about wayward women—must have found root in his soul. He couldn't imagine what would drive a woman to live as a prostitute. He'd heard there was good money in it, but the price was too high. A shudder sent a cold chill through him to think Keri could have endured what her mother did, if not for Grace's selfless sacrifice.

"Is Nate still at the ranch? And Jess? Or did you bring in your own crew?"

"They're still there. Don't know what I'd do without them."

They rode along in silence for several miles, and Brooks watched the colors of the setting sun saturate the sky. Pink. Orange.

"It's beautiful, isn't it?"

"I never tire of watching it. God was good to give us such things to enjoy."

She peered at him from under her hat. "So, you're a God-fearing man then?"

Noose-fearing might be closer to the truth, but he nodded. "I'm getting to be one. I've drifted for a long while, but I think I'm finally reaching the end of the trail."

"That's good. Everyone needs something—or Someone to believe in."

He wondered what she believed in. Had the hope of one day seeing her daughter again been the thing that kept her going all these years?

What would Keri say when she discovered he'd brought Grace home? He chuckled. Good thing he owned the ranch, or he'd probably be fired.

"I can't thank you enough Mr. Morgan—for thinking that

a woman like me could be good for Keri."

He looked at her. "God is all about second chances. I'm finding that out more and more. I ran away from home when I was sixteen, and I can't tell you how many times I was sorry for that."

"Did you ever go back?"

He shook his head. "No. So I know a bit what it's like to lose my parents. Keri's a beautiful, capable woman, but in many ways, she's just a lost, lonely girl. I hope you can stay for a while, because having you around will be the best thing for her—short of her giving her heart to God."

"I know a woman who talks about God like you do. She's a good, kind woman—Emma Perkins. She took me in several years ago when I got . . . um . . . with child again." She looked away and stared out at the countryside. "I was terribly ill from the very beginning. I lost the baby and nearly lost my life. It was an eye-opener for me. I quit the brothel and stayed with Emma, and tried to change my life, but there was always one thing left undone."

"And now you have the chance to make amends." He pointed up at the new sign. "Raven Creek. We're home."

"Home. I like the sound of that, and I sure hope my daughter doesn't cast me out as soon as the sun rises tomorrow."

"She can't. I own this ranch, and you're my guest."

Grace's smile was wide, and Brooks caught a hint of the pretty woman she must have been at one time. He glanced at the house up ahead. Smoke rose from the kitchen chimney, so that meant someone was cooking dinner. His stomach growled, but he tried not to get too over eager. Once Keri saw his passenger, he was more than likely to get sent to the bunkhouse without any supper.

CHAPTER SIXTEEN

rooks squirted the last of the milk from the cow's teats and stood. He bent backwards, stretching out the kinks from being hunched over for so long. He rolled his shoulders and noticed Nate standing at the barn door, staring out. Nate wasn't one to lollygag, and that piqued his interest. He grabbed the pail and walked over to stand beside him.

"Nice day, isn't it?" The day was like most early summer days—warm and sunny, not a sign of rain.

"Uh-huh." Nate looked to be staring at the house.

"Bacon sure smells good. I'm ready to go eat. How about you?"

Nate grunted. It wasn't like him to not perk up at the mention of food. He was definitely out of sorts for some reason.

"Looks like we'll get a gully washer today. We can sure use the rain."

"Uh-huh." He blinked several times then turned toward Brooks. "What?"

"Fess up. What's on your mind?"

Nate finally looked fully at him. "How long is Grace gonna stay here?"

Ah, so that's what was bothering him. Brooks had kept his attention on Keri last night at supper. After he'd carried Grace's satchel upstairs, Keri had lambasted him for bringing her ma home. Well, he'd expected that. Suddenly it dawned on him that Nate had referred to Keri's ma by her first name. "You know her?"

"A long time ago. Before she . . . went away."

Brooks searched his mind. Something didn't fit. "I thought you started working at Raven Creek after Will came back with Keri in tow."

Nate rubbed the back of his neck. "I was raised near here and worked for Will when he and Grace first moved here. Was still in my teens. After Grace left, I did too for a time. Joined the army, but I came back once I was done with my roving years."

"I certainly can't fault you for wanting to see more of the country. Until I came here, I drifted for ten years. Didn't mind it so much at first, but I have to say it feels good to settle down." Brooks clapped Nate on the shoulder. "I may own this place now, but you have the years invested. I hope you know you're welcome here for as long as you want to stay."

Nate stared into his eyes for a moment then nodded. "Gimme that bucket. I'll carry it up to the house."

He couldn't help noticing the red that had crept up Nate's neck. The man wasn't much for talking about himself. He strode to the well and saw Jess in the paddock and whistled at him. Shaking off the wash water, he smiled. Life at Raven Creek sure had gotten interesting the past twelve hours.

———— ★ ————

Keri rubbed her gritty eyes and stretched as sleepiness ebbed away. The sun shone bright, and the delicious aroma of bacon cooking wafted through the open window. She bolted upright. Someone was cooking, and that was her job. She threw off the covers and her nightgown and quickly dressed in a tan shirt and her trousers. After wearing the split skirt, they felt uncomfortably tight.

She ran the brush through her long hair for a couple of strokes, then tied it back with a ribbon. Looking in the mirror, she saw that one side of her cheek was red where she had been lying on one of her hands, but there was nothing to do about that.

She hadn't slept much last night after *she* moved in and Keri had an argument with Brooks. He told her that *she* was *his* guest for as long as *she* wanted to stay. Keri no longer had a say in her own home. Carl's offer of marriage was looking better and better.

In the kitchen doorway, Keri paused. Her mother stood at the stove looking like a regular mother, dressed in the apron her uncle wore when he had cooked. And her mother didn't looked disheveled like she did, but perfectly put together in a pale blue calico with tiny pink-and-red flowers and splashes of white and green. Her hair was braided and pinned in a tight coil at the base of her neck. She looked just like her dreams of a real mother would.

Keri didn't know what to do or what to say to her. She didn't want her there and yet the thought that she might leave frightened her half to death. Last night she'd tossed and turned, cried and railed at Brooks in her dreams for bringing her here. What was she going to do? She blew out a loud sigh.

Her mother turned, spatula lifted in midair, her uncertainty obvious. "I hope you don't mind that I started breakfast."

Keri gave a quick shake of her head and headed for the

pantry to grab a cup. She poured some coffee and sipped the hot brew. A cup of Arbuckle's always helped wake her up. She poured her second cup, then set the table and sliced the loaf of bread her mother had baked.

Her mother tapped the spatula on the side of the skillet. "I know this is awkward, but I hope you'll give me a chance. I so want to get to know you better."

"All my memories make sense now—the women in frilly dresses, the big house, the monsters that came out at night . . ."

Grace laid a hand to her chest. "You remember all that?"

Keri nodded and set the butter bowl on the table. "I remember having to stay hidden away at night, too."

Grace sucked in a deep breath and turned around. "I should have sent you to Will sooner, but parting with you was the hardest thing I've ever done."

Gripping the back of the chair, Keri thought about all the hard things her mother must have been called upon to do as a lady of the night. What a horrible, miserable life that surely was. No wonder her mother had sent her away. For the first time, she fully understood her mother's sacrifice and how she had protected her. "When Uncle Will came and got me, why didn't you leave and come too?"

Grace turned and walked over to her but didn't touch her. "I wanted to, oh so badly." She ducked her head and twisted the towel she held. "But that's a hard life to leave."

Her response horrified Keri. "Surely you don't mean you enjoyed that kind of life?"

"No. But I'd made commitments that were not easy to get out of."

Keri shook her head. "I don't understand."

Her mother reached out and cradled Keri's cheek in one hand. "And I'm ever so grateful that you don't. I just hope you can forgive me one day."

The back door banged and they jumped apart, both staring at Nate. His cheeks grew red as he obviously realized he'd interrupted something. "Uh, sorry. I brought the milk." His gaze flitted between Grace and the floor, his neck, ears, and cheeks turning bright red.

Keri had never seen the man so flustered before. Could it be he was attracted to her mother? The spark of an idea ignited in her mind. If her mother were to fall in love with Nate, maybe she'd never leave.

——— ★ ———

After the noon meal had been cleaned up, Grace went upstairs to rest, still weary from her travels. Keri trotted Bob toward the windmill, glad to be out of the house for a while. Jester stood near the tower, his head down, and a movement high above snagged her attention. What was Brooks doing up there now that the tower was done?

She sat there watching, and soon he began to climb down. Keri didn't like the uncomfortable thoughts swirling through her. What if he fell? No one was even around to ride for help, providing the fall didn't kill him. She didn't want to like the confounding man, but she did—more and more. Brooks jumped down the last few feet, then walked toward her, pulling off his leather gloves and grinning.

"Well, now that's the prettiest thing I've seen since lunch."

She ducked her head, fighting a smile. The man was the biggest charmer she'd ever seen.

"What brings you out here? Everything all right back at the house?"

"Grace is resting, so I thought I'd take a ride."

"How about a short walk? I want to go down to the pond."

"All right." He held Bob's head while she dismounted, then

they followed the water trail downhill. "It looks higher than the other day."

"It is. That's why I was up on the tower. I set it so the fan wouldn't spin. Don't want to use the underground water if we don't need it."

She glanced at his profile. His face was tan from working in the sun, and his thick lashes would make any woman jealous. Brooks Morgan was a handsome man—if a person could get past all that grinning. "I don't think you should be up there alone. What if you fell?"

He turned, a wide smile creasing his cheeks. "Afraid there'd be no one to catch me?"

"No."

He chuckled, and she nudged him in the side. "Don't laugh at me."

"I'm not."

"Yes, you are." She turned and faced him, her heart sprinting. She didn't like the feelings racing through her, making her antsy as a calf just separated from its mother. She winced at the thought. "Are you ever going to give the ranch back to me?"

Brooks's smile faded and he pursed his lips. "No. I've come to believe it's God's will for me to be here." He looked away, staring at the pond, as if he could no longer face her.

She would have to make some plans, sooner or later. She could not continue to live here knowing that. With no money, Carl was her only option.

Brooks cleared his throat. "If you want to share ownership of the ranch, you can marry me."

Keri jerked her gaze back to his, to see if he looked as serious as he sounded, but Brooks seemed more stunned than she was at the proposal he'd blurted out. "You can't be serious—you sure didn't sound like it."

"Well, I surprised myself, but the idea is growing on me."

"Growing on you! That sounds like a rash or something contagious." She stomped back up the hill, hurt that he didn't want her because he loved her or cared. The idea of marrying Brooks didn't sound all that bad, but the fact that he made it more of a joke than a real proposal annoyed her. It wasn't any better than Carl's had been. She couldn't deny that she was attracted to Brooks, but she was afraid. Afraid that if she gave him her heart, he would leave—or die—and she couldn't bear that, so the only other alternative was to keep him at arm's length. "I'd rather leave the ranch than marry a sidewinder like you."

She mounted Bob and urged him to gallop, giving the horse his head. Why did things always have to change? She'd halfway gotten into a routine and used to sharing the ranch with Brooks; then he brought her mother home and now he halfheartedly proposed. It wasn't fair to take her frustration out on Bob, so she reined him back to a walk. Glancing up at the sky, she wished she could trust in God—that there was Someone—Something—bigger than her. Someone she could lean on for once. Being strong and independent could be exhausting. Bob stopped, and Keri stared out across the land she loved. *Marrying Brooks might not be so bad.* At least she wouldn't have to leave.

She rode Bob toward the fence line that bordered Raven Creek and the Double D—Saul Dengler's land. The fence looked intact, so there was no fear that their cattle had wandered onto Dengler's property. She guided the horse along the fence line, then rode into the valley the creek used to run through. The zigzagging brown section that marked the empty creek bed marred the landscape. The grass along the dry bed had already started turning yellow. If Brooks hadn't been successful with the windmill, they'd be forced to sell some of their cattle by now.

A small herd of steers grazed quietly, making a serene scene. The girls at the school never understood her love of horses and cattle. They'd wrinkle noses and turn up their lips in disdain.

Across the valley, near a line of shrubs, several steers bolted away from the shrubs and back toward the herd. A loud bawling erupted. Keri nudged Bob forward, curious as to what had caused such a ruckus. She drew near the frightened calf, whose leg had gotten lodged in a bush. "You poor thing."

Keri lifted her leg over Bob's back and heard a snarling growl. Bob squealed and bolted, throwing her off balance and spiraling through the air. She hit hard, pain ratcheting through her. Glancing up, she spied a coyote less than six feet away. She sucked in a breath. The creature growled again, its eyes half-closed, foaming slobber drooling from his mouth. Keri's mouth went dry and she froze; the only thing moving was her racing pulse.

The animal snapped at her, then sidestepped, as if having trouble keeping its balance. The calf bawled. Keri's heart pounded. Coyotes were generally scared of humans and avoided them. Only one thing she knew would cause one to be so aggressive—rabies.

She was in trouble.

Her rifle was with her horse.

CHAPTER SEVENTEEN

rooks followed Keri as she rode toward the edge of their property. He didn't like the thought of her riding alone so close to Dengler land.

He also didn't understand her reaction to his proposal—a proposal that had stunned him as much as it had her.

Still, he was an affable enough guy; at least most folks he encountered seemed to like him. He was doing a decent job running the ranch, even though he still leaned on Nate a lot. And most women found him good looking, although Keri sure seemed immune to his charm.

But marrying her just makes sense. That way they could share ownership of the ranch and he could finally live in his house. A smile tugged at his lips at the thought of him and Keri married. She was beautiful, spirited, stubborn, could shoot the seed out of an apple at fifty paces, and would make the perfect rancher's wife. Somehow he had to make her see reason. He muttered a prayer for God's help.

He heard a rustling noise and turned. Bob nickered, trotting through a cluster of tall bushes toward him. Brooks's heart lurched. Keri was an excellent rider and not one to be unseated easily. Had she fallen or had Bob wandered off after she dismounted? He reined Jester to the left, guiding him through the bushes and into a wide valley he'd ridden through a few times.

Brooks's gaze darted around the clearing, searching for any sign of her. A calf bellowed nearby. "Keri! Where are you?"

Jester pulled at the bit and sidestepped, and Brooks saw the calf, jerking and yanking, frantically trying to free his hoof, which had gotten caught in a bush. A snarling growl just to his right made Brooks jump. He jerked out his rifle and turned in the saddle, and his heart lurched. On the far side of a downed tree entangled with honeysuckle, Keri lay on the ground staring down a coyote with its teeth bared, only a half dozen feet separating them. Ever so slowly, she turned her gaze on him, terror etched in her eyes. Brooks aimed and fired. The coyote leaped sideways and fell. Keri shot to her feet and limped toward him, and he bolted out of the saddle and wrapped her in his arms, his hand pressing her head against his chest. He could have lost her. *Thank You, God, for getting me here in time.*

In that moment, the depth of his love became real. He honestly, truly loved Keri. His heart would have been ripped in two if something had happened to her. For the first time since they'd met, she seemed truly vulnerable. *Needy.* He tightened his embrace and wished he could kiss away her fear and trembling, but she'd probably scalp him before she'd kiss him back.

"Are you all right?"

She nodded against his shirt. "I was so scared—and so mad that I'd fallen off Bob and didn't have my rifle."

Brooks chuckled, allowing the last of his panic release. Reluctantly, he lowered his arms. "I'd better get you back; then

I need to get a shovel and bury the carcass before other critters start eating on it."

She nodded and glanced back at the coyote. Brooks turned her face back to his and brushed some dirt off her cheek. "I don't know what I'd have done if something happened to you."

Keri held his gaze. "If you hadn't shown up when you did, I'd have been coyote bait." She leaned up and kissed his cheek. "Thank you."

Brooks smiled. "Happy to oblige." He took her hand, led her to Jester, and lifted her up into the saddle. He freed the poor, half-crazed calf and smiled as it limped back to its mother across the field. He walked over and poked the coyote with the muzzle of his rifle to make sure it was dead, then he swung up behind Keri and headed home.

His marriage proposal may have been impetuous, but it was sounding better and better all the time.

←—— ★ ——→

She had nearly died—and what a horrible death that would have been. Keri shuddered and sipped a cup of tea that her mother had made for her. In that moment when her life hung in the balance, she realized two things: she wasn't ready to meet her Maker, and she wanted to live and spend her days with Brooks.

Grace pulled out a chair and stared at her with concerned blue eyes. "Are you certain you're all right?"

"Just a bit rattled. I've always been careful to make sure I was armed whenever I went out riding, and I felt so . . . impotent staring down that coyote without my rifle."

"Thank the Good Lord that Mr. Morgan came along when he did."

Keri nodded. "His timing couldn't have been better. I

thought for sure that coyote would jump me any second." She stared into her cup for a long moment then looked up. "Do you believe in God?"

All manner of expressions crossed her mother's face. "There was a time I didn't—no, that's not true. I was angry and often railed at Him for the life I was forced to live."

Keri felt the skin on her face tighten and she closed her eyes, unable to consider the dreadful things her mother had endured. Why hadn't she left that place and come to Raven Creek? Surely Uncle Will would have welcomed her.

Grace reached out and touched her arm. "I'm sorry, sweetie, I shouldn't have mentioned my former life."

"How did you get out of it?" *And why didn't you sooner?* she wanted to ask but didn't.

Her mother's lips pressed tight together, and pain creased her brow. She was still a pretty woman though she looked older than Keri knew her to be. "I got pregnant again."

Keri blinked, stunned by her mother's revelation. And yet, why shouldn't she have expected that, all things considered. "I have a sibling?"

"No. He was born too soon and didn't survive. The doctor didn't expect me to live either, so Mel, the owner of the . . . place where I worked, allowed a woman who lived in town to take me in."

Keri couldn't believe that she'd nearly had a brother. All her life she'd wanted siblings—a family.

"Emma Perkins was the woman, and she was the most kind-hearted, God-fearing person you'd ever met. She didn't give a hoot as to what I'd done in the past, but only cared about me and my future. A month later, after I recovered, she helped me slip away in the night and sent me to her sister's home."

"And how long were you there?"

"A year and a half."

Her statement stabbed Keri. "Why did you wait so long to come here? If you'd come sooner, Uncle Will would have still been alive."

Her mother looked toward the open door. "For one, a few of the people I had lived with knew about you and where you were. I was afraid if I came here, they'd find me and force me to go back."

Keri's stomach swirled. "How could anyone force you to go back to such a life?"

Her mother shook her head. "You don't understand. They're cruel people, and they have their ways."

Grace was right. She didn't understand. She would have run away from such a place the first chance she got. "Did you ever try to get away?"

"No."

"Why not, for heaven's sake? How could you stay in such a place?"

Grace winced, but then her expression grew stoic. "At first, I was carrying you and had nowhere else to go. Once you were born, I needed a place for you."

Her gut clenched. "So, it's all my fault." Keri pushed her chair back and started to stand, but Grace grabbed her arm.

"No, of course not, but I had you to consider. They threatened to steal you away, and I couldn't bear the thought of anything happening to you." Her mother's eyes pleaded with her to understand.

"Why didn't you come to Uncle Will's?"

Grace ducked her head. "He's the one who sent me away—because I wasn't married and got pregnant. He was trying to protect me from the gossipers, but his plan went horribly wrong. The home for young women, whose advertisement he answered, turned out to be a brothel, but I didn't know that until it was too late."

Keri gaped at her mother, struggling to digest all she'd said. "Did you write Uncle Will and tell him?"

Pursing her lips, Grace shook her head. "I couldn't bear to tell him—not until years later, when the manager started pressuring me to—" Tears swam in her eyes. "That's when I knew I had to send you away."

For so many years she'd pined for her ma—railed at her for abandoning her. But now she knew the truth. Her mother had been the victim of a horrible scheme. Yes, she'd done wrong by getting pregnant in the first place, but she'd paid a dreadful price. Keri felt the wall she'd built around her heart crumbling. "Poor Uncle Will. He must have felt awful when he learned the truth."

Grace nodded. "He was heartbroken."

"I'm sorry . . . Mother—Ma. It's been so long since I've called you that."

A sweet smile lifted Grace's lips, and tears pooled in her eyes. "It's all right, sweetheart. I'm just glad to be here now—to be with you."

Keri laid her hand on her mother's. "Me too." And she really meant it.

Grace clung to Keri. "Emma is the one who told me about God. I listened, but I didn't really believe that there could be a God who loved us when He'd allowed me to endure such awful things. But once I got away and to her sister Betty's house, I saw that things in my life could change. Now that I've gotten back with you, I feel hope in my life again."

Keri smiled. "You can stay here. You don't ever have to worry about going back to that place."

Instead of smiling, her mother stood and walked back to the teapot and poured some more hot water into her cup, then added some fresh tea leaves. "I can't tell you how many times I've dreamed about you saying that . . . but I don't know as it's the best thing for you."

"Why?" She stood and crossed the room, standing in front of her mother. "This is your home now. Stay." Keri took the teacup and set it down, then grasped her mother's hands. "I don't want to lose you again."

Tears coursed down Grace's cheeks. "I don't either, but there are so many things to consider."

"Like what?"

A tiny smile tugged at her mother's lips. "For one, this is no longer your house. Mr. Morgan might have something to say about me staying permanently."

She didn't honestly think that would be much of an issue, especially not after Brooks's rash proposal, but she wasn't ready to share that news with anyone yet. "What other reasons?"

Grace pursed her lips and exhaled a deep breath out her nose. "There's always the chance someone from my past will recognize me."

Keri stiffened. Her reputation was already in question because folks frowned on her desire to wear pants, but what would they think if they learned her mother was a . . .

"I can see how the thought disturbs you. I should probably leave soon."

"No! It doesn't matter what others say."

Her mother cocked her head and gave her a wistful smile. "You know it does. A good reputation is important to a woman."

"Well, just don't go running off yet. We'll think of something."

"Thank you for listening and being so gracious." Grace cupped her cheek. "I want you to know that I never stopped loving or missing you. My life was empty not having your sweet hugs and warm smiles. I know a person can't go back and redo things, but if I could, I would have. Emma told me that God can wash a person clean and make them new—pure. I've been reading the Bible she gave me for a long while and am starting to believe what she said is true. Maybe we can both start over."

Keri didn't know about the God part, but she was more than willing to forgive her mother and begin again. "I'd like that."

"Good." Grace smiled. "Now I'd better get those clothes off the line before they get covered in fly specks." She moved away from Keri and reached for the door.

"Ma. There is one thing I'd like to know."

Grace turned and lifted her brows. "Yes?"

Emotion tightened her throat, so she cleared it. "Who was my father?"

◄──── ★ ────►

Brooks strode into the barn, his thoughts still on his impulsive proposal. "I'm an idiot."

Jess popped his head out of the tack room. "You just now finding that out?"

"Look who's talking," Brooks muttered under his breath. Jess's horse was tied up outside its stall even though it was midday. "What are you doing back already? I thought you and Nate were out riding herd."

Jess carried a spare saddle out of the tack room. "Girth strap broke. I liked to crack my neck when I fell off Beans."

Brooks certainly knew what that felt like. "I'm glad you weren't hurt bad. Everything all right out there?"

Jess nodded and fastened the cinch strap. "Yep."

"Had an incident over near our border with Dengler. I shot a coyote—a rabid one."

Peering over his saddle, Jess's eyes widened. "You sure?"

He nodded. "You and Nate keep a watch out for critters acting odd. Cattle too. Shoot them if they show signs of the rabies."

Jess swallowed and nodded. He mounted, then pulled out his rifle and checked its ammunition. "That's a bad thing. We'll keep an eye out." He nudged his horse forward.

Brooks grabbed a shovel and headed back to where he left the coyote. Ten minutes later, he arrived at the spot and gazed at the carcass. A shudder raced through him and goose bumps rose on his arms. Keri had a close call—a very close one. She was normally so in control that he hadn't known how to react to her trembling, and he'd been half scared to death himself upon finding her in such a predicament. He hoped she never came that close to death again.

He leaned his rifle against a tree trunk, keeping it close at hand just in case it was needed, and then rammed the shovel into the ground. It was stupid of him to hope that Keri wouldn't encounter death. Everyone died—he ought to know, being as he came just about as close to dying as one could without it actually happening.

But God had spared him.

That much he knew for sure.

He tossed a load of dirt to the side and scooped up another. A passage of verses from the Psalms that he had memorized after hearing the pastor share them last Sunday popped into his mind.

The Lord is nigh unto all them that call upon him, to all that call upon him in truth. He will fulfill the desire of them that fear him: he also will hear their cry, and will save them. The Lord preserveth all them that love him: but all the wicked will he destroy.

He paused and leaned on the shovel's handle. He didn't want to suffer the fate of the wicked. From attending church when he was young, he had heard all about heaven and hell, and hell wasn't a place he cared to go. He'd been a foolish, spoiled kid when he left home and had pretty much wasted the past ten years of his life. Wasting the next few decades—or however long he had left—didn't sit well.

Brooks dropped to his knees, his heart ricocheting in his chest. He gazed up at the sky. "Dear God, Your Word says that You hear the cries of those who call on You. Hear me now. Forgive me of my sins. I confess that I believe in Your Son Jesus Christ, who died for my sins. Save me, God, and make me a new man."

Tears scalded his eyes, and he wiped them on his sleeves. His hands were grimy and his pants covered in dirt, and a dead coyote lay four feet away, but for the first time in his life, his heart felt pure. He threw back his head and laughed, joy filling his whole being.

⟵ ★ ⟶

Keri shuffled from foot to foot, worried that maybe she shouldn't have voiced her question. She hadn't put all that much thought in the past into who her father was, but now she had a festering ache to know.

Her mother blinked several times, mouth gaping. "Your uncle never told you?"

"He knew?" She crossed her arms and gnawed on her lower lip, feeling betrayed. Why would Uncle Will have kept such important news from her if he knew? Did he not think she'd want to know? Or maybe . . . "Was my father a bad man?"

"No, of course not." Grace turned and looked out the back door. "I know this will be hard for you, but I don't feel it's my place to say."

Keri grabbed her ma's shoulder, forcing her to turn and face her. "Why not? Don't I have a right to know?"

"Of course, but I would have thought he'd have said something to you if he wanted you to know."

Keri gawked at her ma, not wanting to believe the thought taking form in her mind. "You mean I know him? Does he live in Shoofly?"

Grace nodded.

Her mind raced. She thought of all the men she knew in town and tried to think if any of them had looked at her differently. She tossed her arms out sideways. "Why wouldn't he have told me? Didn't he want to know me?"

"I don't know." Grace reached for her. "I'm sorry."

Keri stepped back. "Surely it wasn't Uncle Will? Is he truly my uncle?"

Her mother lifted a hand to her mouth. "No, of course it wasn't him. And, yes, Will honestly was my older brother."

Anger and hurt roiled through her. It was bad enough to know that her mother had sent her away for protection, but to know that her father lived right here in a house nearby and had never once approached her—it was more than she could bear. She sucked in a sob, ran upstairs, and slammed her bedroom door. She collapsed on the bed, tears gushing from her eyes. After nearly dying today and learning about her mother's awful life, this news was more than she could endure.

CHAPTER EIGHTEEN

A knock sounded on Keri's door. She rolled over and yawned. Why was she in bed in the middle of the day? She sniffed and rubbed her gritty eyes, and it all came rushing back.

Tap. Tap. "Keri, you have a caller."

"Tell them I can't see anyone today."

"I don't think he'll take no for an answer."

"All right. Fine. Tell him I'll be down in a few minutes."

Keri pushed off her bed, dug around in her dresser for a handkerchief, and blew her nose. She glanced in the mirror and gasped at her red nose and eyes. How could she entertain guests looking like this? She poured some water from the pitcher into the basin and soaked one end of a towel in it and washed her face. She still looked like she had a bad rash, but there was nothing more she could do, so she straightened her blouse and headed downstairs.

Her mother waited at the bottom of the stairs and held out her hand toward the parlor. She smiled, albeit an uncertain smile. "I'll fix some tea for you and your guest."

Curious, Keri entered the parlor, and her heart sank like a blacksmith's anvil dropped into a pond. "Carl."

He stood, smiling wide, but then he frowned and hurried toward her. He took hold of her shoulders in a far too personal manner. "Keri, whatever is wrong?"

"Nothing you need to be concerned about." She twisted loose and hurried to the nearest chair.

Carl walked over to the mantel and parked his elbow on it. "I was hoping you'd come to town and see me."

"We've been busy."

"We?"

Heat warmed her cheeks at the odd tone Carl used. What was he imagining? "Yes, there is much to do on a ranch."

He pursed his lips. "So, let me get this straight. You not only live on a ranch you no longer own, but you also work here? With the cattle? Out with the men?"

"You make it sound dirty. But, yes, I do. Mainly, I fix the meals, but sometimes I ride out and help with the cattle or work with the horses." She lifted her chin. "I like helping out."

Carl barked out a harsh laugh. "That Mr. Morgan is a lucky man."

"What does that mean?"

"It means he gets a free cook—a beautiful one at that—and a free wrangler. A very lucky man indeed."

Keri jumped up, unable to sit in the face of Carl's accusation. "It's not for free. He allows me to stay in my home, and in exchange I work here." They'd never actually talked about such an arrangement, but that's how it had worked out, and that was fine with her.

He picked up an old photo, taken at her uncle Will's request when she was ten, and stared at it. "You were lovely even as a child."

She didn't want his compliments or his presence, but she wouldn't be inhospitable. The rattling of dishes preceded her mother into the room. Grace entered and set the tray on the table. Besides tea, she had added two slices of peach pie. She started to leave, but Keri grabbed her arm, and Grace lifted her brows in a questioning gaze.

"Carl, I'd like to introduce my mother, Grace Langston. Mother, Carl Peters, an old acquaintance."

"Your mother?" He was obviously taken off guard, but he recovered quickly and pretended to tip his hat, which lay on the coffee table. "A pleasure to meet you, Mrs. Langston."

Though Grace blanched at the mention of *Mrs.*, she managed a smile. "Nice to meet you, Mr. Peters. I hope you enjoy your visit. If you'll excuse me, I need to start supper preparations."

Carl nodded. Her mother smiled then left the room.

He turned on Keri. "Mother? I thought your mother was dead?"

"Why would you think that?"

"Oh, maybe because you were raised by your uncle."

She walked over to a window and stared out. How could she explain things in a way that would satisfy Carl? Maybe it was best to avoid the topic altogether. "What did you say was the nature of your visit?"

He walked up behind her then slipped his arms around her waist. Keri stiffened as he nuzzled her ear. "A man doesn't need a reason to visit his fiancée."

She spun around and suddenly realized her mistake. Carl grinned down at her like a snake eyeing a mouse. She swallowed and pushed at his arms, which still encircled her. "I have not agreed to marry you; thus I am not your fiancée."

A muscle ticked in his jaw. His hands tightened on her waist. "I'm not a man to trifle with. I've waited a long time to marry you, and I will."

She'd never been afraid of Carl, but she'd never seen him like this before. "Why do you want to marry me?"

His expression softened, and a wistful smile replaced his frown. "I wanted to the day I first saw you marching down the street, trying so valiantly to keep up with your uncle. You were unlike any young lady I'd ever known. I knew then that I wanted you for myself."

"You didn't even know me then."

"Didn't matter. I know what I want, and I get what I want."

She shoved him hard, slipped out of his grasp, and hurried across the room before she turned back to face him. "You might want to take some lessons in deportment. A lady likes to be wooed, not ordered to marry. I think it's time you leave."

Grace walked into the room. "Is something wrong?"

"No, Mother. Mr. Peters is leaving."

"This isn't over." He singed her with a glare, snatched his hat off the table, then paused in front of her mother. "Have we met before?"

Grace's face paled. "I . . . uh . . . not that I know of." Her worried gaze flicked toward Keri.

"Hmm . . ." Carl glanced down at Keri. "I can give you anything you'd ever want. I'd reconsider if I were you."

"Good day, Carl." Keri opened the front door, and after a long, hard stare, he walked out.

"That man gives me the creeps." Grace wrapped her arm around Keri's waist. "Are you all right?"

She desperately wanted to ask her mother if Carl had looked familiar, but instead she nodded. "Yes, but I'm afraid of what Carl might do."

"We'll face that if the time comes, but most of the time men who are riled just spout off and never follow through."

Keri closed her eyes. She didn't want to know how her mother knew that, but she hoped it was true.

But deep down inside, she had a feeling that more trouble was coming.

———— ★ ————

Keri stared out the train window at the countryside passing in a blur. "I can't believe I let my mother talk me into this."

"Aw, relax. It will be fun," Brooks said.

"You're like a child sometimes, you know that? How can a staged train crash be fun?"

Brooks turned on the seat, his eyes gleaming. "Don't be such a stick-in-the-mud, Missy. What's not to like about two trains speeding down the rails and crashing into each other? Think of the explosion it will make."

"I am, and I feel a headache starting all ready. And don't call me Missy."

Brooks chuckled. "Well, at least try to have fun for your mother's sake. She wanted to do something special for you."

So she'd bought the train tickets for Keri and Brooks to attend the Crash at Crush that was sponsored by the Katy railroad. Keri shook her head. "I'd have rather had a new pair of pants—or boots. And what kind of a name is Crush for a town, anyway?"

Brooks laughed, drawing a curious glance from the lady in the seat across the aisle. "This coming from a woman who lives near a town called Shoofly? Now that's a strange name if I ever heard one." He shook his head. "Besides, from what I read in the newspaper, the town is just a temporary one, set up special for the event and named after that man who thought up the idea. Crash at Crush. It's rather catchy, don't you think?"

"I think it's crazy that this train is so crowded they allowed people to ride on the top." Keri held up a finger and shushed him. "And quiet down. People are gawking."

Brooks winked at her then turned toward the gaping

woman and tipped his hat. "That's a mighty pretty dress you've got on, ma'am, if you don't mind me saying so."

The woman fanned her face as a scarlet blush rose to her cheeks. Keri leaned back in her seat and pinched her forehead. What a charmer Brooks Morgan was. And he had asked her to marry him.

"So, why is the Missouri, Kansas, and Texas Railroad hosting this event? I don't get it." Keri watched a small herd of buffalo grazing, but the train barreled past the huge animals.

"It's a publicity stunt, from what I've heard."

"How can a railroad crashing trains be good for business?"

Brooks waved his hand in the air. "Just look how crowded this car is—people standing in the aisle and even riding on top. With the discount rates for the train tickets and free admission, I imagine this will be a popular event."

She shrugged, still not understanding how such a day could be considered entertaining. A train crash wasn't her idea of fun, but it was something different, and walking around on Brooks's arm with other women green with envy wouldn't be too bad either. A smile pulled at her lips.

After fifteen minutes of watching the landscape flatten out, Keri yawned. Brooks sat with his long legs stretched out under the seat in front of him. His head dipped forward. Keri needed something to help her stay awake and nudged him in the side. "Tell me something about your past."

He yawned and stretched. She couldn't miss the tightness of the fabric across his chest. Her mouth went dry. Brooks turned toward her again, his knees pressing into the side of her dark blue skirt—the skirt her mother had loaned her and had insisted she wear.

He grinned. "I was my mother's favorite child."

Keri rolled her eyes, but the image of a young Brooks charming his mother with his pretty eyes and wide smile came easily.

"Josh is my older brother. My parents adopted him when he was three. He's probably a doctor by now." Brooks shrugged, but the thought of Josh being so successful when he had wasted the last ten years of his life left a bad taste in his mouth.

"I also have an older sister named Melissa. I guess I like calling you Missy because that's what we often called Sis. I often conned my naïve younger brother Phillip into doing my chores with promises of things that never materialized." He cocked one side of his mouth up, as if he now regretted his actions.

"Guess I wasn't too great of a big brother to Phillip." He glanced past her, staring out the window. "My pa thought I was lazy, but I just saw it as outsmarting my brother. Pa pushed me hard, and I didn't like it. I left home at sixteen, wanting nothing more to do with my father's ranch or his religion. I drifted for the past decade, doing almost any job I could find." He blew out a sigh and looked at her again then smiled. "But I'm older now—and wiser."

"That's a rather sad story." She couldn't help comparing how he'd had what sounded like a good family and walked away from it when all she ever wanted was a family.

"I've wanted to stop drifting for a long while now, but I never had anywhere to go. Raven Creek is my chance to do that."

No wonder he refused to give her the ranch. It still hurt that her uncle hadn't saved it for her as he'd always said he would, but if she couldn't have it, she was glad someone like Brooks, who wanted it so badly, got it. She thought of his family again—another mother out there wondering about her child. A father who bore the heartache of a lost son. Siblings who never saw their brother fully grown. "Why have you never gone home?"

He shrugged. "I guess mainly because I'm ashamed of how I acted back then."

She turned and touched his arm. "Oh, Brooks. You need to go home and reconcile with your family. Trust me when I say how much that will help you."

"You know the ironic thing?"

"What?"

"They live just outside of Waco."

"Waco? Why, that's not far from where we'll be."

"I know."

"Maybe we should—"

"No." His deep blue eyes darkened, and the charmer had been replaced by someone she didn't know. "I'm not ready yet. I want to make something of myself before I face them again. I want to prove to my pa that I'm responsible."

Keri leaned her head back and stared out the window. Now she understood why Brooks smiled so much—he was trying to keep the hurt away.

←——— ★ ———→

Brooks knew they'd be in Crush soon, but he scooted down in the seat and hung his hat over his face. Why had he suddenly turned chatty and told Keri his life story?

Because he wanted her to know the real Brooks Morgan, not the phony, grinning rascal she thought him to be. But nothing he'd said today would make her want to be harnessed to him for the rest of her life. She'd be smart to run the other way.

Instant chastisement beseeched him to not put himself down. He was now a precious child of the King, God the Father. He had a lot to learn about God's ways, but he knew making Keri feel sorry for him wasn't the right thing to do. If he truly loved her, he needed to make her feel special—cherished. Maybe now that she was away from the ranch and with just him all day, he could do that.

The train slowed and the brakes screeched as it stopped. The people who had stood in the aisles for most of the trip headed for the doors.

Keri sucked in a breath. "Look! They've got a circus tent, and I can see the trains. They're painted green and red. How fun!"

He leaned against her shoulder and stared out the window. "Look over there—see the hills on opposite sides of the tracks? That's where all the spectators will sit. And have you ever seen so many people?"

She shook her head. "There must be thousands of them. Why, this little town must be the most populated one in the whole state of Texas." She giggled and glanced at him.

His gaze locked onto hers, and he couldn't look away. His breath caught in his throat. She was so pretty. He wanted to kiss her, and he allowed his gaze to drop to Keri's lips. A lady behind him coughed, pulling him back to reality. "Guess we'd better go."

"Um . . . sure."

Outside the train, the air was abuzz with excitement. Brooks held Keri's arm and moved with the crowd toward the tents. "If we happen to get separated, let's meet at that small wooden building."

Keri nodded. "Can we see what's in that huge circus tent?"

"Sure." Brooks kept her close, and soon they were at the tent—a restaurant. Stomach-tingling aromas wafted out the open flaps. "Are you ready for some dinner, or would you rather see what else there is first?"

She looked around. "The line here isn't too bad. Why don't we go ahead and eat?"

After passing through a line and selecting their food, they sat down at a table and were soon joined by two other couples.

A thin man with a long face and big eyes pointed his empty fork at Brooks. "Where you folks from?"

"Shoofly." He speared a fat sliced carrot. "How about you?"

"Austin."

"That's a mighty long ways to come." He shoved a quartered potato in his mouth.

The man and those with him all nodded. "This is the biggest thing to happen in Texas since the war ended," said the other man, who looked to be a brother to the first man.

Brooks wasn't sure he agreed with him on the importance of the day, but it was something different, that was for certain.

"So . . ." a woman Brooks guessed to be the thin man's wife gazed at him and Keri with a warm smile. "How long have you two younguns been married?"

CHAPTER NINETEEN

arried? The piece of meat Keri just swallowed lodged in her throat. She coughed and coughed. Her eyes watered. She grabbed her glass of lemonade and took a big swig, washing down the bite.

Brooks turned and rested his arm on the back of her chair. "You all right?"

She nodded and wiped her tears with her napkin, embarrassed to her boot tips at the spectacle she'd made. "Sorry."

"That's all right. You ready to go and see the rest of the tents?"

"Yes," she said, very appreciative of his offer to make a quick exit. She did not want to explain to those people that they weren't married. Not that it was a problem, but some folks would look down their nose at an unmarried couple traveling together.

When they were outside, Keri reached out and squeezed Brooks's hand. "Thank you for getting me out of there. I'm mortified."

"Nonsense. Everyone chokes once in a while." He wrapped her hand around his arm. "Shall we?"

Several hours later, they stood on the hillside in a swelling crowd of what had to be twenty thousand people, and across the tracks on the other hill stood just as many folks. Some people stood on wagon beds and some had even climbed the few trees within sight. The two trains, one painted red with green trim and the other green with red trim, were in position. The engineers waved at the crowd, arousing loud cheers as the trains crept forward and touched cow-catchers. Aptly named, the V-shaped metal grids on the front of the trains were used for clearing debris off the rails. Both engines pulled six boxcars with colorful ads on their sides promoting the Katy Railroad, the Oriental Hotel in Dallas, and the Ringling Bros. Circus.

The heat of the late September sun was stifling, especially with everyone packed together as they were. Sweat trickled down Keri's back, but even with the discomfort, the excitement was infectious.

An ear-splitting roar rose up as the trains backed away to their two-mile starting points, from which they'd make their final run. A few minutes later, here they came! The behemoths churned out ebony smoke, and the steam jets spewed vapor. Whistles shrilled. The trains barreled toward one another at a frantic speed, unlike anything Keri had ever witnessed. Both engineers and firemen jumped from the speeding trains, did a barrel roll or two, regained their footing, and bowed to the crowd. Keri jumped with each succession of explosions of torpedoes that had been placed on the track. Brooks grinned, waggled his brows, and wrapped an arm around her.

A grand roar rose from the crowd as the two engines barreled toward each other. Keri bounced on her tiptoes. Closer and closer they came, and the crowd hushed, waiting for the crash of the steel monsters.

And then they hit. The roar of the crowd was barely heard over the thunderous crash as the two powerful behemoths collided. Box cars and flat cars climbed atop their leaders and disintegrated. The engines reared up like battling stallions and then fell slowly back to earth, each telescoping the other.

Brooks hugged Keri. "Wasn't that a sight to behold?" he yelled.

Suddenly, another deafening roar sent the crowd running. The one bad thing that Keri had speculated about all day had happened—the boilers had exploded. Thousands of chunks of metal flew through the air like bullets. Fiery shards rained down on the helpless spectators. As the people behind them turned to run, Brooks shoved Keri to the ground and fell on top of her, his body sheltering hers. Others tumbled over them. Someone stepped on her hand. A rock stabbed her cheek and she couldn't breathe.

She lifted her head and saw a smoke stack, blasting skyward before it fell back to earth. She couldn't see where it landed, but prayed that nobody was nearby. All around her, moans and cries of the wounded rang out. If only she could get free, she could help, but she couldn't move. Brooks's heavy body pinned her down. "Get off," she wheezed.

He didn't move. Not a speck.

Keri's heart thundered. *Is he hurt? Dead?*

The thought of never seeing the rascal's smile again brought a strength to her that she'd never had before. Pushing with all her might, she managed to ease out from under him. She spun around and gasped. Blood seeped from a wound on the side of his head, but it was the twenty or so dots of blood on his back that drew her gaze. The debris had rained down on him as he'd protected her. One slit in his shirt smoldered.

She grabbed the edge of her skirt and smothered the life out of it. What if she'd lost him?

Blinking back tears, she reached out and touched him. He was warm—still alive. She searched for her handbag and found it a few feet away. She pulled out a clean handkerchief and dabbed Brooks's forehead. It was the worst of his injuries, she suspected.

She looked around, and as far as she could see, people lay or sat on the ground, tending one another. It looked like she imagined a Civil War battlefield would look. She needed to get help for Brooks, but how could she in this mess?

"Help!" she screamed. No one even so much as glanced at her.

She turned back to Brooks and shook him. "Wake up, please. You need to wake up."

He didn't move.

She needed to get him back to their train before it left without them. The crash had started late because of the spectators crowding the tracks, which meant they hadn't much time left before it pulled out.

A man rode by on horseback, dodging the injured. Keri chased after him. "You, hey. Wait!"

He reined to a halt and glanced over his shoulder. She ran up to him and grabbed his leg. "I need your help."

He lifted a haughty brow and stared down.

"Please. Help me."

"What do you need?"

"My friend is injured. We've got to get to the train before it pulls out."

He blew out a sigh and nodded. Relief made her limbs weak. "Oh, thank you so much."

She spun around and rushed back to Brooks. Too late she realized the stranger could have ridden off, but when she looked back, he was there.

He peered down at Brooks and harrumphed. "If you'd told me your friend was a man, I'd have probably ridden on." Still, he bent down and tugged on Brooks's arm. "He's a large man. I don't know that I can lift him myself."

"I'll help."

Keri spun around to find a soldier carrying a piece of metal debris from the crash. "I'd be ever so grateful." She batted her eyes at the man, just as she'd learned from friends at finishing school.

"It'd be my pleasure, ma'am."

A short while later, she and Brooks were finally aboard the train. "I can't thank you enough for your assistance, sir. You may well have saved his life."

"My pleasure. I just hope that one day I find a woman who's willing to manhandle a stranger should I ever need help." He tipped his hat and smiled, then slipped out the door.

Keri touched Brooks's face—still warm, but not hot. Good. She hoped he didn't fall off the seat where the stranger and a depot clerk had laid him.

"Here, ma'am." A lady carrying a basket shoved a roll of bandages under her nose. "Looks like your man needs some doctoring." She shook her head. "Pitiful thing this crash is. So many hurt, even children."

Keri glanced around the train car. Everywhere were people with bloodstained clothing, people comforting one another or trying to calm a crying child. This day had looked so promising, but had turned out so disastrously.

She wrapped Brooks's head, but the nicks on his back would have to wait. The train whistle blasted, the passenger car shuddered, and then they started moving. She'd get Brooks home and tend him there—send for the doctor if need be.

With her head against the warm windowpane, she watched the grasslands roll by. The sun was preparing to set, but still cast plenty of light. Keri sighed and closed her eyes, just wanting to be back home at Raven Creek and for Brooks to be all right.

The screech of the train's whistle made her jump, and Keri realized she'd fallen asleep. The conductor stepped into the car. "Waco, in two minutes."

Keri blinked and stared at him. Waco? That was the opposite direction from where they needed to go.

← ★ →

Brooks struggled to open his eyes, but a room finally took shape. It smelled like an apothecary. Where was he?

He started to sit up, but the room swam like a top some youngster had spun. His back stung, as if a hundred nails had been driven into it. What happened?

"Brooks!" Keri hopped out of a chair and hurried across the room. "Don't get up. The doctor says you have a concussion from the blow you took at the train crash."

"Where are we? This isn't Doc Brown's office."

Keri nibbled her lip and looked away. "Well, you see, there was a lot of confusion right after the crash. Lots of people wounded—two even died. All I could think of was getting you away from there and to a doctor."

His gaze roamed up and down, as if searching her body for something. "Were you hurt?"

She smiled and shook her head. "Nothing more than a few bruises. You protected me when you threw me to the ground and fell on me."

"I did that?" He grinned to hide his concern. He didn't remember falling on her. Surely that's something he'd remember if he was in his right mind. "Where are we, Keri?"

She wilted and cast him what looked like an apologetic grimace. "Um . . . Waco."

He bolted up. "Waco?" A thousand spears pierced his head,

and he grabbed hold of it. The room swirled again. He closed his eyes.

"Lie down, son," a man said. "You took a bad hit to your temple. You need to rest."

He pressed the palm of his hands against the side of his head. "I can't rest. I have a ranch to run."

"You'll do no one any good like you are now. Just rest."

Brooks groaned.

"Oh, don't be such a baby." Keri pressed him down and held him there. "Don't make me have the doctor restrain you."

He peeked out one eye. "You wouldn't."

She lifted both brows, giving him a schoolmarm glare. He closed his eyes and tried to relax, not sure whether she was teasing or not. But she didn't understand that he couldn't relax in Waco—not when his family was just a few miles away—the family he hadn't seen in ten years.

———— ★ ————

Keri guided the buggy she had borrowed from the doctor over another rise, hoping she hadn't gone taken a wrong turn. She'd driven over a dozen of these little hills without finding what she was looking for, but this time she was rewarded. A well-tended clapboard house sat in a copse of trees, and not too far away was a tall, red barn with a paddock off to the side. The house rested in a lovely valley with a creek running through it. A dozen horses grazed on the far hill. A serene setting if she ever saw one. So this is where Brooks grew up. If she lived in a place like this, she wouldn't ever want to leave.

Now that she'd seen his former home and knew it existed, she ought to just turn the buggy around and go back to town, but she was curious. She wanted to meet his mother. His father. His siblings.

But she feared he'd hate her for it.

Still, he deserved to reconcile with his family, like she had. To know his family again. To see how they all had changed. Ten years made a big difference in people's lives. She knew all too well.

A woman stepped out onto the porch and shook a rug. She laid it across the railing and started to go back inside, but she shielded her eyes with her hand and glanced up the hill, right at Keri. She lifted her hand and waved.

Caught.

Now she couldn't turn back.

Her heart pounded and hands shook as she drove the buggy down the hill and pulled to a stop in front of the house. The woman left her porch and walked over to her, a welcoming smile gracing her face. "Afternoon."

Keri gave her a tight-lipped smile in return and climbed out of the buggy. She stood facing a woman whose light-brown hair was starting to gray, but her kind brown eyes looked curious. "I'm Annie Morgan. Are you looking for someone?"

"I—I'm a friend of your s-son's."

"Oh? I'm sorry, but Phillip is out working with his father today. They'll be home for supper, but that isn't until later. You're welcome to wait if you'd like."

Keri couldn't stop shaking. But after being separated from her mother for so long, to have been in the same town and not seen her would have been impossible, even if she had to go to the cat house to do so. She took a deep breath and strengthened her resolve. "I'm a friend of Brooks, ma'am."

Mrs. Morgan gasped a cry and lifted her fingers to her mouth. "Brooks? Is he—safe? Alive?"

Keri relaxed and smiled. "Yes, very."

Mrs. Morgan collapsed on the porch steps, tears pouring from her eyes. "Thank you, Father. I've prayed so many years for Brooks. We've missed him terribly. Since we hadn't heard anything in so long I feared he must be dead." She wiped her tears on the edge of her apron. "I'm sorry for not being a good hostess. Would you care to come in and have some tea?"

"Yes, thanks, but I can't stay long. I need to get back." She followed Mrs. Morgan into the nice, two-story house. A large parlor sat on her left with a smaller office/library on the right. They passed both rooms and stepped into a nice-sized kitchen, one twice as big as the one at Raven Creek. A pale yellow color on the walls gave it a cheery atmosphere. Things were tidy and in order. Somehow she'd expected Brooks's family to be less than perfect. Why else would he have been so determined to get away from them?

"Please, have a seat at the table. It won't take long to reheat the water."

Keri perched on the end of her seat. Now that she was here, she didn't know what to say. She hadn't asked Brooks if he wanted to see his parents. He had mostly slept the past two days, but he was sitting up for longer times. The doctor said they could leave in the next day or two if he continued to progress. She knew if she was going to talk to his parents, it had to be now.

Mrs. Morgan set a plate of cookies in front of her. "It's funny, I must have had Brooks on my mind, because I baked oatmeal cookies today. He loved them the first time I made them, but then he left before I made another batch. I always wished he'd come home so I could make him some more." She wiped away her tears and sat down. "Please Miss—"

"Oh, I'm sorry. My name is Keri Langston, and I'm from Shoofly."

"Why, that's not all that far from here." She leaned forward. "Is that where my son is?"

"It's where his ranch is."

She sat back against her chair, eyes blinking. "Brooks owns

a ranch? I thought he hated ranch life. That was why he left us."

"Things change in a decade. I think you'll like the man he's become." Keri smiled, hoping to reassure the woman.

"I'm so glad you've come here, Miss Langston, but why now? Why didn't Brooks come too?"

Keri told her the story of the Crash at Crush, of the explosion, and how Brooks had been injured trying to protect her. "And when the train pulled to a stop, we were in Waco, not Shoofly. I got Brooks to the doctor so his injuries could be treated and sent a telegram home so my ma wouldn't worry about us."

"How bad are his wounds?" Suddenly she jumped up so fast, her chair fell backwards, banging against the floor. "Wait! You mean to say that Brooks is in Waco?"

Keri smiled and nodded.

"Oh!" Mrs. Morgan pressed her hands to her chest. "We have to see him." She spun and ran out the back door and pounded the clangor on the metal triangle. Then she rushed back inside, grabbed a rifle that had been hidden behind the open door, went back outside, and fired three shots in the air.

She hurried back inside, put the rifle away, and stripped off her apron. She patted her hair. "How do I look? Should I change dresses? This one has some smudges on it."

Keri took her hands. "You look fine."

Tears made Mrs. Morgan's brown eyes shimmery. Keri could see little glimpses of her expression in Brooks. "I didn't tell him I was coming out here."

Mrs. Morgan stiffened. "What if he doesn't want to see us?"

"He might say that and even be angry at me for taking you to see him, but deep inside, I know he misses his family. He doesn't feel worthy enough to return."

"Surely he knows all is forgiven. We just want our son back."

"He's not the boy you knew back then." Although as soon as she said the words, she wondered if she wasn't wrong. Brooks would always be a cocky teaser. That was just his personality. But she felt certain he had matured. Just the fact that he wanted to make a go of the ranch proved that.

The sound of galloping horses approached the house, then footsteps rushed toward them. A tall man came in, an older version of Brooks from his dark hair with silver accents to his square face and blue eyes. He glanced at her, a rifle in his hand, then at Mrs. Morgan. "Annie, what's wrong?"

She rushed to him and grabbed his arms. "Oh, Riley. Something wonderful has happened."

The man relaxed his rigid stance and the wariness in his eyes vanished, replaced by curiosity.

"What is it, Ma?" A tall, thin young man—Keri guessed to be a few years older than she—stepped around Mr. Morgan. Phillip, she suspected. He had his mother's brown eyes, but had gotten his stature from his father. He glanced at Keri and smiled, much like his brother.

"This woman—" her voice caught, and she dabbed her eyes again. "She's a friend of . . . Brooks. He's here. In Waco."

The man blinked. "Brooks is in Waco?" His stunned expression hardened. "Why didn't he come to see us?"

"He's been hurt. He's at the doctor's office."

Phillip nudged his pa's shoulder. "Can we go see him? C'mon, Pa."

Keri could see the struggle in Riley Morgan's eyes. He longed to see his son, but the hurt from the past was still there. She reached out to touch him, but stopped short of her goal. "I think you'll find Brooks to be different. He's a good man, Mr. Morgan."

"He owns a ranch now, up near Shoofly," Mrs. Morgan said.

The man was obviously surprised, but then his expression

changed. "How could he live so close to us and never tell us? Didn't he realize we've been wondering if he was even still alive?" He crossed his arms and walked to the back door and stared out.

Keri sipped her tea, uncomfortable with witnessing the emotions of the Morgan family at the news their prodigal son had come to town. She needed to get back before he awoke from his nap, or he'd probably find his clothes and be gone when she returned. He made a grumpy patient.

"Well, are we going to see my big brother or not?" Phillip stepped farther into the room, and Keri could see similarities in the brothers, although they were different more than they were alike. "Someone needs to tell Melissa."

Mrs. Morgan snapped her fingers. "That's right. Phillip, you ride over and tell her what's happening, and you can meet us in town."

"Yeehaw! Can't wait to see Missy's face." He shot out the kitchen door.

"Miss Langston, if you're ready to go back, I'll ride with you, and my husband can come on his horse when he's ready."

Keri noticed the woman didn't say "if and when." She seemed to know her struggling husband would follow.

Mrs. Morgan grabbed a tin can off a shelf, shoveled in a dozen cookies, then hurried from the room. By the time Keri caught up with her she was at the door with her sunbonnet on. "Ready?"

Keri smiled at her eagerness. She may be the only woman left in the house, but it was easy to see who was the boss. They climbed in the buggy, and Keri started it down the road, then glanced back at the cozy house. Mr. Morgan stood on the front porch, all by himself.

"Don't worry about Riley. He'll be along. He's just struggled all these years with thinking he was too hard on Brooks. Riley fought in the war for nearly four years, and that makes a man tough. Hard. But he's a good man with a big heart. He can just be stubborn at times."

Keri chuckled. "That sounds a lot like Brooks, except he tries to joke and charm his way out of problems."

Mrs. Morgan nodded. "That sounds like my son. Always the charmer." She wrung her hands—the only outward sign of her nervousness. "I want so much for things to be good between us again. I've prayed thousands of prayers for Brooks, asking God to keep him safe, to help him to be happy and find a place to call home."

Keri guided the wagon to the left where the road split. "I believe God must have answered some of those prayers. Brooks has been going to church regularly lately."

"Oh, blessed be the name of the Lord." Mrs. Morgan pressed her closed fists against her mouth. "I've prayed so hard that Brooks would make peace with God."

Keri followed the road back to Waco, filling Mrs. Morgan in on how she and Brooks met and the status with the ranch.

"My son always had a good heart. I'm glad that he's letting you and your mother stay in the house. Dare I hope there could be something more than a business relationship between the two of you?"

Keri's cheeks, already warm from the hot afternoon sun, heated even more. "I don't know. Maybe. One day." She pulled up at the doctor's office, grateful for the timing and for not having to talk any more about her relationship with Brooks. She hardly understood it herself.

But seeing him lying in that field, bloody and hurt, had changed something. It made her realize just how fast she could lose him—and she didn't want to lose him.

As she climbed down from the buggy, Mr. Morgan rode around the corner on his horse. Mrs. Morgan glanced across the buggy at her and winked.

CHAPTER TWENTY

rooks leaned against the wall, trying to read the Bible the doctor had loaned him, but the tiny print kept blurring together. He slammed it shut and set it on the table. He needed to get back to Raven Creek. Who knew what kind of problems Saul Dengler could be causing?

And where is Keri? She was supposed to be here when he awoke to keep him company and tend to him. He smiled in spite of his grumpiness. What a lovely nurse she had made. If he didn't know better, he'd suspect she cared for him. He'd seen her worried glances over the past few days.

He fiddled with a frayed edge on the sheet. His feelings for Keri had taken him by surprise. He'd never been in love before and didn't know how to act. If Keri would just marry him, things would be perfect. They could share the ranch, and he could move into the house, although they'd have to do something with Grace. He snapped his fingers. That was it. She could have Keri's room, and he and Keri would take Will's bigger room. Perfect.

If only the stubborn, pigheaded Miss Langston would say yes.

The bell on the doctor's door jangled, and the object of his affections walked in. She smiled, but he noted a hesitancy—not her normal smile. Was something wrong at the ranch? He had to get out of here. He grabbed the sheet to toss it off and realized that all he wore was his drawers. Quickly, he pulled the sheet up, and forced himself to be content with Keri's company. But this was his last day in bed.

A man and woman entered after Keri, to see the doc most likely. But they didn't seek out the man who sat at his desk across the room. Instead they focused on him. His heart pounded like Indian war drums, and he couldn't take his eyes off them. *Ma. Pa.*

He ducked his head, ashamed of the way he'd worried them and the trouble he'd caused everybody. Why had Keri brought them here? He pinned her with a glare, but his mother stepped in front of her, blocking his view. Ma looked so vulnerable. So hopeful.

"It's really you, isn't it, son?"

"Yep, the prodigal son has come home. Are you going to kill the fatted calf?" He grinned because he couldn't let his folks see all the emotions swarming him like mad hornets.

"How about some chicken and dumplings instead?" his mother asked. She held out a small tin. "And this."

He took it, opened the lid, and sniffed. His eyes blurred with tears, and his throat tightened. "Oatmeal cookies?" he rasped.

She nodded, tears coursing down her cheeks. "The Good Lord must have known you'd be here and gave me a hankering for oatmeal cookies. I baked them this morning."

He set the can on the table next to the bed and swung his feet to the ground, keeping the sheet around his middle. He cast a glance at Keri, hoping she could read his request for help. Keri pushed around his mother and came to his side, but as she reached down to help him, his father stepped forward. Brooks gazed up at the man he'd hated for so many years, and for the life of him, he couldn't remember why he'd despised him. "I'm sorry, Pa."

His mother sucked in a sob as his pa lifted him to his feet. His father turned and wrapped him in a bear hug. "I'm sorry too, son. Forgive me if I was too hard on you."

His pa slapped him on the back several times, and Brooks gritted his teeth from the pain, then his mother embraced him, and they stood together, a family united again.

He glanced at Keri and smiled then gazed up at the ceiling. *Thank You, Lord.*

Three hours later, after the doc had given him permission to walk across the street and eat supper with his parents, his brother, and his sister and her family, Brooks couldn't remember ever being so exhausted. He sat on the edge of the bed, reluctant to say good-bye but wishing he could lie down and go to sleep.

"We need to head home," his pa said. "It will be dark soon."

"We'll be back tomorrow." His mother bent and hugged him around the neck, then kissed him on the cheek. "I'm so glad to see you again and to see the man you've become." She leaned up against his ear. "Don't let that pretty gal get away from you." She stood and winked.

Next Melissa bent and hugged him. "Don't stay away so long next time, little brother."

Five-year-old Abby and two-year-old Mikey both hugged their father's legs, staring at him. Brooks waved, and Abby waved back, but Mikey ducked behind his pa's leg. Melissa pried them off, and Jarrod Banks, her husband, walked toward him. Brooks forced himself up off the bed and shook the man's hand. "It's good to meet you. Thanks for taking such good care of my sister."

He nodded. "My pleasure. You're welcome at our house anytime." He winked. "And bring your lady friend," he whispered.

Brooks glanced at Keri, who stood back, leaning against the doctor's desk. She glanced at him and smiled.

Next, Phillip walked up and stared at him, nearly eye-to-eye. Brooks shook his head. "I still can't get over how you've grown up, little brother," Brooks said.

Phillip grinned. "I still can't get used to how old you've gotten, big brother."

Chuckles filled the room, and Phillip wrapped him in a big hug. "It's really good to have you back, Brooks."

His pa was the last to say good-bye. He'd been quiet much of the evening, and Brooks wasn't sure if he was glad he'd returned or not. He wanted a relationship with his father. With the train running between their two towns, a weekend trip on occasion wasn't out of the question. Maybe they could even spend Christmas together—if his pa was willing. And maybe Josh could come home then too and bring his family. He shook his head, hardly able to believe that his older brother was married and was a doctor in a small town in South Dakota. He hadn't thought about it before, but he was an uncle now.

Keri pushed away from the desk, and she followed the others outside. The door shut, and he and his pa were alone. Brooks swallowed the lump in his throat.

Riley Morgan stood with his head ducked and fiddling with the hat he held. Brooks didn't know what to say to make things easier for his father. The only thing he could think of was, "I'm sorry, Pa."

His pa's lips tightened, and he glanced up with tears shimmering in his eyes. "I'm sorry too, son. I responded in anger when forgiveness should have been foremost."

Tears burned Brooks's eyes. "It wasn't you, Pa. I was a stupid, rebellious kid. I wanted to come back home so many times, but I was stubborn and immature. I hope you and Ma can forgive me for all the pain I've caused you."

He shook his head and shrugged, stealing Brooks's hopes.

"Done. We forgave you years ago, but we never stopped missing you."

He struggled to hold back his emotions, but it was in vain. Brooks fell against his pa's solid chest and felt as if he'd come home again. His tears wetted his father's shirt, just as his father's tears did his. A peace that Brooks hadn't known before—except that day he asked God into his heart—flooded him.

He was home.

←——— ★ ———→

Two days later, Brooks tugged on his boots. He was ready to get back to the ranch but hated leaving his family. At least his parents were riding back on the train with him and Keri. His father had taken care of the doctor's bill—a big relief since he had no money. The Katy railroad was offering them free passage home because he had been injured at Crush. He just wanted to get to the ranch and see how things had fared while they had been gone.

He buttoned his shirt and walked to the door, looking for Keri. She should have been here already. They were scheduled to meet his parents at the café for breakfast, then catch the train. Ah, there she was, looking pretty in her new blue calico dress.

She hiked her skirts, revealing her boots underneath, and

jogged across the street. When she cut in front of a wagon, his heart jolted. Crazy woman. He pulled the door open. "What's the big hurry? We're not in so much of a rush that you need to risk your life." He grinned but the expression on her face stole it away.

"Look at this."

He opened a piece of paper she had shoved at him—a telegram from Nate that read, "Trouble."

← ★ →

Brooks drove the rented buggy as fast as he dared. Keri clung to the seat with one hand and the side of the buggy with the other. His ma and pa somehow hung on in the back-seat as the matched pair of blacks galloped down the lane. As soon as the train had arrived, they'd headed to the livery, and now home loomed just around the next corner. The thin trail of smoke and dark clouds over the ranch didn't bode well. He prayed no one was hurt.

They pulled into the yard, and Brooks sawed back on the reins, slowing the snorting, lathered team to a walk. Nate and Grace jumped up from the porch rockers they'd been sitting on and hurried toward them. Relief washed over Brooks to see that the house and barn were intact. So what was burning? He stood and looked at the smoke in the distance. The windmill was gone!

"What happened?" Brooks jumped down and helped Keri, while his pa assisted his mother.

Nate stared at Keri with an odd look on his face and shook his head. A stark white bandage had been wrapped around his hand and lower arm. "It happened just before dawn. I'm guessing Dengler's men snuck in while we was still asleep and set fire to the tower."

"They'd have had to use kerosene to burn it down that

fast." Brooks stood with his hands on his hips, staring at the ground. He'd just reconciled with his parents and with God, and things were going good. Why did this have to happen? And why now when he had his parents along? He wanted his father to see him as successful, not beaten down.

Grace walked toward his mother, smiling. "Welcome to Raven Creek. I'm Grace Langston, Keri's mother, and this is Nate Connelly. He works for Brooks."

His mother walked up to Grace and smiled. "How very nice to meet you. This is my husband, Riley. We're Brooks's parents."

Stunned was the only word Brooks could think of to explain the expressions on Grace's and Nate's faces. Grace recovered first and embraced his mother in a warm hug. "What a pleasure it is to meet you both. Why don't you come inside, and I'll fix some tea and coffee? We can let the men talk."

Brooks glanced at Keri. She seemed to be barely containing her fury. He walked over and squeezed her hand. "It will be all right. We can rebuild."

She glanced up, hurt and fire in her eyes. "And what's to keep them from burning down the next one?"

"We'll hire night guards."

She leaned up close to his ear. "And did you forget that we have no money?"

"What about contacting the marshal?" Riley asked.

Nate shrugged. "There ain't no proof of who did it. We had a witness . . ." He ducked his head and kicked a rock and sent it rolling.

Apprehension crawled up Brooks's neck like spiders on a wall. "What witness?"

Nate glanced up and back down, an expression of anger and pain unlike any Brooks had witnessed affecting the man before smoldered in his eyes. "It was Jess. He heard them and rode out before I could get my pants—" he glanced at Keri, his ears reddening—"and . . . uh. . . my horse saddled. I found Jess down by the tower. They hung him."

Keri sucked in a sob and fell against Brooks. His heart twisted. "This isn't right. Jess never hurt a soul. Did you see who did it?"

Shaking his head, Nate pursed his lips. "Sorry, boss. You know I don't see well at night. I managed to get Jess cut down before the fire got too bad, but he was already gone." Nate breathed in a deep breath. "We buried him over in the South pasture on that hill with the little redbud tree."

Brooks looked at his pa with tears blurring his eyes. "Jess never did harm to anyone. He didn't deserve this."

"No, he didn't." Keri jerked away from him and ran toward the barn, but at the last minute, she swerved and jogged down the lane toward the tower.

Riley stepped up to Brooks and placed a hand on his shoulder. "I'm sorry, son. Tell me what I can do to help."

He nodded his thanks. "Would you mind cooling off the horses and seeing to them?"

"Of course."

"I'll help," Nate said, glancing up at Brooks's head. "What happened to you?"

"Had a run-in with a train."

"How bad is the train?" Nate obviously tried to lighten the mood as he headed toward the team.

Riley paused halfway to the horses and turned back. "There's something I need to tell you. I hope you'll listen to me and not get angry."

Brooks felt his nostrils flare. Would his pa lecture him about something he'd done wrong? He forced that thought away and relaxed, then nodded.

His pa walked toward him and stopped in front of him. "I always hoped you'd come back to us. But when you didn't and knowing how you hated ranch life, I groomed Phillip to take over our place."

Anger flared at being left out, but Brooks doused it with a pail of common sense. It was his own fault. They hadn't known if he was dead or alive. His pa had done the right thing.

"I started a fund in the bank a few years after you left. Each year that we made a profit, I'd deposit one-third of the money there. It's your money, son. The account is in your name."

Brooks blinked, unable to comprehend what his father had said. He wasn't broke? Though he deserved nothing after he'd abandoned his family, his pa had the grace to save a portion of the ranch's profit's for him.

"There's enough to rebuild the windmill, if you want." Riley grinned. "In fact, there's probably enough for fifty of 'em, and maybe more."

Brooks yanked off his hat and ran his hands through his hair. "I don't know what to say. I don't deserve such a kindness."

His pa wrapped his arm around his shoulder. "You deserve it because you're my son. It's the same with God—not that I'm comparing myself to God. We don't deserve His love and the sacrifice He made in giving His only Son to die on the cross for our sins. We can never do enough or be good enough to deserve His favor. We have it because we are His children."

A month ago, his pa's analogy would have angered Brooks, but not now. Not since he'd made things right with God. It made perfect sense. He grasped his father's hand and shook it. "Thanks, Pa. I don't deserve it, but I'm sure thankful to know it's there. Times have been tough here."

"Let me help with the horses, and I think you have a pretty, little lady to check on." Pa winked and hurried over to help Nate unhitch the horses.

Brooks watched him jog away, still unable to grasp that he'd made peace with his family—with his father. What a fool he'd been to waste so many years. He couldn't afford to waste any more. He strode to the barn and saddled Jester. He needed to survey the damage and make sure the fire was completely out and that Keri was all right. He thought of the rabid coyote and how she didn't have a gun with her now. He led Jester out of his stall and climbed on. As soon as he cleared the barn, he urged the horse to run.

✦

Keri stomped toward the smoldering windmill. She knew Dengler was responsible, but how could she prove it? Why did this have to happen now, when things were going so well? An ominous thought made her stumble. She gasped and regained her footing. What if Carl had done this? He'd warned her that he wasn't someone to trifle with.

She walked down the hill, tears pooling in her eyes as she stared at the charred remains of the windmill. It had been so majestic the day they left Raven Creek, and now it was nothing but rubble—and poor Jess had died here. She thought of the happy man. He may not have been the sharpest pencil in the box, but he was always kind. Nate would miss his company something fierce. And now they were a man down and had no money with which to hire another one.

Maybe she should encourage Brooks to sell out before he was killed too. He'd already had a close call. But then he'd go away, and she didn't think she could bear that. In spite of trying so hard to resist him, the man had gotten under her skin and into her heart. She wasn't certain if she loved him— she'd had few examples of love—but she cared deeply. She'd been so scared at the crash when she thought he was dead. She folded her arms and rubbed her hands on them, even though the hot afternoon sun bore down on her.

Quickly approaching hoofbeats thundered in her direction. She didn't have to look to know it was Brooks. After her close call the other day, he wouldn't leave her out here knowing she was unarmed. Still, she glanced over her shoulder, and her heart leapt at the sight of him.

He dismounted and walked up beside her and took her hand. He squeezed it and blew out a loud sigh.

"What are we going to do?" she asked.

"We'll rebuild."

"But how? And what about finding out who did this?"

"I think we both know who that is."

She paused a moment, considering whether to tell him or not. "It might have been someone else."

Brooks faced her, brows lifted. "What does that mean?"

"It may have been Carl."

"Carl Peters? Why would he do such a thing? I thought he liked you."

"He did—or does, but I told him I wouldn't marry him."

Brooks grinned. "Found someone you liked better, did you?"

She scowled and shoved him. "Don't be a ninny. This isn't something to joke about. Jess was murdered! Our windmill has been destroyed. We have precious little water left. Even if we started rebuilding tomorrow, in this heat, we won't have enough water for more than a few days."

As if to emphasize her point, a cow down at the pond mooed.

"I have to return the horses to the livery tomorrow, so I'll see if the same crew is available to build another windmill." He walked over to a smoldering hunk of wood and kicked dirt over it. "Once this cools down, we can sort through it. There's quite a bit of wood that didn't completely burn. We can use it this winter for firewood and won't have to hunt for so much wood."

"Do you always see a silver lining in every storm cloud?"

He shrugged. "I didn't used to. If I had, I never would have left home."

"What changed?"

He rubbed the back of his neck and stared past her. "I guess I did. My mother spoiled me, no doubt about it. I know she meant well, but it still happened. I grew into a sullen adolescent who didn't want to work. My pa tried to make a man of me, but I rebelled and ran off, thinking I knew more than him." He gazed down at Keri and brushed the back of his finger across her cheek. "I was wrong. It took me nearly ten years of hard knocks and growing up to learn that."

Keri stared up at him, a smirk dancing on her intriguing lips. "You're a slow learner, aren't you?"

He grinned. "In some things. But there's one thing I was good at right from the start."

She blinked her long lashes, a smile pulling at her tempting lips. "What's that?"

"Kissing." He tugged her closer, and dipped his head, enjoying how her eyes widened, but then he closed his and pressed his lips against hers. He'd wanted to kiss her since the first time he'd seen her mounted on Bob and pointing a rifle at the men bent on killing him. He pulled her up against him and deepened the kiss, breathing hard out of his nose. He didn't want to pull away, but he knew he should and did.

Keri wobbled, her lips red, her eyes half glazed over. He grinned.

She shook her head and turned her back to him. Either she was embarrassed, angry, or both.

"What about Carl?"

That unexpected question sure doused his passion. "What about him?"

She spun back around, still looking thoroughly kissed. He stood a bit taller.

"He said that he wanted to marry me and that he always got what he wanted. What if he did this because I refused him?"

Brooks wouldn't put it past the man. His gut instinct had sensed something the first time he met Carl Peters. "It's possible, I guess, but it sounds more like Dengler's work." He fingered his throat. "Especially the hanging part."

"We need to make him pay. How do we get even with him?"

"You can't get even with a man like Saul Dengler. They don't play fair. You have to bide your time and hope they make a mistake. Besides, I think this is something we need God's help with. It's too big for us to handle on our own."

"What did God ever do for us?"

"Oh, He saved me from hanging and from getting killed at that crash. He saved you from that coyote."

"You saved me, not God."

Brooks pressed his lips tight and shook his head. "I don't think so. I was ready to ride the other way and let you walk off some steam, but then I felt this overpowering desire to find you. That was God impressing on me that you needed help."

She crossed her arms. "Maybe. But I haven't seen much of God's hand in my life."

"Maybe you aren't looking hard enough."

She glared up at him. "Just what does that mean?"

"I can see God's hand in many things that happened to you."

"Like what?" She pursed her lips in a pouty manner that made him want to steal another kiss, but he resisted.

"Well, for one, your uncle sent your mother away when she became pregnant. If he hadn't done that, life here would have been difficult for you. You know how people thumb their noses at—well, children born out of wedlock. Two, he brought you back here, gave you a home, and raised you the best he knew how. Will loved you, I'm sure of it."

"You don't know anything. Since when did you start taking things seriously? You always laugh and joke around. You're a clown, Brooks Morgan. What makes you think I'd ever want to marry you?"

She spun around and stomped back up the hill. He stood there speechless, with his hands resting on his hips. What had he said to set her off like that? He'd just been trying to help her see how God had worked in her life when she hadn't known He was there. He shook his head.

Women.

CHAPTER TWENTY-ONE

en. None of them confused her like Brooks Morgan. *And that kiss. Oh my.* It had reached in and stirred up her insides worse than a butter churn. It made her—feel. Warmth, delight, anger. *Why did he kiss me?*

And why was she disappointed when he stopped?

She thought about kissing Carl, and her stomach churned in a different manner—like it had that time Uncle Will made her drink milk. Only he didn't know that it had gone blinky. After she retched all over the kitchen floor, he sent her to bed, and never made her drink milk again.

Keri washed her face at the well, wiped it off, and shook the water off her hands. She paused at the kitchen door and heard voices.

"You have a lovely daughter," Mrs. Morgan said.

"And you have a handsome, charming son," her mother replied.

The two women giggled. Keri plastered herself against the back of the house so they wouldn't see her out the window or the back door.

"I guess maybe you're hoping what I'm hoping," Grace said.

Keri couldn't for the life of her wonder what her ma's dreams were. They hadn't had time to talk about them yet.

"Is that horseradish in that dish? And sugar and vinegar?" Brooks's ma asked.

Keri couldn't hear her ma's reply so she assumed she'd nodded. Several times a day, her mother took a bite of the odd concoction that made Keri shudder.

"Isn't that combination a treatment for a heart condition?"

Keri's own heart clenched. She burst in the back door and stared at her mother. "A heart condition? You mean you're going to die?" Keri couldn't stand the thought that she might lose her mother when she had just gotten her back.

Both women jumped.

"For heaven's sake, Keri. Were you eavesdropping?" Her ma held on to the bib of her apron, as if hiding her heart.

"Don't change the subject. Are you going to die?" She couldn't bear the thought.

"Everyone is going to die, dear."

"Don't patronize me."

Mrs. Morgan backed up and slipped out of the room.

Grace sighed. "I have a heart condition, but the doctor has assured me that if I continue the treatments he gave me and don't overly tax myself, I could live to a ripe old age."

Keri's lip quivered. "So you're not dying?"

Her mother smiled. "No one knows for certain the day they will die, but I feel fine. I'm strong, healthy. I'll be all right." She cupped Keri's face with her palm. "I've never had more to live for than I have now."

Keri closed her eyes, immensely relieved. "I just couldn't bear to lose you when I just got you back."

"I fully intend to live long enough to see my grandchildren grow up."

Keri pulled back. "Grandchildren? But I'm not even married."

"Well, I hope to remedy that situation soon."

After all the tenseness and problems of the day, Keri laughed. "Leave it to two women to put their heads together and start matchmaking. I suppose we'd better go find Mrs. Morgan and move you into my room so they can stay in Uncle Will's."

She locked arms with her mother. Keri's emotions had run the gamut today. Even having to share her bed, she would have no problem sleeping tonight.

— ★ —

Brooks thought he'd never get to sleep last night. He yawned and stretched, giving the horses their head. They certainly knew the way back to town. Hitched to the back of the buggy, Jester nickered, as if jealous that he wasn't being ridden. "You'll get your turn, boy."

Breakfast had been a crowded affair in his little kitchen with his parents there, and yet it was difficult not seeing Jess, making his odd comments and wolfing down his food. Brooks's heart ached, just thinking about what those vigilantes had done to that poor man. He fingered his neck. If God hadn't intervened in his hanging, he'd be dead now, and his parents would never have known what happened to him. He would have never met Keri.

"Lord, there's got to be something folks like me can do about a powerful man like Saul Dengler. Can't You let him step on a rattlesnake or something?" Brooks chuckled at the thought of that sidewinder killed by a rattlesnake. He instantly sobered as he realized what an un-Christian thought that was. "Sorry, Lord."

He returned the buggy, then led Jester down the street to the marshal's office. He passed the café where he'd first met Will, and he paused to remember the old man and to consider how his life had changed since arriving in Shoofly. If he didn't know better, he'd think God had orchestrated the whole thing.

Will needed him, and he needed friendship and a home—a hope for the future.

He needed to find God and make things right with Him, and he needed Keri in his life.

He knocked on the marshal's door and stepped inside. The office was empty, except for a man lying on a cot in one of the cells in back. "Hey, when's a fella s'posed to get somethun to eat around here?"

"Don't know," Brooks hollered.

He stood on the boardwalk and looked around. There ought to be a way to get folks to band together to fight Dengler. He rubbed the back of his neck and decided it was time for a haircut. Maybe if he spiffied up some, Keri would be more inclined to marry him.

He crossed the street and strode into the barbershop. A man sat in one of four chairs that lined the wall, while Earl sat in his barber chair. "Well, lookie there, Curtis, the whelp decided to come and pay his respects. How you been, kid?"

"I've been better." Brooks took off his hat and laid it over his knee.

Earl draped a cape over Brooks's shirt and secured it at his nape. "What'll it be today?"

"Just a haircut."

Earl grabbed his comb and shears and began snipping. "What's got you so low in the mouth?"

Brooks really wanted to tell the marshal first, but more than likely, word had already gotten out. "Someone burned down our new windmill early this morning, and they hanged Jess Baxter."

Pausing with the comb and shears in midair, Earl gawked at Brooks in the mirror. "I'm sure sorry about that. Jess was a good-hearted man that wouldn't hurt a fly. Any ideas who did it?" He snipped along Brooks's neckline.

"I have my suspicions, but no proof."

Curtis, a man Brooks had seen around town, harrumphed. "Only one yahoo around here causing problems for folks." He spat on the floor. "Dengler—and his cronies."

"There ought to be something we could do to put a stop to his cruelties." Brooks scratched at a tickle on his neck. The tightness of the barber's cape against his throat reminded him of that noose and his close call.

"There was some trouble out at O'Malley's last night too." Earl moved around front and trimmed around Brooks's face. The man smelled of cigar smoke, as he always did.

"Was anyone hurt?"

Earl pursed his lips and nodded. "Yup. They killed Tom. Strung him up like smoked ham."

Brooks closed his eyes and sighed. Tom O'Malley wasn't much older than he was and he had a wife and three young'uns. "What's gonna happen to his family?"

Curtis sat up and leaned forward. "Probably sell out to Dengler now. What else can a widow woman with a flock of youngsters do?"

"We need to form a committee to do something about Dengler," Brooks said.

Earl barked a laugh. "Sure, and they'll kill you like they did Will."

"They already tried to murder me once, but they didn't succeed."

Earl ran the comb through Brooks's hair. "And you won't succeed in finding anybody to head up that committee. Ever'body's got too much at stake."

Brooks mulled over the idea of a committee, but what would be the point? The people of town were good, law-abiding citizens, not a frenzied crowd of vigilantes. *Lord, we need some help here. How do small-town folk stand up to a bully like Dengler?*

———— ★ ————

Keri rummaged through the trunk of clothes that she'd brought home from Georgia. She tossed dress after dress onto the bed then turned and stared at the mountain of fabric and ruffles. What was she going to do with all these?

She tugged out a pale green dress that she halfway liked. She spread out the wide skirt and tapped her lip. "Hmm . . . I wonder."

"Wonder what?" Her mother carried Keri's pitcher over to the stand and set it in the bowl. She brushed her hand across her brow.

"I told you to let me do the heavy lifting. You need to take things easy."

Grace walked over and lifted the skirt of a blue gown. "What are you going to do with all of these?"

"I don't know."

"If I might offer a suggestion . . . you should pick out the ones you like best, and we can make some adjustments so that they look more like a dress a woman would wear than a girl and keep them for special events, like barn dances, or church socials."

"I suppose we could do that, although I rarely go to such events."

Her mother flashed a knowing smile. "I have a feeling

you'll be going to more of them if a certain man has his way."

Keri scowled as she thought of how demanding Carl had been. "I have no desire to go anywhere with that man."

"Why? What has he done?"

Keri threw out her arms. "You were there. I'm sure you heard some of what he said. Threatening me if I didn't agree to marry him."

Grace laid her hand on her chest and laughed. "I didn't mean him. I was talking about Brooks. Surely you can see that he cares deeply for you?"

Heat rushed to Keri's cheeks, and she turned and walked to the window. Nate and Mr. Morgan were sorting through the rubble of the tower, looking for anything salvageable. Their pile was small so far.

"Keri, do you have feelings for Brooks?" Grace coughed and cleared her throat. "I mean, if you'd rather not talk to me about that, I understand."

Keri turned and glanced at the door. "Where is Mrs. Morgan?"

"She's downstairs, washing their travel clothes so they'll be clean when they return home."

"Brooks will hate to see them go. It's been really good for him to spend time with them—after all that happened."

"Yes, this seems to be the month for reconciliations."

Keri cocked her head. "I noticed you and Nate are getting rather chummy."

Her ma ducked her head and shrugged. "I guess it's just natural. You've got Brooks, and Riley and Annie have one another, that leaves Nate and me. He's a nice man."

"Do you think you'd ever consider getting married? Not that I think Nate would ever find the nerve to ask you."

An embarrassed smile danced on Grace's lips. She shrugged again.

Keri's eyes widened. "You don't mean you two have actually talked about it—I mean you hardly know the man."

Grace walked to the window and stood beside Keri. "Actually, we've known each other for a very long time. Don't forget I lived here before I went away."

"And Nate worked at Raven Creek back then? But I remember him coming here after I did."

Grace shoved the dresses to the back of the bed and patted the blanket. "Come and sit here with me, sweetheart. I want to tell you a story."

She did as told, her mind racing as she struggled to make sense of things. Her mother had known Nate over twenty years. How could she not know that? What hadn't Nate told her?

Keri settled on the edge of the bed and turned to face her ma.

Grace stared down at her hands for a long moment. "A long time ago, there was a young woman—about your age, in fact—who terribly missed her parents. They'd been killed in a stage holdup when she was fifteen. Her older brother raised her, but she was a wild, rebellious girl who sought to quench the pain of loss in the arms of men."

Keri closed her eyes. Grace was talking about herself.

"There was this especially nice and handsome young man who came to work at our ranch. He treated me with respect and protected me from those who'd try to take advantage when Will wasn't around. I fell in love with him."

Keri gasped. "Nate?"

Grace nodded.

"But . . . so what happened?"

Grace stared toward the window and sighed. "Will didn't think Nate was good enough for me. He was just a ranch hand, you see. He owned nothing of his own and couldn't even give me a home."

"So? Uncle Will could have built one on the ranch for you."

Grace shrugged. "Will was overprotective—didn't think I was old enough to be in love or get married. He fired Nate and told him to never return here."

Keri frowned. "But then why did he rehire Nate later?"

"I don't know. I suppose he had remorse for treating us so harshly. I do know they made amends with each other, because Will wrote and told me."

"Why didn't Nate come to you later?" Keri picked up her pillow and hugged it.

"I don't think Will ever told him where I was."

Grace paused a moment and then continued. "I need to finish my story, so there will no longer be any secrets between us." Her mother stood and paced the room, twisting her hands. "Nate came to me one night to tell me he was leaving. He wanted me to go with him, but I couldn't leave Will all alone, not after losing our parents and all."

"So, you just let Nate go?"

Her ma blew out a sigh that puffed up her cheeks and looked at Keri. "Not exactly."

"Then what?"

"I stayed with him that one night. I know it was wrong, but I never regretted it, because he gave me you."

Keri blinked. "But—that means . . ."

Grace nodded. "Nate is your father."

CHAPTER TWENTY-TWO

*K*eri raced Bob across the open range, trying to outrun the hurt—the pain of all the people who had run her life. Her mother—who gave her away. Her uncle—who knew the truth and hid it from her. Her father—who had helped care for her, taught her to fish and hunt. A father who'd never had the guts to tell her who he was. Finally, she reined the exhausted horse to a walk. Lather had formed on Bob's sides, and the tired beast heaved as he struggled for breath. She dismounted and walked him down a faint trail that she didn't remember ever traveling on before. They'd long ago left Raven Creek land.

She wiped the dust from her eyes—dust that had collected on her tears.

She didn't know what to do, or where to go. All she knew was that she couldn't go back home until she'd sorted things out.

A short while later, she came to a small pond and let Bob drink. She took a slurp then sat down under a tree, as tuckered out as her horse. If she had any money, she could hop the train and go somewhere else, but in truth, there was no place she wanted to go. Raven Creek had always held her heart. She loved the land, the cattle, and mostly, the horses.

And she might even love Brooks—if the tingles in her belly when he came near were any indication.

She yawned. They needed to head back soon, even though she wasn't ready to face all of them. Her ma would probably have told Nate that she knew the truth, and that would change everything. She wouldn't know how to act around him now that she knew he was her father. Still, hadn't she loved him almost from the start? When she'd been furious at Uncle Will for taking her from her ma, Nate had been there to comfort her and distract her. He made her laugh.

She sat up and wrapped her arms around her knees. Had anything really changed?

Her gaze lifted to the sky. The preacher at church said that God loved her and cared about what was important to her. "Can you make this all turn out right, God? Are You really up there?"

Blowing out a sigh, she stood, stretched, and mounted Bob. She loped him back to the east, back toward home—but she still didn't have any answers. She would just have to face things head-on and see what happened.

Thirty minutes later, she ran across the road leading to Shoofly. Somehow she'd ridden in a huge circle. Keri started to turn toward home, when she noticed a buggy coming over the hill in her direction. She shaded her eyes and realized the driver was Ellen Peters. Thankfully, her brother was nowhere to be seen.

Ellen waved at her. "Oh, Keri. Yoohoo!"

She rode Bob toward the wagon and stopped next to it. She smiled. It wasn't Ellen's fault she had a bossy brother. "Are you headed into town?"

Ellen shook her head. "No, as chance would have it, I was headed out to your place."

"Mine?" Ellen had only been to her house the one time she came with Carl, the day Keri fell and hurt her ankle. "Were you coming to see me?"

Bobbing her head, Ellen reached into her pocket. "I have a note for you from Carl. He was busy with work and asked me to bring it to you."

Keri reluctantly took it. "I can't imagine what it is."

Cocking her head, Ellen smiled coyly. "I bet he's asking you to attend next month's harvest dance with him."

Keri's stomach felt as queasy as if she'd swallowed a slug. She opened the sealed envelope and scanned the note. Her heart clenched.

I know who and what your mother is. Come back to the house with Ellen, or I'll go public with my news.

She held the letter her against her chest. If the townsfolk learned her mother's true identity, Grace would never be able to stay at the ranch. Good, decent folks wouldn't want to associate with Grace, no matter how much she'd changed.

Keri had no choice. She had to face Carl and see what he wanted in exchange for keeping silent. "I need to talk to your brother, Ellen. Could you take me to him?"

"Certainly." Ellen gazed up at her with a knowing smile. "My brother's a handsome man, and he cares a lot for you. I hope things work out for you both, because I'd love to have you for a sister."

"That's nice of you to say." Keri inwardly shuddered at the thought of marrying Carl. Was Ellen really so naïve that she didn't know what her brother was truly like? But who was she to talk, when she had lived with her father most of her life and never even knew it?

Ellen turned the wagon back the way she'd come, and Keri

rode alongside, heading away from town—away from home. She had an overpowering urge to turn around and ride for home, but she couldn't let Carl destroy her mother, not when they had just reconciled.

———— ★ ————

Brooks rode up to the house, wishing he hadn't waited in town for the marshal to return. The task had been fruitless, and he'd missed lunch. His stomach growled just thinking about that. Grace threw open the front door and ran down the steps. Her gaze snapped toward him, then she looked past him and down the road.

"Isn't Keri with you?"

Apprehension raised the hairs on his arms. "Uh, no. I was in town earlier and then I rode out toward the O'Malley place, looking for the marshal. How long has she been gone?"

Grace twisted her hands and ducked her head. "I told her something that upset her, and she rode off early this morning. She didn't come back for lunch. I'm so afraid something has happened to her."

Brooks looked at the horizon, tension tightening the muscles in his neck and shoulders. "That was hours ago." He knew Keri and Grace were still working out some issues from the past, but it wasn't like Keri to get so upset that she'd be gone for hours and especially not be here at mealtime. "What did you say that upset her, if you don't mind me asking?"

Grace stared up at him with a look he'd never seen before. His pulse galloped.

"I told her who her father was."

Brooks lifted one eyebrow. He'd never heard a word mentioned about Keri's father. Of course she had one, but *who* he was had never crossed Brooks's mind. But the bigger question was, why would the news upset Keri so much?

"You'll find out soon enough, so I might as well tell you. Nate is her father."

"Nate?" Brooks thought of the times he'd seen Nate and Keri together, working, teasing, laughing. It made sense, now that he knew the truth. "How come Nate never told her?"

Grace nibbled on her lip. Behind her, the front door opened and his ma stepped out onto the porch. "Nate didn't know— at least not until yesterday."

Brooks clenched his jaw but held his tongue. So many secrets. So many lives hurt. There was lots more to this story, but what had happened in the past was none of his business. And he had to find Keri. What if she had crossed paths with another rabid creature? Or what if one of Dengler's men had captured her?

"Nate and your pa have been looking for her the past hour. They promised to fire three shots in the air if one of them found her."

"Which way did they go?"

"North and west."

Brooks didn't need to tell her to pray. "I need a fresh horse. Then I'll head out."

Grace reached out and touched his leg. "Please find her. I can't lose her now."

He nodded and rode for the barn. Everything in him told him to hurry—take Jester and go, but he had to be calm and think straight. A rested horse would serve him better and help him find Keri quicker.

Please, Lord. Keep her safe. Watch over her and show me where she is.

He unsaddled Jester and turned him loose in the pasture to graze, then slapped his gear on Jess's horse. He had to find Keri. His life wouldn't be complete without her in it.

Keri followed Ellen into a beautiful house, at least six times the size of hers. She stood in the foyer and stared up at one of the most elaborate chandeliers she'd seen this side of the Mississippi. An elegant stairway led up to the second floor. To her right was a parlor filled with ornate carved furniture, and a grand piano sat in the far corner.

Carl's parents must have left him a sizeable inheritance, because he could never afford something this nice working at the bank.

"Your house is amazing." She turned back toward Ellen.

"I suppose it is lovely. I just wish it wasn't so far from town. It gets lonely out here."

"Have you no family besides Carl?"

Ellen shrugged. She pulled a flower from a bouquet on the coffee table. "We have an aunt back east. She's asked me to come and stay with her, but how can I leave Carl here all alone? It's just been the two of us since our parents died last year."

"My condolences. I hadn't heard about that, since I was away."

Ellen stuck out her lower lip and scowled. "Carl didn't like you going away. He said it ruined his plans." She crushed the flower in her hand and gazed up at Keri. "I don't like it when Carl gets upset." She ducked her head. "Sometimes he hurts me."

Keri's heart somersaulted in her chest. Maybe she'd been right in her apprehension about Carl. "Why would your brother hurt you?"

She shrugged. "You have a seat. I'll see what's keeping Melba. We need some tea and cakes. Yes, most certainly some of her little cakes. They are quite delicious."

Keri perched on the edge of the nearest chair. She shouldn't have come here. Something wasn't right, and poor Ellen didn't seem in full control of her faculties. Had she always been so—

"Ah, a lovely flower graces my parlor. What a surprise."

Keri jumped up and found Carl leaning casually against the doorjamb. With his white shirt, gold brocade vest, and neatly pressed tan pants, he looked ready to go to the bank for a day's work; so why wasn't he at the bank?

Keri stood. "Well, you wanted me here, and you got me. What did you want to say to me?"

He wagged a finger in the air. "Ah, ah, not so fast. Whatever happened to making polite social talk? Please, have a seat. Refreshments are on their way."

Shaking her head, she walked toward him. "I don't have time for either talk or refreshments. I've been gone a long while, and folks will be worrying. I have a long ride ahead of me."

He stroked his finger across his upper lip. "What about your mother? Don't forget I know who she really is. Or should I say, *what* she is."

"And just what is that?"

He huffed out a laugh. "Come, come. Do we need to be so vulgar? We both know how your mother made her living for so many years."

She took a step closer to him, wishing she was strong enough to wipe that haughty look off his face. "And just how is it *you* know that?"

"Surely you aren't that naïve, not with a mother who lived in a bordello?"

Keri hauled back and slapped his cheek. He hissed and grabbed her wrist. "Let's not resort to violence, at least, not yet."

"What do you want with me?"

He shoved her back, and she fell against the sofa. "I want you. I've had plans for a long while, but you messed them up when you went away to school."

"I don't understand. I never encouraged you."

"A man has no control over his heart."

Keri struggled to find something to say—anything that would discourage him. "And knowing what my mother did doesn't concern you? You're not worried about your reputation?"

He walked over to the window, his back to her. She glanced toward the foyer, trying to gauge if she could make it to the door before he could reach her.

"Don't try to leave. Remember, I can make life miserable for your mother."

Keri fell back against the sofa. What was she going to do? How could she get out of this frightening situation? She thought about God. Could He help her? Would He?

In spite of everything, she felt a warmth flood her insides. *God, if You're real, please help me.*

Ellen sashayed back into the room with the maid following, carrying a large silver tray. She set it on the table beside the sofa, then poured three cups of tea. She handed one to Carl and then one to Keri, avoiding her gaze. Keri sipped the warm brew, thankful to have something in her stomach. Breakfast had worn off a long time ago.

She ate the almond cakes the maid served, trying to not seem overeager. No one spoke, although Carl cast glances her way, as if proud of having outsmarted her. "What are you going to do with me?"

He stared at her a long moment then shrugged. "Honestly, I'm not sure. I hadn't expected you to respond so quickly, if at all."

"You'd best let me go. Holding a person against their will isn't lawful."

He held his hand toward the foyer. "Leave, if that's what you wish. But just know that word will soon get around about your mother. Or stay and marry me and all will be forgiven."

Thoughts raced through Keri's mind. Her mother could go away with Nate, and Keri could visit her. Wouldn't Grace prefer that to knowing her daughter married a scoundrel just to keep him quiet? And what about Brooks? Could she sacrifice her love for him to save her mother's reputation? She stood, and looked from Carl to the door.

A knock sounded at the front door, and Keri jumped. Carl motioned to Ellen to answer. She quickly complied, and a moment later she ushered Nate into the parlor. Keri's heart leapt. God had answered her prayer.

Relief softened the worried look in Nate's eyes, but suddenly his gaze darted past her, and he reached for his gun. An explosion sounded behind her. She jumped and Ellen screamed, then collapsed on the floor in a faint. Nate dropped his gun and grabbed his arm. Blood pooled on his sleeve and oozed between his fingers.

"Nate!" Keri rushed toward him, and threw her arms around him.

"You all right, Missy?"

She nodded. She longed to call him Pa, to let him know she knew and that she was happy about the news, but she didn't want Carl to know. He might use it against her and harm Nate further. Releasing her hold on Nate, she remained close and turned back to Carl.

He scowled, the gun still in his hand. The scent of gunpowder filled the room. "Well, now, this is a predicament, isn't it?"

CHAPTER TWENTY-THREE

*K*eri wrapped a bandage that Ellen had given her around Nate's arm. Carl had locked the two of them in the cellar and left. "What are we going to do?"

"Brooks and his pa are out searching. They'll find us sooner or later."

"How did you find me?"

"I'd say it was luck, but I suspect there was more to it than that. I found Bob's tracks and was following them. I'd nearly caught up with you when you ran across that snake's sister."

"You saw me?"

He nodded. "But I was too far away. You didn't hear me when I called out."

"Sorry." She stared at him, trying to comprehend that this man—a man she cared so much about—was her father.

"No, I'm sorry." He sent her a look that made her heart clench. Was he sorry for not telling her sooner that he was her father? She glanced down at her hands, and realized she was twisting them just like she'd seen her mother do. "Why didn't you ever tell me you were my father?"

He reached out and clutched her hand. Dried blood stained his callused fingers, but she didn't care. "I didn't know, Missy."

Her gaze shot up to his. "What do you mean?"

"I should have put two and two together, but I didn't. Grace didn't tell me you were my daughter until that day the windmill was burned. She hadn't told you, so I kept quiet." His eyes pleaded with her to believe him. "It's the best thing that's ever happened to me—learning I'm your pa."

Tears pooled in her eyes. "There's no one else in the world I'd want for my pa as much as you."

She moved closer and laid her head on his chest. He wrapped his arm around her and laid his cheek against her head. She was locked away in a dark dungeon with only one small lantern for light and no way of escape, but enveloped in her father's arms, she had the feeling everything would be all right.

Brooks rode into town, his gaze searching every nook and cranny. Neither he nor his pa had found any sign of Keri back at the ranch. It would take days—if not weeks—for the two of them to search all of Raven Creek. He'd decided to check in town to see if maybe someone had seen her, and if not, draft some men to help search for her. He just prayed the marshal was back so there'd be some men to recruit.

More than half a dozen horses stood in the street in front of Marshal Lane's office, and a crowd hovered around his door. Brooks dismounted and hurried up to them, hoping—praying—nothing had happened that involved Keri.

He pushed his way through the crowd and found the marshal at his desk, reloading his rifle. He nodded when he saw Brooks.

"Well, you won't have to worry about Saul Dengler anymore," Marshal Lane said. He laid the rifle on his desk and pulled out his six-shooter and reloaded it.

"What happened?"

"He's dead. In a gunfight." The marshal nudged his head toward the cells, where two men sat, looking forlorn. One man had a busted lip and swollen eye, and the other man's arm was in a sling. "We caught those two stealing cattle from Tom O'Malley's widow, and after an exchange of gunfire and then some encouragement on my part, they started babbling like a couple of women at a sewing bee. Said Dengler ordered the deaths of O'Malley and at least four other men in these parts if they wouldn't sign over their land to him. I went to arrest him, and he drew on me."

Thoughts ricocheted in Brooks's mind. Dengler's death would have everyone breathing easier. Everyone except him. He wouldn't rest until he'd found Keri. "That's good to know, but I'm here on another account. Did any of you run across Keri Langston?" Brooks looked around the room at the men lining the walls, and each one shook his head. "She's been missing since shortly after breakfast."

"Sure am sorry to hear that." Marshal Lane shoved his gun back into his holster. "Wish I could help, but we're headed out to arrest Carl Peters."

"Peters?" Brooks thought about the man who'd come to visit Keri several times. He'd had a gut feeling about him—and it wasn't a good one. "What's he done?"

The marshal headed for the door, and the men in the office backed up to let him pass. Brooks followed on his heels.

"Guess you know he works at the bank?" Marshal Lane untied his horse from the hitching post.

Brooks nodded.

"Turns out he's been working for Dengler. He passed on

information about people defaulting on their loans or having trouble making their payments."

Suddenly, all the pieces fell into place. "So that's how Dengler chose his victims." His thoughts turned to Keri's uncle. "Will didn't owe any money on Raven Creek, but I can't help feeling that he fell prey to Dengler's men too."

"Once the dust settles, I'll question those two in my jail. If they know anything about Will, they'll 'fess up."

Brooks nodded his thanks. "I need to keep searching for Keri. You'll keep an eye out for her?"

"Yep. Let's ride, men." Marshal Lane reined his horse around and the posse followed, thundering down the road and stirring up a cloud of dust.

Brooks walked down the boardwalk toward the store. If Keri had come to town, that's probably where she would have gone. He was glad that Carl Peters wouldn't be able to bother her anymore. Something in that man's eyes just didn't sit right with him.

Suddenly, Brooks paused. What if Peters had stumbled across Keri? He hadn't hidden the fact that he was interested in her. His shoulders tensed. He wouldn't put it past Peters to do something to Keri. He had a gut feeling that's where he'd find her. Could God be guiding him to her as he had prayed He would?

He turned and ran for his horse. Peters's house was as good as any place to look for her. He followed the dust cloud, riding hard for a good half-hour, and then the air exploded in gunfire. As he crested a hill, a massive house—like something that could be found on a Georgia plantation—spread out before him. Brooks stopped and surveyed the situation. The posse had lined up in front of the house, hiding behind trees or lying on the ground. As best as he could tell, only one gun was firing from the house.

Brooks reined his horse around and rode away from the house and the gunfire, and circled around to the back. If only Peters was shooting, it wouldn't be hard to get the drop on him.

He tried the back door and found it unlocked and stepped inside, gun drawn. A huge kitchen with a fancy stove sat empty. He tiptoed through the room, being careful to stay to the side and away from the doors, so Carl wouldn't see him or a stray bullet find him.

The shooting from the inside stopped, and Brooks peered around the door frame into a wide hall that led to the front door. Carl Peters had turned a tall hall tree on its side, blocking the front entrance, and was using it for a shield. Sunlight shone through several holes in the glass in the door. Carl squatted behind the hall tree, reloading his gun.

Brooks had never shot a man before, and he prayed he wouldn't have to now. Heart pounding in his ears, he stepped out from behind his cover. Carl jumped and stood, holding his loaded gun down.

"Take it easy." Brooks held up his free hand. "No one needs to get hurt."

"How'd you know to come here?"

Brooks's gut twisted. "Let's just say I had a hunch."

Carl huffed. "You're not good enough for Keri, and I'm not letting you take her."

"Don't be stupid. There's close to a dozen men outside, and just the one of you."

Carl's eyes darted to the left and then the right.

"There is no escape, Peters. Dengler is dead. Your work with him is over." Brooks held his gun steady, trying to keep his breathing even. He wasn't used to talking down a half-crazed man with a gun. Maybe he could barter with him. Brooks didn't have to think long to make his offer. "Peters, give me Keri, and I'll give you the deed to Raven Creek."

Carl lowered his gun a few inches and seemed to be considering his proposal. Suddenly he heard a shout from outside the house.

"Peters. This is the marshal. Come out with your hands up and you won't be shot."

Carl ducked and spun back toward the door, then he whirled back toward Brooks and raised his gun.

"No. Don't—"

Carl fired, and the bullet hit the door frame near Brooks's shoulder. He fired his gun, and Carl grabbed his leg. Gunfire blasted from outside, hitting Peters in the shoulder. He cried out and collapsed on the floor, moaning.

"Marshal!" Brooks waited for the gunfire to cease. "It's me, Brooks Morgan. Peters is shot. Hold your fire."

"All right, but we're coming in."

Brooks strode up to Carl and kicked the man's gun out of reach. He tugged Carl away from the door then pulled the hall tree back.

The marshal shouldered himself through the opening and surveyed the scene. "Where'd you come from? Thought we left you back in town."

"I got this overwhelming urge to follow you, and Peters all but confirmed that he has Keri."

The crusty marshal smiled. "Glad you did. Might have saved a life or two."

Brooks nudged Carl's foot with his boot. "Where's Keri?"

Carl scowled at him but said nothing. He lay back on the floor and closed his eyes and gritted his teeth. Brooks looked at the marshal.

"You men, get in here and search this house. See if Miss Langston is here." The posse clomped inside, and the marshal waved several men in different directions.

Brooks turned back to the kitchen. There'd been a closet

or door to another room that he wanted to check. As he neared the door, he heard a shuffling sound, and his heart took wing. He jerked the door open. "Ker—"

Ellen Peters and a woman he didn't recognize huddled in the back of the pantry, staring at him with wide, frightened eyes. Ellen whimpered.

Brooks holstered his gun and held up his palm. "It's all right, ladies. It's safe to come out now."

The older woman gently escorted Miss Peters out and over to the kitchen table.

"Is m-my brother dead?"

"No, ma'am. He's been shot, but I believe he'll live."

Instead of looking relieved, she frowned. Brooks didn't have to think hard to imagine what it was like living with a man like Peters.

The older woman nudged her chin toward another door on the far wall that Brooks hadn't noticed before. "There's a man and woman locked downstairs in the cellar. Mr. Peters, he got the key in his pocket."

Brooks didn't bother searching for a key. He jogged to the door and rapped on it with the butt of his gun. "Keri? Are you in there?"

"Brooks? Yes, Nate and I are here. Carl shot him."

"Get back and find cover." He waited until Keri called out, then he fired his gun at the lock three times, and the door fell open. Brooks stormed down the stairs, searching the crates that were stacked on top of each other—and then he saw her.

Keri slipped out from behind several crates and rushed into his arms. He held her tight, pressing his cheek against her head. "I thought I'd lost you. Thank the Lord you're all right."

"I didn't know how we'd get free, but I prayed, and God sent you."

Brooks loosened his hold on her and cupped her cheeks. "Do you know how much I love you?"

She smiled. "No, but you're welcome to tell me."

And he did—with his lips. He kissed her so thoroughly she was breathing hard and her lips were puffy. Then he cradled her against his chest, rejoicing in how God orchestrated the steps that brought him here to rescue her.

"If you're done with your kissin', could someone help me before I bleed to death?" Nate requested.

Keri giggled and pushed back from Brooks's chest. "We need to get Nate to the doctor. It's just a flesh wound, but it's a deep one."

Reluctantly, Brooks stepped back from Keri and stretched out his hand to Nate, who sat on a chair with a broken-off back. "Come on, Pops, let's get going."

"I'm not your Pops."

Brooks grinned. "You will be if I have anything to say about it."

Nate chuckled, and Brooks helped him up the stairs.

Behind him, Keri muttered, "Don't I have any say in the matter?"

Nate glanced over at Brooks and winked.

⟵ ★ ⟶

Brooks held Keri's hand as they stood beside the charred spot where the windmill had been and stared at the water flowing freely in the creek again. "That sure was some explosion when they dynamited that dam Dengler built."

"I wish I could have been there," Keri said.

Brooks wrapped his arm around her shoulders. "I know, but that was a good thing you did by waiting with Miss Peters until the train came."

"I hope Ellen will have a better life with her aunt than she had here."

"Yeah. At least she won't have to worry about her brother hurting her again—not for a very long while, if ever."

Keri turned in Brooks's arms and hugged him around the waist. "It's a huge relief to know he won't ever bother me again."

"It is to me too." He kissed her forehead, then her eyes before tasting of her sweet lips. His kiss deepened, and he crushed her against him, his mouth pressing hard against hers. She moaned a sweet little noise that was almost his undoing. Tomorrow. Tomorrow she'd be his fully, but not today. He moaned himself, inwardly, then stepped back.

He brushed a lock of her hair back behind her ear. "I guess we'd better head back. It is our party, after all."

"And Ma's and Pop's."

"Theirs too." He took her hand and walked her back toward the house. More family than he knew he had had come for the wedding. Uncles. Aunts. And cousins galore.

"Your family sure is nice. I didn't know there'd be so many of them."

He squeezed her hand. "Neither did I."

At the corral, he stopped and surveyed the dozen Morgan horses his family members had brought as wedding gifts. Now he could continue the tradition of raising the beautiful horses named after a distant relative.

The delicious aroma of the pig roasting on the spit filled the air. In front of the house, tables had been set up, and the women had covered them with food. He was starving. He leaned over and stole another kiss. Starving for the affection of his beloved.

Fast hoofbeats approached from the north, and he turned to see his father riding with his cousins Alex and Greg, and a friend of Alex's, who was always spouting scientific stuff; what was his name? Nelson—that was it.

The four horsemen stopped a few feet away, and Pa was grinning like a possum. "Nelson has some news for you, son."

Nelson struggled to get his left leg over the horse's back and half fell to the ground. He adjusted his wireframe glasses and walked toward Brooks, his frizzy hair standing up in all directions like a tangle of broken barbed-wire fencing. The bookish man clapped Brooks on the shoulder. "Congratulations, Mr. Morgan. I predict you'll soon be a wealthy man."

Brooks raised his brow and cast Keri a confused look. She shrugged.

"I give up. Tell me how that's going to happen. I mean, I got lucky in cards the day I won this ranch, but I've sworn them off."

Nelson's grin was as wide as Pa's. "You know that creek with the black water?"

Brooks nodded. "Sure. Raven Creek. It's what the ranch is named after."

"Well, that's not brackish water out there, that's a pool of oil."

"Oil?" Brooks rubbed the back of his neck. "What good is that to me?"

"It's as good as gold—and maybe more."

Brooks shook his head. "Guess I'll have to take your word for that."

Alex and Greg walked up to him and shook his hand. "Congratulations, cuz. Looks like you're having good luck all around," Alex said.

The dinner bell clanged, and they all turned and walked toward the food. Alex fell into step with Brooks, telling him all about the oil industry and how gasoline-powered automobiles would soon replace the horse and buggy.

Chuckling, Brooks shook his head. He doubted that would happen any more than he'd be rich one day. But then again—he wrapped his arm around Keri's shoulders. He was already a rich man. Rich in love with a beautiful woman and rich in love for his God.

———— ★ ————

Grace stood next to Keri's bed, holding a packet of faded envelopes. "I have something I want to give to you."

"What is it?"

Grace caressed the papers then handed them to her. "They're the letters your uncle Will wrote me. At least once a year he'd write me to let me know how you were doing. I followed your life through his letters at least until the last few. I couldn't stand that he sent you away, so I didn't read the last few. I never even knew he was dying."

Keri laid out the missives on her bed. There were probably a dozen and a half. Three of them were still sealed. "You really don't care if I read these?"

"No. Please. Go ahead. Maybe they will help you to understand your uncle better. Will was a good man, even if he didn't always make the right choices."

"Thank you for sharing these."

Her mother smiled. "I thought it might be a nice wedding gift. Are you getting excited?"

Tingles charged through her at the thought of becoming Brooks's bride in less than twelve hours. "Yes. And how about you? You've waited much longer than I have."

"It hardly seems real. After so long, Nate and I will finally be together." She leaned against the bedpost. "He's such a good, forgiving man. Not many men would marry someone with a past like mine."

"The pastor said Sunday that God makes each one of us new

←———— 245 ————→

when we ask Him to forgive our sins, so you're pure. New. Right?"

Grace leaned down and kissed Keri's cheek. "Thank you for the reminder. Now read your letters."

Keri looked at each envelope but the ones that pulled at her were the unread ones. She picked up the newest-looking one and slit it open. Her heart clenched as she read the news where Will told her mother that he was dying. He apologized for sending her away to that horrible place and ruining her life. He apologized for firing Nate and not allowing them to be together. He'd been wrong about Nate. He may not have much money or property, but he had character, which was more than many men had.

She read the next paragraph and gasped.

Her mother lowered her hairbrush. "What's wrong?"

Keri held up a faded parchment. "This is what I've been looking for. Uncle Will left me the ranch and all his holdings. I never found a will. That's because he sent it to you."

"Glory be. Good things just keep happening."

EPILOGUE

*B*rooks paced from one tree to another outside the Shoofly Christian Church. They'd opted to marry in town because the church was bigger than their small church. Jarrod, Melissa, and the children, as well as the other Morgan family members were staying at the only hotel in town, as had the rest of them last night.

He gazed around at the mingling people. The townsfolk stood in small clusters chatting with one another. His pa, Phillip, and Nate were talking to a man and examining a Morgan horse Pa had sold him. Looking at the large crowd, Brooks wished they had decided to have a smaller wedding at the ranch with just family and a few close friends. Too late for that.

He pulled out his pocket watch and glanced at the time. The women were inside, prettying themselves up for the wedding, which should start any minute. Soon he'd be a married man. He had a ranch and enough money in the bank to hold them over through hard times and to build a small house for Nate and Grace.

Fast approaching hoofbeats pulled his attention from his thoughts. The marshal dismounted and looped the horse's reins over a wagon wheel. He took off his hat and slapped it against his leg, sending dust flying. He walked toward Brooks, clapped him on the shoulder, and started up the church steps. Then he paused and came back down. "It's not exactly a good time to be talkin' business, but I thought you'd want to know, those two yahoos in my jail've been chirpin' like hens at a church picnic. Dengler ordered Will's death, and one of his men —who died at Dengler's hand—was responsible for the deed."

Brooks blew out a breath. He'd wait to tell Keri, but it was a relief to finally learn what had happened. "Thanks for letting me know."

The marshal pinned him with a solemn stare. "Will saw something in you, son. He entrusted all he cared about into your hands. Take good care of her."

Brooks nodded and watched the marshal lumber up the steps.

His pa strode toward him, his gaze flicking between Brooks and the marshal as he entered the church. "You all right, son?"

"Yes, I am. Fine and dandy." He wrapped his arm around his pa's shoulders and hugged him. Things couldn't get much better—except if Josh could have attended the wedding, but with his wife so close to giving birth, they sent their apologies. Brooks gazed up at the sky and considered his blessings: The water situation with the ranch was good now that Dengler's dam had been blown up. Brooks had reconciled with his family, as had Keri, and he was marrying the only woman he'd ever loved. He gazed heavenward. *Thank You, Lord, for Your many blessings.*

The church doors opened, and Ma stepped out, shading her eyes with her hand. She looked pretty in her new lavender dress and with her hair done up in a fancy style. She waved. "All y'all can come in now. We're ready."

Brooks chuckled and shook his head and started for the door. Someone grabbed his arm and hauled him back. He reached for his pistol but remembered he'd left it in his room.

"Not you, son." His pa chuckled. "The groom is the last to go in—at least the last one before the bride and her bridesmaid."

"How do you know?"

"I've attended a few weddings in my day." He straightened his jacket, then reached out and adjusted Brooks's bowtie.

Brooks swallowed, not liking the tightness. "These things too closely resemble a noose."

Pa chuckled. "There's probably more truth in that than you realize."

"Do you hate wearing them as much as I do?"

His pa grinned and winked. "You know I do, but we do it to make our women happy. And if that's the worst thing you do to satisfy Keri, consider yourself a lucky man."

Phillip followed the last of the guests as they filed into the church. Brooks and his pa walked around to the side of the church and entered there, while Nate waited at the back to escort Keri. At the minister's nod, Brooks walked in the side door and to the front. His hands shook, but he smiled at his family and friends—Marshal Lane, Doc Brown, Earl, and many others. He'd ridden into this small town, just looking for a shelter from a storm, but he'd found salvation, reconciliation, and romance. He smiled at his father, proud to have him stand up beside him as his best man.

The organist began playing the processional, and he and everyone else looked back to the door, where Keri would enter. Excitement galloped through him, but something nagged at him. Was it possible that God had sent that hailstorm all those weeks ago? Had God been guiding him, even before he'd repented and turned his life around? Had God sent him here—to doctor Will, to take over ownership of Raven Creek, and to become Keri's protector and husband?

It was almost too much to fathom.

A shadow darkened the door, just before Grace entered. She started down the aisle, a big smile on her face, and she took her place at the front. Once Brooks and Keri were married, Nate would join Grace and finally unite their lives.

Brooks's heart thundered as he waited for his beloved to appear. Then Keri glided in on Nate's arm, resembling a fairy princess from a children's storybook. She looked gorgeous in her cream-colored dress with short, poufy sleeves. Her narrow waist looked even smaller with the belt encircling it. Bows were mounted on her shoulders, and the ends hung down a good foot.

Brooks gazed at the lovely smile on Keri's beautiful face and doubted he'd ever be this happy again. And then she stopped in front of him. He trembled and smiled, once again marveling how God had orchestrated events to bring them together. "You're beautiful," he whispered.

"So are you." She smiled, her blue eyes dancing.

The minister cleared his throat. Keri ducked her head, cheeks red. Brooks turned and wrapped her arm around his, and they faced the minister together, ready to become husband and wife.

His journey had been a long, hard one, but he'd finally reached the end of the trail.

The End

A MORGAN FAMILY SERIES

CAPTIVE TRAIL

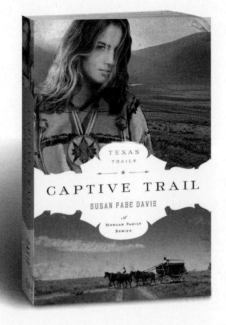

paperback 978-0-8024-0584-5   e-book 978-0-8024-7852-8

Taabe Waipu has stolen a horse meant for a dowry and is fleeing her Comanche village in Texas. While fleeing on horseback she has an accident and must complete her flight on foot. Injured and exhausted, Taabe staggers onto a road near Fort Chadbourne and collapses.

On one of his first runs through Texas, Butterfield Overland Mail Company driver Ned Bright is escorting two nuns to their mission station. They come across Taabe who is nearly dead from exposure to the sun and exhaustion. Ned carries her back with them and begins to investigate Taabe Waipu's identity.

MOODY
PUBLISHERS

MoodyPublishers.com   TexasTrailsFiction.com

A MORGAN FAMILY SERIES

THE LONG TRAIL HOME

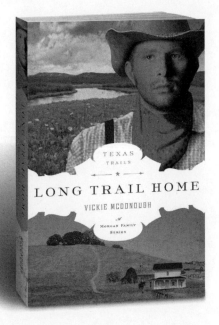

paperback 978-0-8024-0585-2   e-book 978-0-8024-7876-4

Riley Morgan returns home after fighting in the War Between the States and there is nothing he wants more than to see his parents and fiancée again. He soon learns that his parents are dead and the woman he loved is married. To get by, Riley takes a job at the Wilcox School for the blind.

At the school Riley meets a pretty blind woman named Annie, who threatens to steal his heart even as he fights to keep it hidden away. When a greedy man attempts to close the school, Riley and Annie band together to stop him and start falling in love. But Annie has kept a secret from Riley. When he learns the unwelcome truth, Riley packs his belongings and prepares to leave the school that has become his home.

MOODY
PUBLISHERS

MoodyPublishers.com   TexasTrailsFiction.com

A MORGAN FAMILY SERIES

paperback 978-0-8024-0587-6

e-book 978-0-8024-7907-5

paperback 978-0-8024-0586-9

e-book 978-0-8024-7877-1

paperback 978-0-8024-0408-4

e-book 978-0-8024-7892-4

Calling all book club members and leaders!

visit

TEXASTRAILSFICTION.COM

for discussion questions and special features